What Others are Saying

"*The Final Word* is a romantic suspense gem—perfect balance of swooning romance and nail-biting tension to keep your heart racing! Laura Thomas delivers strong, relatable characters who wrestle with questions of belief and ultimately learn to trust God through every twist and trial. A romantic suspense with heart, hope, and high stakes—you won't want to put down!"

—Darlene L. Turner, *Publishers Weekly* bestselling author

"Author Laura Thomas has penned a tale that is, at times, as chilling and suspenseful as the title suggests. At its heart, though, it is author Sophie Brooks' own love story—with Miles, the opera singer who sweeps her off her feet, the sisters with whom she longs to reconnect, and, above all, the God who is wooing her back to Him. Get comfortable because, once you start this one, you'll be turning pages well into the night, desperate to find out who will end up having The Final Word."

—Sara Davison, multi-award-winning author

"From the pen of Laura Thomas comes yet another brilliantly written, compelling page-turner. In *The Final Word*, the highly anticipated second title in her *Bite of Betrayal* series, Laura deftly weaves the themes of romance, faith, suspense and drama in a story that will hook you and not let you go. Highly recommended."

—Glenys Nellist, award-winning children's author of five popular series, including *Love Letters from God: Bible Stories, Bedtime Blessings, Snuggle Time and Little Mole*

"The rolling hillsides of the charming English countryside spell danger for Sophie Brooks and Miles Morgan in Laura Thomas's *The Final Word*. Exploring themes of second chances and healing from the past, Sophie and Miles learn to trust in God in all circumstances—a lesson for all of us to remember. If you love your suspense in idyllic settings, along with a sweet falling-in-love story, then grab your copy of *The Final Word* today."

—Sarah Hamaker, award-winning author of *The Cold War Legacy* and *The Seeking Justice Series*

"Book two in the *Bite of Betrayal* series, *The Final Word*, promises spine tingling suspense and boy does it deliver! If you loved the twists and turns Laura Thomas gave us in *Captured in Frame*, you won't want to miss Sophie's story. More twists, more twisted persons, and even more turns. Seriously, these Brooks women are tough cookies (although Sophie's baking is anything but tough!). If you love a book full of faith, romance, and more twists and turns (and stone walls!) than an English country road, you won't want to miss this book. The only thing that could be better is if I had book three in my itchy fingers right now."

—Chautona Havig, *USA Today* bestselling author

"Intrigue, romance, suspense, drama, grace, and fascinating characters—all woven into one beautiful story. Laura Thomas has done it again! Her latest volume in the *Bite of Betrayal Series* is a satisfying read. Once I started, I could not put the book away. I highly recommend this one!"

—Melanie Redd: Speaker, Blogger, & Author of *Live in Light: 5-Minute Devotions for Teen Girls*

The Final Word

Series

Captured in Frame—Book One
The Final Word—Book Two
Book Three—Coming in June of 2026

The Final Word

by

Laura Thomas

Dedication

To the Author of everything,
who always has the final word.
May this story give hope to every reader
for their own happily ever after.

Acknowledgements

This is such a special story to me! The Final Word is the second book in my "Bite of Betrayal" series, and encompasses many of my own personal passions and connections in life—writing, baking, England, opera, all things Paris, and my favorite Bible verses. I'm immensely grateful to the following who have all been a part of this journey:

Mountain Brook Ink Publishers—to Miralee Ferrell and her wonderful team for their belief and trust in me as one of their authors, and for making this book such a page-turner. I'm thankful to be part of the Mountain Brook Ink family.

Karen Neumair at Credo Communications—my fabulous literary agent, who found my publisher for this series of Christian romantic suspense.

Blossom Turner—my amazing critique partner who always makes time for my manuscripts, even amidst her own writing deadlines. You know I appreciate your friendship so much!

Charlotte, Jameson, and Jacob—my adult children who will always be my greatest joy. Special thanks to our aspiring opera singer, Jacob, for help on my research for "Miles" and for patiently listening to your mother's ramblings!

Lyndon—my phenomenal husband who has been my greatest encouragement in my writing adventures. For walking the streets of Paris, acting out scenes with me in an ancient English pub, and perusing bookstores in the city of Bath to make this story shine, thank you for always being supportive, understanding, and ready for anything! I can only write about true love because of ours.

My heavenly Father—for giving me light and life and words.

Chapter One

THE DESERTED STREET WAS DELICIOUSLY SINISTER in the glow of a solitary lamp—the perfect milieu for Sophie's final nights living in Paris. The clack-clacking of her high-heels reverberated between buildings—*stay, go, stay, go, stay, go.* Was she making the right decision? She gazed up at the dimly-lit, creamy brick buildings and their black iron balconies stuffed with sleeping flowers tucked in boxes. This glorious city was supposed to be her forever home…

A split-second lapse in concentration and the smooth leather sole of her brand-new ankle boots slipped across slick cobblestones. Sophie let out a gasp then steadied herself before she hit the ground. No harm done.

Grateful there was not a soul to witness her inelegance, she buttoned her blazer to stave off the sudden breeze and adjusted her crossbody bag. In the absence of her echoing footfalls, a high-pitched squeal split the night air.

What on earth?

Every muscle tensed as she pulled the phone from the outside pocket of her bag and held it like a weapon. A quick glance behind. Was someone watching her?

Move. Don't stop. Keep walking.

Clutching the phone, Sophie continued in the direction of her apartment building as fast as her impractical footwear would allow.

Why didn't I grab a taxi? So much for clearing my head.

The farewell dinner with her writing friends went on way too long and their crazy brainstorming for a suspense plot now had her on edge. She eyed her phone. Perhaps she should use the voice memo app and record her description of fear in real-time. Her method of capturing details and inspiration on the fly was a source of amusement to some of her friends, but the system worked for her. Paying attention and verbalizing random thoughts gave her ample fodder for her stories.

Another noise rooted Sophie to the spot. Louder. This time more like a kitten mewing.

Oh, for goodness' sake. A cat? Really?

Curious, Sophie chanced a peek down the narrow alley to her left, from where the noise seemed to emanate. Poor kitty. What if he was hurt? Or hungry? She pressed her phone's flashlight and shone its beam into the lane for a quick inspection. The shadows were… human-sized. A struggle. Then a sharp scream.

Sophie's limbs refused to move as her eyes adapted to the dark. Blonde hair of a woman. She was pinned to the brick wall by a man. Much taller, smothering her mouth with his forearm. He let out a low growl. Sophie glimpsed a slice of metal in his other hand.

She dropped her phone.

A clatter on the stone ground.

The man's head snapped up and Sophie's mouth fell open.

No.

She blinked, crouched to grab her phone, and fled without looking back.

No, not him. It can't be him…

Her footsteps matched the pounding of her heart as she

somehow managed to dial 1-1-2. She might be in danger but her apartment building was in the next block and that poor girl needed help right away. If she wasn't already too late. "Hello?"

"Bonjour, hello—what is your emergency?"

Sophie swallowed and held the phone to her ear. "Yes. Police. Maybe an ambulance." She swiveled to make sure she hadn't been followed. The street was empty. Not unusual for one in the morning in this quieter part of the city.

"Are you safe, miss?"

She slowed to a jog to ensure her words were heard loud and clear as she strained on toward the sanctuary of home. "I think so. There was an attack. A man and a woman. She has long, blonde hair. She was… distressed."

"What is the address?"

"Umm, I'm on Rue Camion, Paris. I'm not sure of the name of the side-street where I saw the… the attack…" Sophie dug into her purse for the keyring as she neared her apartment building. "It's opposite the big florist. A narrow alley. I'm sorry."

"Help is on the way. What's your name?"

"Sophie. Sophie Brooks."

"Where are you now, Sophie? I'd like to keep you on the line."

She stopped at the entrance, wrangled the ancient lock into submission with the key, and let herself into the lobby. "I'm in my apartment building. I'm safe." She slammed the door behind her, took several shaky steps, and leaned her forehead against the cool painted wall by the elevator. No stairs tonight. She exhaled, one hand on her heart. "I hope the girl got away. I think I saw a knife. A glint of something shiny, at least."

"I'm glad you're home, Sophie. Police are en-route. Let's get you into your apartment, shall we? Is there anyone waiting for you?"

"No. I live alone." Sophie stepped into the elevator and punched the number for the fourth floor. "I may cut out in the elevator. Reception's bad. One moment."

As the horror of what she witnessed washed over her, Sophie focused on her breathing and waited in the silent rectangular cocoon until a joyful ping announced she was on the fourth floor.

Sophie whispered into the phone. "I'm here. I don't want to wake my neighbors. I think I'm okay now."

"Is there anyone you can call to come and sit with you?" Kindness and concern wove through the French accent of the female voice on the line. A far cry from Sophie's previous experience with the police here. She bit the inside of her cheek at the painful memory.

"It's late. I'll be fine." The comforting aroma of soup filled the air in the hallway as she untangled the smaller key on the ring and then entered her apartment.

"Did you see the attacker? Is there anything about him you remember?"

Sophie let out a ragged breath. She couldn't be sure. Her overactive imagination had to be playing tricks with her. "I'm sorry. Not much. They were quite a way down the alley. He was tall, wore a baseball cap. Caucasian, I believe. Dark clothes. I can't be certain about anything else."

"No problem."

"But will I ever know what happened to… to the girl? Will I be called back? I hope she got away when I stumbled upon them." The immediate warmth of the room was welcome for the chills running through her body, now causing her teeth to chatter. She kicked off her ankle boots. "I'm moving to England on Saturday. Tomorrow's my last day in Paris."

"I see. Well, I have your number on file here, so if there is anything the police need, they'll be in touch. Maybe stay by your phone tonight. Let's hope the attacker got spooked."

Sophie double-checked her locked door and leaned her back against it as if to keep the evil out. "I'm praying that's the case. Thanks."

"Thank you for reporting this. We appreciate it. Stay safe and goodnight, Sophie."

"Goodnight." Sophie slid all the way down to the floor, every ounce of energy drained from her body. The phone rolled from her lap and her hands jittered like they were being electrocuted.

The shock kicked in. Not only of witnessing someone being attacked a couple of blocks from her home. That would have been devastating enough. She wasn't in the habit of being out on her own in Paris late at night. *Mom would be mortified.* She'd never entered into the city nightlife and party scene, even in her early twenties. No, tonight she'd been hanging out with her fellow writers having one last delightful dinner and talking books, and she simply lost track of time.

Sophie wiped wet cheeks with her trembling fingers. She was crying? Of course, she was.

The incident had shaken her, but the real trauma was that although he wore a baseball cap pulled down low, there was something familiar about the attacker. Could it be? Had the one who invaded her nightmares for the past three years come back?

The mere notion sent a shudder through her entire body.

Sophie couldn't leave Paris fast enough.

Chapter Two

A BITTERSWEET BLEND OF NOSTALGIA AND nerves gripped Sophie's chest as she stood in the bakery that had both grounded and inspired her over the years. This was her last afternoon living in the City of Lights.

After eight years in Paris, she was surrendering the quintessential dream she envisioned for herself of being a romance author while falling for her perfect man in the very place that pulsated with love. She blinked back tears, part tired and part terrified…

"Sophie? Come here, ma chérie." Annabelle enveloped her in a tight hug, all vanilla and sugar and butter. "What will Pretty Patisserie do without our favorite Canadian girl?"

Sophie pulled back and stared into the kind eyes of her boss. Her dear friend. She mustered a smile. "You'll have to find someone else to practice your English with, I guess." She kissed both plump cheeks of the woman who was like a second mother to her. "Thank you, for everything. For taking a chance on me and teaching me how to live in this spectacular city and pull off being something vaguely resembling an unofficial pastry chef."

Annabelle dabbed her wet cheeks with the rose-and-white striped apron tied around her ample waist. "We'll miss you. Remember us when you're a rich and famous author living it up in the English countryside with your sisters, yes?"

"Of course." Sophie winced. Her nebulous plan wasn't a complete lie. She *was* going to join her sisters over in England,

and her literary agent *had* found a publisher who was interested in her latest novel manuscript. If only she could share her experience from last night with dear Annabelle. Too dangerous. *Or maybe I'm crazy and imagined it was him.*

She slung her bag over one shoulder and lifted the large rectangular pink box from the glass counter. "My last delivery. The Opera House."

Annabelle bustled around the counter to the front of the small shop and held the door open. "It's who you know, you know."

"Of course, you know everyone who's anyone." Sophie blew a wisp of long hair from her face. "Thanks again for the opera ticket. It's such a generous leaving gift, and *The Magic Flute*'s one of my favorites."

Annabelle shrugged. "It's your guilty pleasure. What better way to spend your final night in Paris? I know your mother always sends you a ticket for Christmas. So, think of this as an early Christmas gift."

"In April?"

"Sure. Why not? And this backstage delivery will be the prelude. A peek into the green room, or whatever they call it. I guess they work up an appetite with all that singing, no? Who are we to deny them a sugar fix?"

"No one of sound mind can resist your profiteroles." Sophie's eyes misted. "I'll miss you. I may have to call you from England when I need a new recipe…"

"I'll be here. Au revoir, Sophie, dear."

"Au revoir."

At risk of collapsing in a flood of tears right there in the bakery, Sophie hurried outside to the waiting taxi, her arms laden with the gigantic box of extravagant pastries. The familiar white-haired driver helped her inside with a courteous nod, half-jogged to the driver's seat, and then pulled into traffic for their short journey. She admired the mint green exterior of Pretty Patisserie one last time and let out the breath she'd been holding.

This is it. I'm leaving the bakery. Leaving Paris.

If only she were leaving the city on a more positive note.

If only she hadn't witnessed the attack last night.

If only she could un-see what she had seen. Whom she *thought* she had seen. She bit her bottom lip.

"Opera House, Mademoiselle?"

The driver's deep voice interrupted her dark thoughts. "Oui. Merci."

Lifting her chin, Sophie pushed the disturbing possibility from her mind, and inhaled the tantalizing aroma of sweet treats encased within the box that perched on her lap. Eclairs nestled next to profiteroles. A rainbow of macarons—and her own personal favorite, gâteau opéra, the opera cake—an elaborate affair of layered almond sponge cake with coffee syrup, French buttercream, chocolate ganache… so luxurious. So opera-esque.

The taxi pulled up at the side of the stunning Palais Garnier Opera House. Annabelle usually made this delivery herself as she knew a couple of the staff members and some of the performers, but today this was Sophie's last task as her employee. There would be just enough time to rush back to her tiny apartment, change into her finery, and return for the evening performance.

Sophie peeked down at her white T-shirt smudged with chocolate buttercream, and attempted to brush flour from her black fitted pants.

At least I look like an authentic baker…

The taxi door opened, and the driver took the box from her while she exited the vehicle. Annabelle had paid him in advance, so at least she didn't need to dig into her bag.

"Merci." Sophie tucked a few wayward strands of hair into the messy bun piled on top of her head, and relieved him of the pastries. Her eyes widened. The opera house was gigantic and somehow, she had to find the entrance Annabelle mentioned. She expelled a loud sigh.

I should have paid more attention.

The driver nodded toward a large black door further along the side of the building. "That's where you'll be wanting to go, Mademoiselle."

"Thank you so much." She would have hugged him if she hadn't been carrying the box.

He tapped his hand to his forehead in a salute, and left her alone.

"Okay. Here come the cakes."

The warm early-spring afternoon invited Parisians and visitors alike to swarm the streets in droves. The general hum of traffic, voices, and music filled the air in a way that had become almost comforting to Sophie. This had been home for so long. She detected a combination of fresh flowers and garlicky steak dinners as she headed in the direction of the doorway, careful to avoid colliding with other pedestrians as her arms ached under the weight of her sweet load. She almost squealed with delight when the black door eased open from the inside.

"Bonjour. Bonjour." Sophie focused on not dropping the delivery, and only when she was directly in front of the open door did she dare raise her head to make eye contact with the person who had given her a way inside. "Oh, h-hello." Why had she reverted to her native English? Why indeed.

She could barely gather her thoughts as she stared up into the chiseled face of a man who struck a remarkable resemblance to the love interest in her work-in-progress novel. She blinked. Mute. Had she imagined him into being?

He raised his dark brows and all that handsomeness broke into a grin. "Thank goodness—you have cakes *and* you speak English?"

Sophie knew she was gaping like a fool, but she needed a second. He was literally Prince Charming. Wore the costume. Had the perfect wavy hair. Eyes the color of a stormy ocean. Plus, he spoke with a soft American accent.

"Miss? Mademoiselle? Can I take the box from you?" His forehead wrinkled.

Sophie blinked several times, willing her cheeks to cool down. "I'm so sorry. You took me by surprise. I'm here with a delivery from the Pretty Patisserie." She nodded at his outfit. "I'm guessing you're in tonight's performance."

He laughed and Sophie felt the warm sound reverberate in her own chest. "I am. You'll be relieved to know I don't usually dress like this. Would you like to come in or should I take the box from you here?"

She bit her lower lip. "At the risk of sounding paranoid, I'd like to be able to make sure they're all perfect and set them out as per the instructions from my boss. Her creations are her babies, and I feel responsible. It's my last day working for her and she bought me a ticket to see the performance tonight." *I'm rambling like a buffoon...*

"Well, in that case—" He stood back and allowed her entrance. "Please, go ahead. I'm awfully sorry, I would come with you and help, but I'm running a quick errand." He pulled at the golden tassels on his shoulder lapels. "It's a costume thing. Are you okay to follow the corridor to the end? You'll want to take the last door on the left. A bunch of the crew are in there. They'll be stoked to see you and your cakes."

Sophie's heart sank a little at the thought of him leaving, which was ridiculous.

"It was lovely to meet you, Miss—?" He tilted his head.

"Sophie Brooks."

He nodded. "Enjoy the opera tonight, Sophie Brooks."

"I will. I might spot you on stage. What's your name? I'll check the program."

"Miles Morgan. No prizes for guessing what I'll be wearing." Another killer grin.

"Well, Miles, I think I can improve on this ensemble." Sophie glared at her food-splattered work clothes.

"No improvement needed. Not at all. Have a wonderful evening."

They stared into each other's eyes for an extra beat, like their connection was the most natural thing in the world.

With that, Miles Morgan left. Sophie turned and scurried down the brightly lit hallway with the pink box of cakes, her heart almost beating out of her chest after the most beautiful encounter she had ever experienced.

What just happened?

Sophie fussed with the flouncy hem of her long, strapless gown as she stood outside the Opera House later that evening. This was turning out to be a surreal day. A phone call to the police station confirmed no one was there when they arrived at the scene of the attack last night, and no one was missing at this point. Good news, at least. Yet she couldn't shake the shadow of fear that fell across the end of an era—her life in France. Surely, the attacker couldn't have been her ex. Not after all these years. Yet the possible resemblance rattled her nerves.

Quit worrying. Your new life in England starts tomorrow.

The plan to move had been in motion for weeks and Sophie had been counting the days to leave—until she happened upon Miles Morgan over the box of cakes this afternoon. When she spoke with the rest of the cast in the back room, she did a little sleuthing as to his character, and they insisted Miles was a single, genuine, humble guy. Salt of the earth. Kind and generous. She wasn't surprised. Their brief encounter was something akin to magical, although the timing was utterly lousy. What she wouldn't give to spend another day getting to know *the* Miles Morgan. Leading role as Prince Tamino in tonight's opera.

Sophie scanned the magnificent Opera House doorway in the most nonchalant manner possible while her insides quivered with anticipation. How long should she stand out here like a proverbial lemon? *Miles is worth it.* True. She was almost packed for her travels in the morning, and it wasn't like she had anywhere better to be at that moment than the steps of the Opera House waiting for Prince Tamino.

After a spectacular performance, Miles had sought Sophie out as she exited the theatre. He asked if she would wait a few minutes while he changed from his costume, and then meet him on the steps outside. He wanted to talk to her. So, of course, here she was. Her palpitations evidence that she was enchanted by this man.

God, why is this happening on the night before I leave this country?

Then again, what right did she have to demand answers from God? She'd not given Him the time of day in months. Okay, years. She sniffed the perfumed Paris air and allowed the muted sounds of traffic, music, and chatter to wash over her. The old Sophie would have prayed for guidance in the massive move from this vibrant city life to a tiny English village, but she'd decided all on her own. Been independent. To ask God for anything felt like a sham now, even though her family presumed all was well in her spiritual life. Much like acting a part, as if on stage like the singers in tonight's performance. Impressive, but not real.

Miles played a phenomenal prince in this fairy tale all about darkness, light, and finding one's way in the world. She could still hear the timbre of his rich tenor voice in her ears, both tender and strong. He seemed to have it all. *This man is certainly out of my league.* Yet he wanted to see her. Really?

Sophie tucked her clutch under one arm and dug nervous fingers into the deep pockets of her black satin gown, grateful to have something to do with her hands. Everyone around her was schmoozing and laughing, huddled in groups or couples. The sophisticated vibe reminded her of the first time she came here to watch her twin sister perform in the *Swan Lake* ballet. They were both so young back then with stars in their eyes. Harriet had reached out and grabbed hers with a success that left Sophie in her shadow. Like always. She stared up at a starless sky the color of ripe plums.

What am I doing here? Maybe I should leave and get an early night.

"Sophie?"

She whirled around and came face-to-face with Miles.

"Sorry to keep you waiting." He took a step back and beamed. "You look stunning, Miss Brooks."

"Thanks. As do you." He had changed into an immaculate black tux. *Hello, Prince Charming.* Or maybe now he was giving off more of a James Bond vibe. She swallowed down the nervous giggle that threatened to erupt—and evolved into an indelicate snort.

His grin broadened. "That was adorable. Did something amuse you?"

Sophie shook her head and wrinkled her nose. "That was slightly mortifying. Sorry." She surveyed the area. "It's just that all this is very fancy and surreal for an ordinary person like me. I guess I'm having a Cinderella moment."

"Cinderella?"

"I usually come to the opera once a year. Most days I'm covered in flour or hunched over a keyboard." She wiggled her fingers to mimic her typing.

"I'd love to know more about both. I can promise you I'm a very ordinary person, too."

"Well, you make a convincing James Bond dressed like that. You know you might try acting, if the singing thing doesn't work out for you…"

His jaw dropped, and his face looked as if he'd been slapped.

Sophie's breath hitched. Had she overstepped? "I didn't mean anything. I'm so sorry, I was joking—of course, I was joking. Oh, my goodness." She buried her face in her hands.

The next moment, Miles's rich laughter filled the serene space. Several bystanders turned at the joyful sound. "I'm glad that was the final performance of the season, otherwise your remark could make me feel somewhat insecure."

"No. No, you were fantastic. Brilliant. I would never dream of suggesting—"

"Hey, Cinderella." Miles put a gentle hand on her bare arm. "I was kidding—and now I'm kinda hoping you were, too." He gasped in mock horror. "Please say you were…"

Now it was Sophie's turn to laugh. "Yes, one hundred percent." She put a hand over his. "I take back the James Bond thing. Let's start again."

He led her down the stone steps. "I'll take that one as a compliment. It so happens that I do have my own little version of a Bond car." He winked.

"You do? Please say it's an old sports car. I adore old sports cars."

A flash exploded in Sophie's face. The next second, she saw the paparazzi were busy capturing the leading man post-performance.

"Now it's my turn to apologize." Miles gave a perfunctory smile and a few more shots were taken. "These guys will get bored and move on before you know it. Yes, my baby is a 1964 Porsche 356, if that means anything. I inherited her and am slightly obsessed."

Sophie squealed. "I know exactly what that means. Is the car here in Paris?"

They reached the wide sidewalk. "In England actually. Long story. If you have time, there's a table open at my favorite restaurant around the corner and I'd love to—"

As traffic slowed, a familiar face came into view across the street. It was him. Her ex-boyfriend, Troy Sanders, stood stock still and met Sophie's gaze. He squinted and placed one finger in front of his lips. *Shhh.*

"No." Sophie expelled the word in a whisper and her stiletto heel gave way causing her to sink into Miles's strong arms.

"What's wrong?" He helped her up. "Do you need to sit?"

Sophie pulled away from him, her mouth dry and her head spinning out of control. She chanced another peek between cars to the sidewalk beyond, but now a group of teens stood in a huddle where she had seen Troy.

"No, I have to go." She cleared her throat. "I have to go right now."

Miles touched her cheek and she almost melted back into his arms. "Tell me what I can do to help?" His forehead wrinkled.

"I'm so sorry, Miles."

Sophie took three faltering steps and nodded at one of the waiting taxis lining the curb. She sank into the backseat, pulled the voluminous fabric of her dress inside, and slammed the door. With one last glance at Miles's shocked face, she waved goodbye to Paris and the possibility of some crazy fairy tale ending coming true.

Chapter Three

MILES GROANED AS HE WATCHED THE black taxi drive away in a stream of loud traffic with Sophie Brooks tucked inside. Talk about a Cinderella moment. He scanned the ground in case she'd left a shoe behind…

"Hey, Miles. You coming for dinner? Everyone's waiting around back."

He turned to see his leading lady surrounded by a few of the other cast members he didn't know particularly well.

"Can I catch up with you later, Veronica?" Celebrating with a crowd was the last thing he felt like doing. Usually, he wouldn't mind, but tonight he'd hoped to have a quiet dinner with Sophie instead. There was something about her that was intriguing.

"Are you kidding?" Veronica set a hand on the hip of her sequined gown. "Come on, it's the last night. Who knows when we'll all sing together again?"

Miles cringed. She had no clue how deeply those words cut. No one knew.

"Miles? Hello? Is this about the beautiful brunette you were talking to by any chance?"

He raked his fingers through his hair. "Yeah, I guess so. Her name's Sophie." He'd felt something in his gut—or in his heart, perhaps—that told him she was special. Worth pursuing. Although something or someone spooked her before he had a chance to know for sure.

"Hmm. It's not like you to be infatuated by the fans." She

pursed bright red lips. "You know we all call you Saint Miles."

"Seriously? That's a stretch." He peered down the street one more time. Was he hoping she'd turn around and come back? She left in such a hurry he didn't have the chance to grab a phone number from her, but Miles never shied away from a challenge. He was in Paris for another couple of days. He had time.

"Okay, okay. You're right." He joined Veronica on the steps. "We should all celebrate together this evening. One last time."

She raised a brow. "What about the girl?"

"I'll track her down tomorrow."

How hard could it be to find Sophie Brooks in Paris?

Late the next morning, Sophie stood on the doorstep of her sister's pink cottage in the heart of the English countryside.

This is it. This is home. What have I done?

She breathed in the damp spring air, all moss and bark, and blinked back tears at the sudden sense of loss that hit like a literal punch to her gut. Paris was now in her past, and although much of her time in the city had nurtured her growth and opened her eyes to unparalleled beauty, she couldn't forget the poisonous sliver that marred everything. Just when she thought perhaps the skin had grown over—

"Sophie?"

Georgia's voice came from the pavement behind her and she turned and pasted on a brave smile. "Hey. I made it."

"Oh, my goodness, you're early. I'm so sorry, have you been waiting long?" Georgia dumped full grocery bags on the gravel path and smothered Sophie in a warm hug.

Sophie inhaled her big sister's familiar classic rose scent and closed her eyes for a moment. Safe. She felt safe. This was good.

"The taxi literally dropped me about two minutes ago. I hadn't even knocked on the door yet." She took a step back and ran a hand down Georgia's long brown hair, a little lighter and wavier than her own. "You look great, as always."

"Thanks, you're not too shabby yourself." Georgia scrutinized her little sister's appearance. "You know, you may have to tone down the Paris chic now that you're a country girl."

Sophie untied the elegant silk scarf from her neck and draped it over Georgia's shoulders. "There you go. We can share clothes again. Like the old days."

"Ah, those glorious teen years we all loved so much. Poor Mom. I don't know how she coped with the three of us." Georgia unlocked the front door and retrieved her groceries. "Come on inside. I'll give you a hand with the cases."

"No worries, I've got it." Sophie hauled one case and her laptop bag into the entryway and then picked up the second case before Georgia had an opportunity to help. "I'm used to lugging this lot across the country today. After a crazy early start, two trains, and a taxi—I'm done in."

"I'll bet." Georgia shrugged out of her denim jacket and took Sophie's blazer from her. "We can get you settled in a minute, but first you know we have to do the English thing. You're a resident now."

"A nice cup of tea." Sophie tried out her best English accent, slipped her boots from her aching feet, and followed Georgia into the kitchen.

"Of course. With milk?"

"Please. No sugar." Sophie stretched her arms above her head and attempted to work the kinks from her neck. "Is Harriet still planning on coming over?"

Georgia flicked on the kettle and unloaded her cloth grocery bags. "She'll probably be here any minute with Lucy. I don't think you realize how excited we are to have you living here, at long last. It's been… let's see, over a decade since we all lived in the same country. How crazy is that?"

Sophie sank onto the kitchen chair. "Wow. You're right. Our Vancouver days seem like a lifetime ago, and now only Mom's left over there." She tapped her chin. "How long do you think it'll be before she takes early retirement and joins us?"

The kettle whistled and Georgia pulled three white mugs from an open shelf. "I'm not so sure." She turned to face Sophie. "She hasn't said anything official, but I think she might be seeing someone special."

"What?" Sophie gripped the edge of the wooden kitchen table. "That doesn't seem possible somehow."

"Why not?"

"Because it's Mom." Sophie shrugged. "She's never been really serious about anyone since Dad died. Although I guess it's been almost… twenty-eight years?" The notion of their mom in a romantic relationship was more than her exhausted brain could fathom. An image of Miles Morgan in his tux clouded her thoughts, and her heart ached at how their connection might have evolved given half a chance. She shook her head to clear her mind. "How about you and Will? Are the wedding plans going smoothly?"

"Oh, yes." Georgia poured boiling water into a vintage china teapot and added milk to each mug. "We've got lots of time but everything's going so well." She shrugged. "I still don't know what I did to deserve a hunky surgeon and his adorable toddler son. I have to pinch myself sometimes to prove I'm not dreaming." She let out a little sigh. "God's been so kind."

"Aww, sis." Sophie padded over and gave her a hug. "You

deserve the very best of everything." Georgia had experienced a horrific time with her ex-husband, and then the whole business with his murder and those dreadful criminals last year… Sophie shuddered. "Seriously, I'm so glad all that scary stuff is in your past now and you can concentrate on a future with Will and little Jack."

"Thanks. Me, too." Georgia tossed her hair behind her shoulder. "So, what's going on with you?" She retrieved a package of chocolate chip cookies from a cupboard. "Anything new?"

"Other than moving to a different country, you mean?" Sophie grabbed a pretty white plate from a shelf and passed it to her sister.

"Other than that." Georgia emptied the cookies onto the plate, which she set on the table. "I mean anything new in the romance department? And I don't mean in your writing. Real life stuff."

Sophie groaned. "You sound like Mom."

The front door creaked open.

"That'll be Harriet." Georgia hurried to the entrance, ever the gracious hostess. "Come on in, you two."

"Where's my favorite twin?" Harriet's voice made Sophie chuckle as she entered the living area. Everyone said they sounded as identical as they looked. Except Harriet always sounded more… in control. Confident. Composed.

"Aunt Sophie." Lucy slammed into her legs before she could reach Harriet.

Sophie crouched down and picked up her four-year-old niece. "You've grown so much since Christmas. Are you taller than your mommy yet?"

Lucy giggled. "No. Not yet. Wanna see my pliés?"

"Sure, sweetie." Sophie set her down and watched a series of ballet moves as she gave Harriet a kiss on the cheek. "Nice work, Lucy."

"It's *so* good to see you." Harriet let out a squeal. "I can hardly believe you're here to stay. Forever."

"I know. It's bizarre." Sophie teared up. Her emotions were all over the place. She wiped her fingers under her eyes before her mascara gave her raccoon vibes. "Ugh. I don't know what's the matter with me."

"Why are you crying, Aunty?" Lucy's huge brown eyes filled with concern.

Sophie forced a laugh. "Don't mind me. I need a nap, that's all."

"I'm too big for naps. Aren't you too big for naps, Aunty?"

Harriet scooped up her daughter and balanced her on one hip. "Aunt Sophie's had a long trip all the way from Paris, remember? How about we set you up with some books and coloring while I have some sister-talk for a while?"

"And then the park?"

"Absolutely. Pinky-promise."

Mother and daughter linked pinkies and then Lucy skipped off and collected a tiny, lilac backpack from the entrance hall before making herself at home in the living room.

"Tea?" Georgia was already getting them set up in the kitchen so they could sit around the table and catch up.

"Yes, please." Harriet dug a juice box and a packet of fruit snacks from her purse and set them on the rug next to Lucy.

"Thanks, Mommy."

"You're welcome, honey." She linked arms with Sophie and they wandered into the kitchen. "So… what have I missed? You know, I'm kind of jealous you two are going to be living here together for a while. I'm going to miss out on all the late-night, deep-and-meaningful conversations, aren't I?"

"You know you're always welcome. You're only five minutes away. As for today, you haven't missed much." Georgia set three steaming mugs on the table and sat on one of the chairs. "I think Sophie was about to share details on her love life…"

"What?" Harriet pulled her twin onto another chair and claimed the remaining one. "Spill."

"You guys…" Sophie's face heated. Her sisters were her best friends. Although they weren't as close as they used to be before Sophie distanced herself three years ago to avoid having to answer questions about Troy. Shame and embarrassment were her companions back then. Life would be different now. Sophie had moved on and knew she could tell them anything, and she would. In time. She bit her lip. She couldn't share about Troy's reappearance yet. They would freak out, for sure. Besides, she'd prefer to at least try to figure this mess out herself…

"I know you said you were making the move to pursue your writing and that your agent was optimistic about the publisher in London, but I had a… feeling." Harriet squinted and placed a hand over Sophie's. "Georgia's going to roll her eyes and say it's our weird twin-thing, but I had a feeling something was off. Maybe you were running *from* something rather than *to* something." She furrowed her brow. "I've been praying for you, in case."

Sophie's pulse sounded in her ears. Why were secrets so hard to keep from her twin? Harriet was suspicious about Troy back when they were dating. She wasn't aware what happened to end the relationship though. She didn't know the ugly truth. Or that he was back in Paris. Sophie cleared her throat and cupped the warm mug in both hands, taking comfort from the aroma of strong English breakfast tea.

"Sophie?" Georgia leaned closer. "*Is* everything all right?"

Sophie glanced from one sister to the other. There would be time to explain about Troy later on. For now, she needed to throw them a bone. They were relentless, and a pivot was in order.

"I sort of met someone. Yesterday. An opera singer." Her cheeks burned. At least she wasn't lying.

"What?" Harriet's mouth dropped open. "Well, that wasn't what I was expecting to hear. This is way better. Although—yesterday?"

"I know, the worst timing." Sophie sipped her tea.

Georgia rubbed her hands together. "An opera singer? Mom will be thrilled. You know you'll have to tell her. First, we need to know everything."

"There's not much to tell. The whole thing was a whirlwind… in fact, it's almost like the start of my novel, which is ridiculous and a tad weird." Sophie's heart stirred as she gave them a play-by-play of her initial meeting over the cake box and then the evening after the opera when she'd felt like his Cinderella. Replaying the details out loud, she realized how much their meeting meant to her. She was a smitten kitten, plain and simple. Until Troy showed up. Seeing his familiar face had almost erased the pure joy she felt in the presence of Miles Morgan. Her ex had ruined her life. Again.

Harriet sighed. "That's so romantic."

"So how did you leave it? Has he called you yet?" Georgia nibbled on a cookie. "Please tell me you guys are going to give this a shot, even if it's long distance."

Sophie narrowed her eyes. "Probably not. I left in a hurry and didn't get his number."

"Why?" Both sisters spoke at the same time.

Think, think.

"Because I knew last night was my last one in Paris and I didn't want to make a goodbye harder than it had to be." She grimaced.

Harriet dug her phone from her jeans pocket. "Not a problem. We can find him if he's an opera singer, can't we? He's bound to have a website or be on social media or something."

Sophie grabbed the phone. "Please, don't. I know it all sounds dreamy—and it was—but I think I need a little time to reorient myself here. Settle in. I don't know where Miles is going to be staying next. He said last night was the final performance in the season, so he could be heading anywhere. Literally."

"But you're into him." Harriet took her phone back and set it on the table. "I know you've always been a skeptic about falling in love at first sight, but I can tell this was special. Promise me you won't write him off? You'll follow up in a few days? What if he's the one?"

Georgia stood. "I say we give the girl a break. Let her at least unpack before we start arranging her marriage." She gave Sophie a wink. "Want to have a nap or come to the park for some fresh air?"

"Park?" Lucy appeared in the doorway, juice box in hand. "Can we go and play now?"

Sophie's head was starting to pound and a nap sounded divine. She only managed a couple of hours of fitful sleep last night after spotting Troy and then not wanting to oversleep and miss the early train. How did that man still have such a hold on her?

"If you don't mind, I'll stick around here and unpack. Maybe have a little rest." She held out her arms and Lucy snuggled in. "How about we play at the park tomorrow?"

"Yes, please." Lucy beamed. "I can bring Bunny."

"You sure can." Harriet led the way to the entrance. "Do you need a hand taking your stuff upstairs, Soph?"

"No, I've got it, thanks. Will I see you guys later?"

"Leo's away with work this weekend so Lucy and I are completely and utterly free. We can order in some Thai from the new place in the village."

Georgia slipped into her jacket. "If I don't have to cook, I'm all for it."

"We'll let our kitchen-friendly sister find her feet before we put her to work." Harriet chuckled in jest.

Sophie balked as her mind darted to her manuscript. She had some serious editing to discuss with her agent. Harriet had no idea… "Umm yes, poor Cinderella over here." She feigned a pout.

"Well, enjoy your nap, Cinders, because your ugly sisters will be back soon enough to crack the whip. Just kidding. Sweet dreams." Georgia waved and the three of them disappeared, giggling and chattering all the way down the front path and onto the narrow country road.

Sophie exhaled and collapsed onto the loveseat in the living room. Unpacking could wait a while. For now, she craved a few minutes of peace and quiet. English countryside style. She closed her eyes and rested her bare feet on the coffee table. The window was open in the kitchen and the sound of chirping birds caused her to let out a deep, gratifying sigh. Spring sunshine streamed through the glass and warmed her face. Yes, this. Peace and quiet.

Her phone beeped a text notification from inside her bag in the entrance. She groaned. Could be important. Sophie forced herself to get up and retrieve the bag and then settled back in her cozy spot on the loveseat.

She checked her texts. A missed message from Mom earlier.

"Hi, sweetheart. Checking to see if you arrived at the cottage safely. Speak soon. Love you. xxx"

Sophie would call her when she had a little more energy and time was reasonable for them both. The eight-hour difference was a pain, but perhaps she'd try her in the evening. *Mom will be delighted to hear I met an opera singer. Even if I never see him again, it'll make her day.*

She would see him again though, wouldn't she? Sophie's fingers took on a life of their own as she Googled his name with the words "opera singer". As if by magic, there he was. Miles Morgan. She stared at his chiseled face—yes, he was movie-star handsome. She hadn't imagined that. His professional headshot showed off those steely-grey eyes she envisioned might change with his mood, and his heartwarming grin that caused her own lips to curve…

She flicked back to her texts to see the other message. An unknown number. Her heart fluttered. Could be Miles. No, she hadn't given him her number. Strange. Only one way to find out.

Oh no, no, no. Surely not.

Sophie read and re-read the text. A lump formed in her throat. She threw her phone onto the other couch as if the device were on fire.

Troy?

Why had she not changed her phone number after their break-up? She'd heard nothing for three years and now… this. She curled into a ball on the loveseat and wept as the message replayed in her head.

"SOPHIE, YOU BETTER KEEP QUIET. YOU KNOW I ALWAYS HAVE THE FINAL WORD…"

Chapter Four

MILES INHALED THE TANTALIZING AROMA OF fresh bread as he approached the delightful little bakery on Rue de la Gare. He would need to pick up a French baguette after he plucked up the courage to ask about Sophie.

He'd been awake for hours last night after his dinner with the cast, but it wasn't the usual course of post-performance adrenaline pumping through his veins that prevented sleep from coming. Nor even the possibility that last night may have been his final major performance. Ever. Rather, he replayed his interaction with Sophie Brooks over and over, hoping he might figure out why she disappeared with a look of terror in her big brown eyes.

An elderly woman clutching a small white box emerged from Pretty Patisserie and held the door open for Miles. He thanked her and ducked inside. He hadn't been to this particular bakery before and the Saturday morning crowd buzzed with activity. He waited in line and took in the ambiance that oozed charm with soft green walls, oversized floral paintings, strains of jazz in the air, and of course, the mouth-watering wafts of chocolate, vanilla, and yeasty bread.

As customers shuffled along and lively chatter filled the space, he wondered if anyone would have time to talk with him about the young woman who worked here up until yesterday. He'd been rather pleased with himself for remembering the bakery name on the cake box from when he first caught sight of the beautiful employee. Would the request sound too creepy if he asked for her address or phone number? She must live locally, but the chances of them giving away her personal details to a complete stranger were slim. He wouldn't blame them.

It's a chance I'm willing to take.

Miles adjusted the collar of his buttoned-down white shirt and pulled his wallet from the pocket of his skinny khaki pants. He'd put in the effort to appear respectable and not some lowlife who'd taken a liking to a gorgeous girl. He was momentarily distracted by the impressive display case boasting extravagant pastries with dainty decorations and names he didn't recognize. Where were the jelly doughnuts? The mere thought was probably sacrilege in this establishment. His sweet tooth was tempted by the offerings set before him.

"Bonjour." A middle-aged woman with light brown hair pulled into a curly bun on top of her head addressed Miles with a no-nonsense nod.

He cleared his throat. He could sing in French, but comprehending the language in regular conversation with the locals was a whole other skillset he didn't yet possess. "Bonjour. Parlez-vous—"

"English? Yes?" Her kind eyes crinkled as she raised one side of her mouth. "Or you may point to what you want, Monsieur."

He nodded. "Awesome." He noticed her name tag. "Thank you, Annabelle." He tapped the glass in front of something resembling a chocolate eclair. "One of those, s'il vous plaît? And…" He recognized the pink macarons he'd tried from the box yesterday. "Two of those… and a French loaf. Thank you. Merci."

She worked with efficiency and Miles knew he had to speak up before she went on to the next customer. Especially as she understood English.

"Umm, I'm also looking for Sophie. Sophie Brooks?"

The older woman's head snapped up. "She no longer works here."

"I know. I realize this sounds strange and maybe a little suspicious, but I only met her yesterday and she had to rush off before I got her phone number." He tried dazzling her with his most charming smile. "Annabelle, I know you don't know me from Adam, but is there any chance you might be able to give me her number? Anything. Please?"

"Adam?" Her face scrunched. "I can't give my sweet Sophie's phone number to any guy who comes in here."

"No, I'm not Adam. I'm Miles. Miles Morgan. I'm a tenor with the opera, and Sophie came to the performance last night and—"

Her eyes widened and she called back into the room behind her. "Suzette." Annabelle bustled toward the cash register and gestured for him to follow. "You are in the opera? *The Magic Flute*, no? So beautiful. So whimsical."

An opera lover? *Thank You, Lord.* Miles chuckled and pulled his credit card from his wallet while Annabelle waxed lyrical about her affection for opera and how *she* had gifted Sophie that very ticket last night.

After paying for his items and autographing one of his business cards for her, Miles's heart soared when Annabelle left the other customers in the hands of young Suzette and pointed for him to stand to the side.

Annabelle pulled her phone from a pocket in her apron. "My dear friend is one of the managers at the opera." She shrugged. "This is why I give them my best cakes. If you want my Sophie's phone number, I'll call him to check you out. No?" Her gaze flitted from Miles's face to his business card in her other hand.

"Of course. I'm fine with that." Miles moved out of the way of other customers and watched Annabelle's animated face as she waved his business card and spoke into the phone in rapid French. Thank goodness the manager picked up.

"Okay, Miles Morgan. My friend says you are a trustworthy man. Saint Miles, no? I'll get Sophie's number for you, and let her decide if she agrees with him."

"Thank you." He expelled the breath he'd been holding. "Thank you so much."

Annabelle scurried into the back room and returned brandishing a small piece of paper, which she presented to Miles.

"You know she moved today, yes?"

"Moved house? Today? No, she didn't mention it. Is she still in Paris?" He took the paper with the phone number scribbled by Annabelle.

Her hands flew to her face. "Non. Non, Monsieur Miles. She has gone to England to be a famous writer."

What? "I guess we didn't get into details." His stomach dropped. "England. I have family there. I was planning on visiting now the opera has finished."

Annabelle clutched his arm. "Do it. Go and find her. You would be so, so beautiful together. I can tell you are a good man." She leaned closer and her voice dropped to a whisper. "Sophie is like a daughter to me, and you cannot break her heart. Please, be gentle with her, oui?" She patted her chest.

Miles swallowed. "I promise, I will be kind and gentle. I'll try my very best to find her. Thank you so much for this." He tucked the paper into his wallet. "This, too." He held up the white paper bag filled with baked goods. "God bless you, Annabelle. I'll call in here again if I'm ever back in Paris."

"Merci." She blew him a kiss. "Give Sophie my love. Be safe."

"I've changed my cell phone number." Sophie held her silver phone in the air as she padded into the kitchen. "I thought it would make sense to have a UK provider and a fresh start as a Brit. I sent you both my new number." She attempted to sound casual and upbeat, but recognized her keenness sounded more like she was overcompensating for something.

Harriet frowned. "You don't waste time, do you? You've only been here a few hours. What's the hurry?"

Sophie focused on pouring herself a glass of water. "Oh, no hurry. I found out I could change my number online, and it was relatively straightforward, so now it's done. One thing checked off my to-do list. I may not be quite as organized as Georgia, but I like to think I'm a close second." She returned the frown. "No offense."

"Ha. None taken. I don't suppose you've actually got a passcode on that thing yet. Heaven forbid you should think about phone security."

Sophie wrinkled her nose. "I like to be able to click and go when I use the voice memo. It's how I roll."

Harriet put her hand to her throat. "Capturing the muse. The life of a writer…"

"Okay, you two, food is on the way." Georgia's sing-song voice interrupted them. "I'll grab plates and napkins if you can get the waters poured. Are we all good with eating in the living room? The kitchen's a bit cozy for the six of us."

"No problem. I'm looking forward to seeing Will and Jack again. It's been… hmm, let me see… four months since I was last here. I'll bet Jack's grown."

Georgia glowed. "I fall for that sweet boy more every day. He's turning into quite the little chatterbox."

"I help him with his chatters." Lucy raised her chin.

"I bet you're a great teacher, Lucy." Sophie slid her phone in her back pocket. "It's too bad Leo's out of the country. Does he go away a lot these days?" She found several more glasses and began filling them.

"Yeah. To be honest, more than I like. We're fine though. Everything's fine." Harriet smiled but she couldn't fool her own twin.

Sophie's chest tightened. The atmosphere surrounding the Duval family had felt off for a while now, even to someone who only visited on occasion. They had always been the perfect pair—Harriet, the beautiful ballerina, and Leo, the devilishly handsome French finance whiz. When Lucy was born they seemed to grow closer and as usual, Sophie watched on with equal measures of joy and jealousy. She tried not to allow comparison to creep in as she lived in her twin's shadow, and writing her latest novel had been cathartic in some small way—but she would have to share its details with Harriet if it was to be published. *I'm going to have to make some changes. I can't do this to her.*

"Hey, Soph, you did remember to send Mom your new phone number, right?" Georgia bumped her with her hip. "You know she'll stress if she can't get hold of you."

"Yes, yes, I went through all my contacts and sent it to anyone who needs to know."

"Your literary agent?" Harriet carried the full glasses to the living room.

"Of course." Sophie would be in touch with her very soon about reaching out to her editor with the possibility of making those manuscript changes.

Georgia put an arm around Sophie's waist. "We're all so proud of you. I know it's not a done deal yet but a publisher liking the full manuscript is a good sign, isn't it?"

"It is. Although I've also learned over the years not to count my chickens before they're hatched." She winked. "See how countrified I am already?"

"When do we get a sneak peek of this fairy-tale inspired novel? I can't wait." Harriet caught Lucy as she trotted into the kitchen and swung her around until she squealed. "We love fairy princesses, don't we?"

"I'm Snow White." Lucy curtsied in front of her aunts. "Because I love animals. Who are you all?"

"I'm definitely Cinderella." Sophie picked up a cloth and scrubbed the granite countertop. Goodness, this was hitting too close to her manuscript.

"And I'm Sleeping Beauty." Georgia gave an exaggerated yawn.

Lucy clapped in delight. "Who are you, Mommy? Are you Beauty because you're beautiful and Daddy can be the Beast because he's…" Her little forehead crinkled, "… a grump."

Everyone was silent for a second too long.

"Silly goose." Harriet ruffled her daughter's hair. "Daddy's not grumpy. Besides, Grumpy belongs in your Snow White story, with a shovel and a pick and a walking stick."

Sophie watched Harriet's smiling face for a chink in her armor. *Something is definitely not right.*

"I think I can hear Will's car." Georgia's face lit up. "Or it could be the guy from the Thai place with the food." She hurried off to check and was followed by Lucy, who'd been asking after little Jack all afternoon.

The twins leaned against the counter side-by-side until

Sophie's phone buzzed in her pocket. She flinched. A text message.

Harriet touched her arm. "Hey, you good? You jumped out of your skin there."

"I'm fine. Tired, that's all."

"You're not going to check to see who's texting you?"

Sophie's stomach clenched. This couldn't be Troy now she'd changed her number. Why had he contacted her earlier? Surely, he knew she would stay quiet about what she saw in the alley. Silence was a learned behavior around him. That awful phrase about having the final word. He would use it when he thought she was being a little too friendly with another male or someone complimented her on anything from her baking to her writing to her shoes. The phrase was code for *be careful or you'll get hurt—by me.*

The last words he said to her before the incident.

The last words he spoke to her before he crossed the line, and then disappeared from her life.

She shook her head and her hair tumbled over her shoulders. "It's fine, I'll check it later."

"Could it be your man?"

"What?" The word came out louder than she intended.

Harriet stepped back. "Hey, sorry, I was only teasing. I'm holding out hope for you and the opera guy."

Sophie sighed and pulled her sister in for a hug. "I'm the one who's sorry. Bit of a nervous wreck at the moment. Can we talk later?"

Voices sounded from the front door.

"Sure. I'm here for you."

"Thanks." Sophie straightened her shoulders. "I don't think it's my opera guy. Like I said, I didn't even get the chance to give him my old number."

"Then it's good we can track *him* down. Don't think I didn't stalk him online already. He's utterly dreamy."

Sophie's jaw dropped but her sister wasn't wrong. Their initial connection was like nothing she'd ever experienced and the thought of never seeing him again was like a stab to her heart.

Although as much as Miles could be the man of her dreams, Troy was her biggest nightmare—and now he was back in her life.

"Let me do this in my own time?" Sophie blinked.

Harriet didn't know how Sophie had been wounded. Physically. Emotionally. Spiritually.

"Of course. Come on, let's join the others."

Thai spices permeated the cottage as Sophie led the way to greet the soon-to-be new male members of the family.

So many males in her life all of a sudden.

Including one who had broken more than her heart.

Troy had broken *her*.

She raised her chin.

I'm not giving him the opportunity to break me again.

Chapter Five

Sophie spotted her favorite park bench and made a beeline for the seat, grateful for a few minutes of alone time with a sumptuous novel to read. Living in Paris, she'd grown accustomed to having her own space in her little apartment, and yesterday was a full-on family day. The evening with Will and Jack adding to the girly mix had been fun, but as an introvert, she needed to recharge.

Georgia gave Sophie a *Mom* look when she said she would give church a miss this morning, but as she inhaled the smell of freshly cut grass and heard the sweet birdsong from wrens and blackbirds in the ancient trees, the guilt slid from her shoulders. She was enjoying God's creation. He would understand. She was still taking baby steps after Troy rocked her once-stable faith life. Would she ever get back to where she was?

Sophie drew in a deep breath, and then released it until her lungs were emptied. Amazing how the simple act of breathing with intention could calm her racing heart and still her spinning mind. The unseasonably warm morning added to her general sense of wellbeing as Sophie lowered herself onto the slatted wooden bench and ran a hand across its familiar smoothness. She had the park to herself for now.

Close enough to walk from Bramble Cottage, this was a popular childhood destination when she and her sisters had stayed with their grandparents while visiting from Canada. She crossed her legs and squinted up into the massive oak tree. *Dad's climbing tree.* Her father had been raised in this sleepy English village before he emigrated to Vancouver as an independent nineteen-year-old seeking adventure. Their mom often joked—with tears in her eyes—that her girls all inherited his sense of wanderlust.

Now we've come full circle. All of us living in Bramble Downs.

What would he say about that? The phone buzzed from her bag and her stomach clenched. Although she hadn't heard anything more from Troy, she still feared he may have some way of tracking her down. She found the phone buried beneath her novel and checked the screen. Another buzz caught her attention.

A text from Annabelle. *Relax, girl.* Sophie leaned back and read her friend's message.

"Bonjour, Sophie—I miss you already!

Thanks for sending your new number. Someone is looking for you, chérie... Call me when you have a chance? Speak soon."

Sophie held her breath. Troy? She clutched the phone and scanned the park. An elderly couple ambled along the gravel path toward the rose garden, hand-in-hand. A young woman dressed in exercise gear jogged past, her long blonde ponytail swaying in the breeze.

I'm fine. I'm in sleepy Bramble Downs. The person Annabelle was talking about could be anyone. Could the mystery person be Miles Morgan? She chewed her thumbnail as the possibility took root. Was he captivated by her as she was by him? There was only one way to find out.

Sophie dialed Annabelle's number and prayed she wasn't too busy to talk. Annabelle usually took Sundays off and left her business in the capable hands of her employees, so she may be in luck.

"Bonjour?"

The comforting French accent was a balm to Sophie's soul. "Hi, Annabelle. I got your text."

"Yes, yes, it is good to hear your voice. I have to tell you. The opera man, the handsome one, Miles Morgan, he came in yesterday."

Sophie clutched the phone tighter. "He did? What did he say?"

"Ah, I can tell you are smiling about this. Yes? He is very charming. I think he is a good man, Sophie. My dear friend from the opera vouched for him. I hope you are happy I gave him your phone number?"

A chuckle burst from Sophie's mouth. "Yes, yes, I'm very happy about that."

"But there is a problem. He has your old phone number because you changed it."

"I did, didn't I?" Sophie groaned. "At least I know he's interested." Harriet's suggestion from yesterday came to mind. "Actually, don't worry about it. I can contact him online through his website. If he still wants to talk to me, I'll give him my new number."

"Bravo. Yes. Let me know how you get on."

"I'll keep you posted. I should let you get on with your Sunday…"

"Umm, there is something else. *Someone* else actually." Annabelle's tone was tender. "That man who broke your heart and then disappeared. Troy. He came to the bakery yesterday afternoon before we closed. I remembered him from… before."

Sophie stood. "Troy? Troy was looking for me?" She paced in front of the bench, nausea rising from the pit of her gut.

"I'm sorry, chérie. I know he is bad news. I didn't trust his eyes back then and I don't trust them now."

"W-what did you tell him?" Sophie's hands shook as she held the phone close to her ear. "I need to know everything."

Annabelle huffed. "I told him nothing. I said you no longer worked at Pretty Patisserie, and if he didn't wish to buy any of my delicious baked goods, he needed to leave."

"Thank you." Sophie sank back onto the bench. "And please, if he comes back in…"

"Do not worry. Only I have your new number and he would need to pry my phone out of my cold, dead fingers to get it from me."

Please, God, don't let it come to that.

"I appreciate the sentiment, Annabelle, really I do, but don't put yourself in danger on my account. I don't know what he's doing back in Paris." *Other than the fact I'm pretty sure I saw him attack a girl the other night.*

"Well, I didn't mention it to you before as I didn't want to upset you, but I did hear he'd returned. I heard through the grapevine about his engagement. Which made me more suspicious why he is asking about you."

"Wait, Troy is engaged? This makes no sense. Do you know any details?" Sophie fiddled with a strand of her long hair. Did she even want to know?

"Yes. After he came in yesterday, I searched him online. Do you know the Clement family? They are old money. Everyone in Paris knows them."

"No, I've never heard of them."

"I have. They are how-you-say *billionaires*? Very, very rich. Troy, he is now engaged to one of the daughters. Camille Clement. They are to be married in three weeks. This is interesting, yes?"

Three weeks? Sophie's skin prickled and she made a mental

note to do some digging into the Clement family later. Did he want to make sure Sophie kept his past quiet if he was about to be in the spotlight? What on earth was he doing with the girl in that alley the other night—presuming it was him—if he was now running in elite circles?

"Sophie? Are you still there?"

"Yes, yes, I'm here. Don't worry about all this. If Troy's about to get married, I'm sure he's got more important things to do than track me down now that I've left Paris. Thank you for looking out for me, though. I miss you."

"I'm always here for you. You will tell me if you get your happily ever after with the opera singer?"

Sophie managed a chuckle. "Yes. Of course. Take care."

"You, too. Stay safe, chérie."

Sophie slid the phone back into her bag and watched a red squirrel at the base of the old oak tree. His beady eyes darted around the park in all directions, his ears twitching like antennae before he darted up the tree and hid among the leafy branches.

I can relate, buddy.

Although running and hiding was not how she'd planned to begin her new life in England.

In his tiny temporary Paris apartment, Miles finished watching the online Sunday service which broadcasted from his home church in New York, and he stretched out on the velvet couch. What now? He didn't mind a little personal space, but he was a people person and missed the community of his friends and family back in the States. A sandwich? Yes, he craved the French loaf he'd picked up yesterday. He selected Vivaldi's *Four Seasons* on his laptop, and soaked in the glorious strains of "Spring" as he plodded into the kitchen area and pulled Havarti cheese and fresh tomatoes from the fridge. Classical music always managed to both ground and energize him.

He found a bread knife in the drawer in his well-appointed kitchen, and pulled the aromatic loaf from its paper bag. *Sophie Brooks.* The bakery reminded him of this mysterious woman. He'd been so optimistic after visiting the place, but either Annabelle gave him a wrong number or Sophie had already changed it with her move to England.

He'd prayed this morning about Sophie. That God would make a way for them to connect if his gut was to be trusted, and whether or not he should pursue her. If it was a no, well he had some big decisions he needed to make. His life was about to change radically, and fear battled with frustration while he waited for answers regarding his future.

Lord, there's so much up in the air right now. I could do with a little good news for a change.

He cut through the crusty bread and realized too late that the knife was sharper than he thought. He winced as blood oozed from his left thumb onto the butcher-block cutting board. "Great. Just great."

He grabbed the roll of paper towels from next to the sink and wrapped a piece around his hand. He'd live.

An email pinged from his laptop on the coffee table. He popped a small ripe tomato in his mouth, and then wandered back to his spot on the couch. He needed a distraction. He didn't do well with blood, especially his own. He sank onto the soft cushion and went to his emails. Something from his website—that was a rarity. Not many people checked out his website. It could be something spammy. He clicked to investigate.

"Hi Miles, it's Sophie Brooks..."

Miles's heart raced, his bleeding thumb forgotten.

"I'm so sorry I had to rush off on Friday night—I've actually moved to England. Yes, I realize how crazy that sounds.

Anyway, my boss from the bakery mentioned you dropped by yesterday, and that she gave you my old phone number. (I changed it as soon as I arrived in England!)

So... if you are interested in talking or maybe meeting up again someday if you happen to be in the UK, my new cell number is below.

Hoping all is well with you,
Fondly—
Sophie."

"Ha." Miles fist pumped the air. *Fondly.* She wasn't avoiding him or blowing him off. She really had changed her number—understandable with her living in a different country now.

What to do first? He checked his thumb. The bleeding had stopped but he needed to wash the cut. He grabbed his phone and added the new number Sophie had given him, then rushed to the kitchen sink where he discarded the paper towel, bandaged his thumb, and prayed.

Lord, I don't even know if she's a Christian, and you know how important that is to me. We didn't exactly get very far in our conversation, but there's something about her, some light in her eyes, and a connection that feels so right. I want to explore the possibility of seeing her again.

Joy filled Miles's chest as the music from his laptop played out Vivaldi's "Summer". Taking a deep breath, he opened the French doors that led onto the narrow Juliet balcony overlooking the city. The sweet smell of spring filled his senses while he dialed and then waited.

"Hello?" Her voice was cautious.

"Sophie? Hi, it's Miles Morgan. From Paris. I got your message on my website."

"Miles? Oh, it's really you."

He detected a chuckle, and his shoulders relaxed. "It's really me."

"Thanks for calling. I spoke with Annabelle at the bakery and she said she'd given you my old number. I—I'm glad you stopped by there to follow up after I left rather abruptly on Friday evening. Sorry about that."

He leaned against the black iron railings and grinned. "No problem. Listen, I know you moved to England—Annabelle told me—but I have an idea. If it's too ridiculous, feel free to say no."

"Okay." Another chuckle. "I may be up for ridiculous."

He rubbed the stubble on his chin. "I was planning on coming to England in a few weeks anyway. I have family there."

"You do?" Was that excitement he detected?

"Uh huh… but I think I can change my plans around and come sooner rather than later."

"Sounds great. How much sooner?"

Miles took courage from the magnificent view before him of one of the most romantic cities in the world. "I was thinking maybe… Tuesday?"

Chapter Six

"Are you sure you don't want me to come with you?" Georgia emerged from the bedroom she used as her dark room, a huge mug of coffee in hand. "I can edit these black and white prints this evening. Will has a nightshift at the hospital, so I won't be seeing him."

Sophie paused at the top of the stairs and checked the contents of her bag. "Honestly, I'll be fine. I'm meeting Miles in a public place and I'm fairly sure he's not an axe murderer."

"I know I'm totally overstepping but you barely know him." Georgia pursed her lips. "And you might get lost."

Sophie let out an exaggerated sigh. "I had a text from Mom last night and she's already given me the stranger-danger lecture. I've got to call her when I arrive at the pub, even though it'll be ridiculously early Vancouver time."

"Since when does Mom get up at the crack of dawn?"

"Since she started worrying about my safety again. I think she's forgotten I lived in Paris on my lonesome for almost a decade and I'm thirty years old." *She'd have a conniption if she knew about my troubles with Troy.*

Georgia sighed. "You'll always be her baby, Soph. You *are* the youngest."

"By five minutes. Good grief, I thought you guys would all be thrilled to bits that I'm actually going on a date."

"We are. Absolutely. We want you to be safe, that's all—and to not get lost. In my car…"

"I promise to take good care of your wheels, and I have the address plugged into my phone." Sophie waved her cell in the air. "The whole point of getting together with Miles is to become better acquainted. Preferably, without my big sister there as a chaperone."

Georgia sipped her coffee. "At least text me when you arrive, and then when you're on the way back home. It's about an hour-and-a-half each way. Please? Also, watch the winding roads. Plus, cows, sheep, and donkeys. Seriously, they have zero road sense."

"I will. Promise. I'll text everyone." Sophie walked over and gave Georgia a hug. "I'll be back well before dark. Thanks again for the loan of your car."

"No problem. I won't need it." She turned to head back into her dark room. "You can fill me in over dinner tonight. Drive safe."

"Will do. Don't work too hard." Sophie trotted down the stairs, tugged on her navy blazer and ankle boots, and opened the front door. Rain. Giant drops splattered on the gravel path and drenched the lawn.

Fantastic. The drowned rat vibe will really impress Miles.

She grabbed an umbrella from a pretty white stand in the entrance, slammed the door behind her, succeeded in opening the umbrella on the third attempt, and then sprinted to Georgia's red Mini, which was parked on the roadside.

With no small amount of effort, she closed the umbrella and settled into the car without getting too wet. How could the weather have been so beautiful and balmy yesterday? This morning was dreary and dull with little promise of a break in the heavy rainclouds overhead... *welcome to Britain.*

Sophie started the engine, input her phone details to sync

with the GPS system so she didn't have to worry about checking her phone, and then figured out where the windshield wipers were.

"Here we go then," she whispered to the empty car. After checking the rear-view mirror, she began the journey to The George Inn, an ancient pub suggested by Miles and given the seal of approval by Harriet. Of course, her twin had been ecstatic to hear she was meeting up with the elusive opera singer but was disappointed he wasn't venturing all the way to Bramble Downs so they could vet him. Miles explained that he had an appointment in the city of Bath later in the afternoon, and so it made sense to find somewhere to meet that was close enough for him to catch a taxi. Apparently, he owned a car—the old sports car he'd talked about—but it was on the south coast somewhere with his family. The details were all rather confusing.

Sophie settled for the comforting swish-swash soundtrack of the wipers on her windshield rather than listen to a podcast or music. She gripped the steering wheel and paid attention to the verbal cues from the GPS as she navigated slippery narrow roads edged in bushy hedgerows. Driving in this weather was not for the fainthearted. Probably a good thing Miles was taking a taxi after an early train from Paris to Bath via London this morning. He was sure to be tired.

Sophie's stomach gave a little flutter at the thought of seeing Miles again, this time for a real date. She'd spent way too much time perusing his website last night and eventually fell asleep listening to his phenomenal voice as he sang familiar operas she'd grown up with. *Imagine ending each day by listening to him singing in real life.* She shook her head to clear such ridiculous thoughts, and attempted to concentrate on the wet road rather than her hot date.

Last night, Harriet raved about The George Inn and assured Sophie the pub was cozy but not too romantic if the vibe was awkward. The food was delicious and there was a roaring fireplace if the weather was chilly. She'd rattled off some facts about the Duke of Monmouth using the inn back in 1685 for something or other. How did she know these things? Harriet was good at everything. Sophie bit the inside of her cheek. She wasn't fourteen years old anymore. The fact that her twin always knew more, did better, looked lovelier, and was generally an all-round shining star shouldn't sting—but the contrast between them rankled. She loved her sister, but sometimes trying to keep up was plain exhausting.

The obnoxious honk of a horn from the car behind stopped Sophie's mind from wandering again, and she joined a roundabout to get onto the dual carriageway. This would be a straightforward section, as long as she stayed in the inside lane and avoided the huge lorries that barreled along like bowling balls down a bowling lane. A tiny red Mini was no match. She concentrated on the road ahead and rotated her tense shoulders. The anticipation of seeing Miles today had woken her way earlier than she'd anticipated. They'd chatted on the phone for almost half an hour on Sunday and the conversation was so… easy.

Since Troy, her dating life had been nonexistent. Oh, she'd been out a few times taking a tentative shot at finding a decent man, but she knew she needed someone gentle who put her at ease after her last experience. Trust was not going to come easy. Hence the meeting in a public place with Miles.

"This is only lunch." Her voice filled the vehicle. The advantage of today's technology was that no one knew if one was talking into a phone or was plain bat-crazy chattering away to oneself. "If you get freaked out, leave. If he's not as genuine as he seems, you don't have to see him ever again. If he makes you feel unsafe…" A shudder snaked all the way up her spine. "If there are any signs at all that he's cruel or angry, then jump back into this car and head home." She lifted her chin, satisfied her pep-talk had calmed the anxiety that niggled her nerves.

Out of nowhere, a massive lorry whizzed by, causing surface water to spray the entire car and drenching the windshield so visibility was minimal.

"What on earth?" Sophie flicked on the wipers full-speed and held the steering wheel in a death grip as her vehicle aquaplaned out of control.

"God, help me. Please'?"

Within seconds, she felt the grip of the wet road beneath her tires again and the muscles in her neck relaxed. Crisis averted. She enjoyed driving in normal circumstances—perhaps because of the novelty factor, not having a car of her own. Getting around in a torrential downpour was going to take some practice.

A white SUV appeared and rode her bumper so close she expected to feel a jolt any second.

Now what?

She glanced in the rear-view mirror. A man in a baseball cap and shades. She looked again. Why did he have sunglasses on today?

"Overtake, for goodness' sake." She scowled and slowed down to give him space to get around her comfortably.

He stayed on her tail.

"What's with everyone this morning?" Sophie gritted her teeth and glimpsed her side mirror to see if he was trying to get away from another vehicle behind him. Nothing. The road appeared deserted behind his SUV. Her wipers squeaked in protest and she noticed the rain had subsided to a drizzle so she flicked them back to a reasonable speed.

The SUV flashed his lights at her.

"What?" She was doing nothing wrong. She checked her speed. Totally acceptable. Did he want her to pull over? He wasn't police or anything, as far as she could tell.

Another flash of his headlights.

Sophie squinted at the upcoming stretch of open road where the lorry faded into the distance. She was approaching a hard shoulder where she could pull over and let him go ahead. She pressed gently on her brakes and he held back a little. She tapped the indicator so he would know she was getting out of his way, whatever his problem was. He indicated, too.

Nope. She didn't want him to pull in and stop behind her, thank you very much. There was no legal reason that dictated she had to communicate with him, right? He was a guy and she was a girl. A couple of cars sped by on the other side of the wide road, but there was minimal traffic on this regular, rainy Tuesday. Something was off.

Her heart hammered in her chest cavity. The hard shoulder was getting closer. Closer. She slowed down and noticed another car was coming along behind them. *Perfect.* Almost to a complete standstill, Sophie waited for SUV guy to tuck in behind her and then gunned it out of the layby in front of the next car. The maneuver was worth the honk she received from that poor, frustrated driver. She now had a vehicle between her and the suspicious SUV, and she was not going to slow down. If the police caught wind of her speeding, all the better. They could pull her over and she would report the unnerving encounter she'd managed to avoid.

The rain stopped, but the sky was still bloated and gray when she pulled off the dual carriageway and returned to winding country roads. Checking behind every minute or so, she seemed to have lost the white SUV. Or he'd given up on her. Had he even pulled out or was he still in that layby? Whatever the reason, she was grateful to be rid of him and pushed all sinister thoughts to the back of her mind. She was here to meet Miles. This was their first official date. The last thing she wanted was to make him believe she was some paranoid mess—especially after her disappearing act last Friday evening.

Sophie's shoulders softened as she drove along the next stretch of road. With nothing ominous following her and a delightful lunch ahead, she marveled at the tree tunnel created by a canopy of branches that grew up on either side of the road, leaned over, and met overhead as if holding hands. A smile played about her lips as she drove over several smooth bumps in the road, her stomach doing gentle flips. The sensation triggered a joyful memory. *Grandad drove us up here when we were kids.* Yes, they visited Bath numerous times, and a young Sophie must have travelled over these bumps and marveled at the trees way back then. The vista appeared to be almost magical and she half-expected fairies to flit from the branches.

A quick check of the time on the digital display showed she was twenty minutes early. Perfect. She'd have a chance to call her mom as promised and have a quick freshen up in the ladies' room before Miles arrived. She slowed down upon entering the tiny village of Norton Saint Philip, according to the road sign. *Wow, this makes Bramble Downs look like a metropolis.*

The narrow main street was flanked with cottages and terraced houses, which opened onto the pavement. An elderly woman in green Wellington boots shook an umbrella out before disappearing inside one of the tiny homes. Other than a postman in rainwear and a fat ginger cat, the village was deserted. When she rounded a corner, two pubs sat on opposite sides of the road and looked as if they had been facing off for centuries. The GPS announced The George Inn was on the left.

Several cars were already in the parking lot and Sophie pulled into an empty spot nearest the door in case the rain returned later on. She waited a few seconds and stared back at the opening to the lot, worried the wretched white SUV might turn up again. Nothing. In fact, no other cars even passed by the inn.

I'm fine. Everything's fine.

Except everything wasn't. She turned off the engine and noticed her trembling hands. She clasped them together and willed them to calm down. Why had that vehicle wanted to pull her over? Was she being totally paranoid—or had trouble followed her from Paris?

Chapter Seven

Once Sophie stopped shaking, the urge to record her worrisome experience on the road made her pick up her phone. She flicked on the voice memo and spewed out a flurry of words.

"Monday April the 29th. I think someone was following me on the drive up to meet Miles Morgan. Still feel nauseous. Vulnerable. Unsafe. My heart was in my throat for a while there… the pelting rain did me no favors. Whoever was in the white SUV—with no number plate on the front—either gave up on me for another day or decided he had better things to do. Troy has resurrected all the fear and pain I thought I'd managed to bury a long time ago and I—I hate him for that…"

Sophie poured out her emotions in short, sharp bursts and recalled as many specific details as she could while everything was still fresh. Even if she was being unnecessarily skittish, this information could all be rehashed and used in a future novel. Although the situation wasn't dissimilar to the storyline in the manuscript the publisher was currently considering… love at first sight and a dangerous ex-boyfriend. Not that she'd really fallen in love at first sight with Miles. Love at first sight was pure fiction. Right? Yet something about that man warmed her heart like a steaming treacle pudding doused with lashings of creamy custard. Her stomach rumbled. Time for that lunch date.

Satisfied her heart-rate was now normal and everything important had been recorded, she sent a quick text to Georgia and then called her mom.

"Sophie, sweetheart."

Sophie forced a little extra lightness into her voice. "Morning, Mom. I've arrived for my lunch date. You can quit worrying and go back to sleep."

"I'm up now with my cappuccino. I'm sorry to fuss, sweetheart, only sometimes I have these unsettled feelings, probably because we're all so far apart. You're new in the country. We don't know much about this opera guy—except Harriet sent me a link to his website." She let out a low whistle. "He's incredibly handsome."

Sophie smirked. "And he can sing."

"I know. I spent ages listening to all the clips I could find. He's fantastic, and still so young to be this well established in his career, from what I could tell. Did I mention he was handsome?"

"Mom." Sophie couldn't help laugh, which felt like a soothing balm after her stressful drive.

"You would make the most beautiful babies. I'm just going to throw it out there…"

"Okay, slow down there, Nanny. I've spent all of ten minutes with the man. If I don't get a wriggle on, I'll be late to meet him on our first real date." She checked her hair in the rear-view mirror.

"You go ahead and have a wonderful lunch. Thanks for calling. Love you."

"I miss you, Mom. Have a great day. Love you, too." Sophie slid her phone into her bag, and stepped outside the car. The air was heavy and damp. A shiver ran through her insides—part fear, part chilly, part excitement—and when she turned back to lock the Mini with her fob, she noticed the glorious view at the end of the parking lot. She paced across the wet gravel and stopped at the edge of a beer garden. The vista was like something from a

Jane Austen book.

There was nothing but rolling hills of emerald green grass divided by rustic stone walls and clumps of trees huddled as if gossiping. A beautiful ancient church was situated in the center with a tower and four pinnacles that rose to the heavens like arms raised in worship. The type of church Sophie wrote about in her fairy tale romances, complete with stained glass windows and a graveyard. At that moment, bells rang out filling the silence and she couldn't resist capturing the ambience on her phone camera. Upon zooming in to video more detail, she realized the little black dots in the churchyard were people. A funeral.

Sophie swallowed and tucked away her phone. Funerals always made her chest ache. Losing her own dad when she was a toddler affected the way she observed loss for other people. She felt their loss, too. Her mom said she was empathetic even as a child.

God, would you comfort them in their pain? Just because she was in a precarious relationship with God these days, her lack of communication didn't mean she couldn't pray for others.

She peered across the perfect patchwork countryside one last time. *I'll show Miles this slice of British beauty after lunch.* Or maybe she'd come back on a sunny day. Now, she had to hustle if she wanted to appear relaxed and calm by the time Miles arrived. Ever the researcher, Sophie read online that there was both a dining room and a more casual bar area inside, and she thought the smaller cozy bar with its fireplace would be perfect. Careful not to slip on the slick ground, she left the stunning yet solemn view behind, located the solid wooden door for the bar entrance, and stepped inside.

"Hi, love. Know where you're going?" A woman around Sophie's age with a sharp, blonde bob walked toward her carrying a tray laden with dirty plates.

"Umm, the washroom?" She peered past her down the narrow hallway. "And the bar?"

"American?" The woman's face broke into a smile.

"Canadian, actually."

"Well, there's a dishy American bloke sitting in the bar on his own and he said he was waiting for someone…"

Sophie winced. "Oh dear. I think he could be waiting for me. He must be early."

"Well, lucky you. He's a keeper." She winked. "The bar's first door on your right, love. If you need the loo, it's a bit out of the way. Down the end, through the courtyard, past the dungeon, and on your right."

The dungeon? She closed her gaping mouth. "Never mind." How could she keep him waiting any longer? "Thanks, I'll go straight to the bar."

The woman scurried off into a side room and Sophie tucked her long hair behind her ears and pressed her lips together, hoping the pretty shade of pale pink would suffice without another application. As she walked through the open door to the intimate bar area, the acrid smell of a lit fire tingled her nostrils. She turned to see flames curling upwards from a bundle of logs inside a large fireplace. Cozy indeed.

"Sophie?"

At a mahogany table for two, Miles scraped his chair back and turned to face her, his full six feet accentuating the low-ceilinged room. He grinned and opened his arms for a hug like it was the most natural thing in the world.

"Hi, Miles." *Here goes nothing.* She walked into his embrace and closed her eyes as a sense of peace and safety enveloped her. She breathed in his woodsy cologne, a musky scent with a hint of smoke that lingered in the air. The letting go of him held a measure of reluctance. He looked good in his blue, buttoned-down Oxford shirt and dark jeans. Really good.

"Please, take a seat." He gestured to the oversized carved wooden chair opposite his, and she settled her bag next to her.

"Miles, I'm so sorry to keep you waiting. Have you been here long?" She shrugged out of her blazer and unwound her silk scarf from her neck.

"Not at all. I was a few minutes early. It didn't take the cab long as traffic was surprisingly light this morning. How was your drive up?"

She took a big sip of water from the glass already in front of her. "Oh, you know. Wet. I'm borrowing my sister's Mini, so it's a bit hairy on the main roads."

His grin faded. "You not a fan of driving? Now I feel awful. I could have met you closer to where you're staying."

"No, no." She waved one hand in protest. "I actually love driving. I'm a sports car fan, remember?"

"I remember." His lips twitched.

"Only I haven't driven this little vehicle before and the rain was particularly crazy today." Sophie shrugged. "To be honest, I've never actually owned a car of my own."

"I get it. Living in a city, there's not much point in having a car, right?"

He was a New York native. Of course, he understood. "Exactly."

"Maybe I can persuade you to take my little lady out for a spin sometime?" He raised his brows, eyes full of mischief.

Sophie chuckled. "What did you say she was again? Porsche?"

"A 1964 Porsche 356. She lives down on the south coast, not

terribly far from your neck of the woods. That's my next port of call after my meeting this afternoon."

"I feel like there's so much I want to know about you, Miles. Opera singer. Sports car enthusiast. British roots. Born in New York. How am I doing?"

He leaned forward, his hands clasped on the table. "I think we have enough overlap in common to understand one another, yet plenty of differences to keep things interesting."

Her insides flooded with warmth. Could this man be any more perfect? "I'm hoping we'll know a lot more after our lunch. Speaking of which, do you know what you'd like to eat? I peeked at their menu online last night and it all sounds delicious. They use locally sourced ingredients, and my sister assured me everything is extra special but not in the least bit pretentious."

Miles picked up a paper menu from the table and studied the list. "I was browsing through this before you came in. Anything you can suggest?"

"Honestly, I'm not a huge lunch person. More breakfast and dinner. I'll admit, my mouth was watering at the beer-battered fish and chips, but I think I'll stick with something lighter instead. Oh, and I definitely need a skinny cappuccino to drink."

He set the menu on the table. "I'm more about big dinners, too. Another thing we have in common. As I'm not singing for a while, I'm going all out on dairy so I'll join you with a cappuccino. Do you feel like maybe sharing the cheese plate or charcuterie?"

"Perfect." Her comfort level with this guy caused her to exhale. She'd known from the start he was easy to like.

"I'll go and order up at the bar then. I'll see which she recommends." He stood and walked over to the other side of the room.

Sophie tried not to stare at his broad shoulders and the way he stood with perfect posture. He looked after himself, that much was evident. She'd read somewhere about classical singers being much like athletes. Made sense. Their bodies needed to be kept in immaculate working order at all times, and the dairy thing wasn't great for singing. She'd read that, too. *I'm full of useless facts.*

A ping sounded from her phone and she weighed up whether or not to ignore the notification. She was expecting to hear from Dorothy, the owner of Brambles and Berries tearoom, where she'd be working part-time. They were supposed to meet tomorrow and iron out the details of what Sophie would be doing and the best hours that worked for them both. She hated when people got distracted with their phones when they were out with her, but Miles was busy talking at the bar. Another ping. Fine.

She delved into her bag and checked the screen of her phone. Two text messages. Yes, the first was from Dorothy saying tomorrow at nine would be great. The second was from an unknown number. Sophie's pulse sped up. The message could be a random marketing thing. Her thumb hovered over the button to check. She'd be wondering the whole time she was with Miles if she didn't put her mind at ease. Just a quick peek.

Her hand shook and she gripped the phone tighter. *How? How did he have her new number?*

She blinked and stared at the message, willing the words to disappear. The truth was there on the screen, loud and clear.

"YOU CAN'T HIDE. I ALWAYS HAVE THE FINAL WORD."

Chapter Eight

MILES STROLLED BACK TO THE TABLE carrying their frothy cappuccinos lightly dusted with cocoa powder. He managed to set both on the scarred table without spilling a drop.

"I hope you like a little cocoa powder." He lowered himself into the ornate chair, feeling for a second like a king-of-olde. "It seemed like a no-brainer."

Sophie's frozen glare unnerved him to the core.

"What is it? You look like you've seen a ghost." Which, in this establishment, seemed like a real possibility. "Sophie?"

Color returned to her face and she stuffed her phone into the bag on the seat beside her. "Nothing. W-what were we talking about before?"

Miles reached a hand across the table and touched her arm. The silkiness of her emerald green blouse did nothing to hide her trembling beneath the fabric. "Hey, did you get bad news? Please say if you need to go."

She shook her head and her long, dark hair fell over her cheeks like a pair of heavy curtains. "I-I." She took a moment. "I'm sorry. The last thing I wanted was for you to think I'm some kind of drama queen who keeps running away." She eyed the door next to them. "I'm not like that and I have no intention of leaving."

She lifted her chin and forced a smile, which looked more like a grimace.

Miles's heart clenched. "It's none of my business. I realize this is our first date but I feel like I know you already. Everyone has stuff to deal with." He shrugged. "That's life, but tell me if there's something I can do to help. Please? Or if I can be a listening ear at the very least."

Sophie took a long sip of her coffee and then set the cup back in her saucer, every movement slow and measured. A small crescent of foam remained on her pink lips and he couldn't help but stare. She noticed, and this time she broke into a genuine smile that reached her eyes. She pulled a paper napkin from beneath her cutlery and dabbed at her mouth.

"You don't have to talk about it though. No pressure. We could chat about… the weather." He tried his coffee and made sure to dab his mouth with a napkin afterwards.

"Please, no. Weather is the favorite topic of conversation for everyone here and it invariably ends in the deepest depression." Sophie leaned her elbows on the table and tented her fingers.

"Then tell me about your move from Paris to England."

"Sure. I can hardly believe this is home for me now. I've been planning it for the past year or so—you should see my spreadsheets with all the pros and cons."

"Really?" He leaned closer. This woman was fascinating. "Can I ask what was on the cons side?"

"That's easy… I adore Paris. I've lived there for eight years and thought it would be my forever home. I was going to be a wildly successful author, bake for fun, and have a perfect family. Clearly, that hasn't panned out as planned." She tucked a strand of hair behind her ear. "Also, I have some great friends there. You met Annabelle, my boss, who pretty much adopted me and taught me all things French baking. I'm part of a wonderful writing group. Up until recently, I had a vibrant community at church, too."

Miles nodded. He'd been on the right track about the faith thing. "Can I ask what happened? If it's not being too forward. With the church, I mean."

Sophie picked up her cup, which she held like a shield in front of her. "I got burned. Not by the actual church—they were and still are a great community of good people. I guess I got burned by a guy, and in turn, by God."

"I'm sorry." Didn't see that coming.

"Ever since, I've been deathly suspicious of men who call themselves Christians and want to date me. I guess I'm the same with the One whom I trusted with my heartfelt prayers in all things love. It may sound crazy but I feel betrayed by God." Her last words spilled out in a strangled whisper.

Miles swallowed. This may not be the best time to tell her he was a Christian, too. "I don't know what to say. I hate that you've been hurt."

"Thanks." She sat back. "But on the bright side, the pros list is a lot more joyful."

A woman with short blonde hair arrived at their table carrying a wooden tray laden with three hunks of local cheeses, an array of fancy crackers, a jar of raspberry and habanero spicy pepper relish, and a bunch of fresh greens. "Cheese plate to share, loves?"

"Thanks." Miles took a small plate from the side of the table and set one in front of each of them. "Let's eat while we talk. Tell me about your pros."

Sophie nodded at the woman, who gave a cheeky wink before leaving, and continued talking while she helped herself to some Stilton. "Yes. Well, my sisters are both living in Bramble Downs now. Georgia's three years older than me and Harriet's my identical twin. I guess I always dreamed we would live together and have children who grow up knowing their cousins."

"You get on well with them both?"

"I do, for the most part. They're amazing."

"I love that." Miles broke a cracker in half. "I'm an only child and always wanted a sibling. The nearest I got to a twin was my imaginary friend, Bob." He winced at his sudden confession.

Her laugh was almost lyrical. "Bob? How adorable. I may have had my moments when I would have preferred an imaginary friend over a twin, but we were especially close as kids. Georgia was a nurturing big sister until she went off to college and did her prodigal daughter thing. I love them both dearly. Although I guess Harriet and I aren't as close as we used to be. I'd like to rectify that. Moving here seems like a step in the right direction."

He finished chewing a cracker before speaking. "How are you two different?"

"Hmm." She dumped some relish onto her plate. "She's a ballerina and I'm a bookworm. She's married, I'm not. She has a beautiful daughter, I don't. Everything she does is effortless, while I work extra hard with little to show for it." She lifted a shoulder. "She's an amazing human. It's just that sometimes, I get tired of living in her shadow, I guess. I'm hoping that living in the same village will help." Sophie met his gaze. "I think that was more like a therapy session. Sorry."

Miles was at a loss for words. Again. He cleared his throat. "I'm no expert and I don't pretend to know the first thing about sibling relationships, but is it possible things aren't quite as perfect and effortless as you perceive in your twin's life?"

Sophie stared into the crackling fireplace beside them and for a moment she appeared lost in thought. "Maybe." She turned back to him. "You're good at this listening thing, aren't you?"

"I'm genuinely interested. I want to know what makes

Sophie Brooks tick, that's all. Also, what freaks her out." He reached over and took her hand this time. "The night at the opera when you jumped into the taxi, I saw fear in your eyes. I noticed the same when I sat down with the coffees a few minutes ago. I'm a good listener but I meant it when I said I'm willing to help in any way I can… if you'll trust me with what's scaring you."

She squeezed his fingers. "It's complicated, but it's my ex. Troy. When we dated, something happened and our relationship ended really badly." She stared at the cheese plate between them and dropped her voice. "Horribly. He went home to the States afterwards and I prayed I would never have to see him again. Then last week, I witnessed a girl being attacked. The guy looked an awful lot like Troy, but it didn't make sense as I thought he wasn't living in Paris."

"Oh, Sophie." No wonder she was freaked out. "What a frightening thing to witness. Did you report it?"

"Of course. I didn't mention Troy's name though. It seemed ridiculous and I thought my mind was playing tricks on me. The alley was dark and I wasn't positive the guy was him. The authorities didn't get back to me for further questioning so I presumed the whole nasty incident was over." She shivered even though the room was toasty warm with the fire blazing next to them. "On Friday night, when we were talking on the Opera steps, I saw him. Troy. Plain as day. He stood on the opposite side of the road. Put one finger over his mouth to *shush* me. I was shocked."

"So you ran." That made sense now. "You ran from him."

"Yeah. I was leaving the country the next morning, and figured if I hurried home and laid low, I would be safe."

Safe? Miles scraped a hand through his hair and sat back in the throne-chair. "This is disturbing. Has he been in touch since?"

She eyed her bag.

"Did he call you?"

Sophie's shoulders sank. She explained why she changed her cell phone number with such haste, and then relayed the text she just received from an unknown number with its familiar message.

"What's the deal with him having *the final word*?"

Her eyes misted over. "When we were together, he was super jealous. Possessive. When he thought I had encouraged any attention from another man or he didn't like the way a guy looked at me or pretty much anything at all, he'd grab my arm until it bruised and then he'd whisper how he would always have the final word in our relationship because I was… *his*." She wiped at a stray tear. "I know how pathetic this sounds, but he wasn't always like that. He was a solid *Christian guy*. Charming. Caring. Attentive. Until things went horribly wrong."

As soft jazz music played in the background, Miles clenched his free hand into a fist. If there was one thing that riled him up, it was violence toward women or children. He had his reasons.

Lord, show me how I can help her.

Guilt washed over him as he wrestled with his thoughts. Should he tell her he was a man of faith now? Maybe this wasn't the time.

Later, Lord. I'll tell her later.

Sophie took a tissue from her bag and wiped another tear from her cheek. "I'm not usually this emotional. Maybe it's allergies." She attempted a small smile.

"Right, those allergies." Miles drained the last of his cappuccino. "Are you worried he may have followed you over here to the UK? Or do you think he's pestering you from Paris or the States or wherever he is."

"According to Annabelle at the bakery, he may have good reason to cover his tracks and tidy up his dirty past. For all I know, there could be other women out there that he's hurt." She rubbed at her left arm and a scowl formed on her face. "Apparently, he's marrying into some super-wealthy French family in three weeks."

What was wrong with her arm? "Three weeks? Are you fearful for your own safety now? Here in England, I mean." His late uncle had been pretty high up in the police force in the south of England. Aunt Joyce would be willing to pass on any contacts if he asked her.

Sophie fidgeted in her chair and stared past him toward the street. "I don't know. It could have been nothing, but today there was some jerk in a white SUV who tried to get me to stop on my way here."

"What?" Miles knocked his teaspoon to the wooden floor and she jumped at the clang. "Are you serious?" Why was she only mentioning this now?

"The incident could have been unrelated. It was hard to tell as the guy wore a baseball cap with shades—even though it was raining."

"Weird." His voice croaked and he cleared his throat.

"I know. That's what I thought. Although he didn't come after me when I left him in the dust, so it could have been a regular sleaze and not my ex. Lucky me."

Miles stretched his aching neck from side to side. "I feel bad that I asked you to come all the way here because of my appointment. You have to drive back again in this rain, too. I'm so sorry. I should've been patient and arranged to meet you tomorrow or later in the week."

"Not at all." She twirled a section of hair around her fingers. "I was anxious to get together today. You may not have noticed, but I didn't need much persuading."

He leaned closer. "I did notice." His heart rate kicked up a notch.

"You did?"

The blonde woman reappeared beside them. "Anything else I can get for you, loves?" She batted her extra-long eyelashes at him and gathered their cups and saucers. They hadn't made much of a dent in the cheese plate but their heavy conversation had taken center stage and food seemed trivial.

"I'm fine, thanks." Sophie nodded toward the window. "I'm wondering if I should start back home soon. The rain's hammering down out there and I want to take my time."

"It's going to storm." Blondie shook her head. "Thunder and lightning and everything, apparently. A bit much even for our spring showers." She turned to Miles. "How about you, love?"

"The bill would be great, thanks."

"Follow me to the bar? We'll sort you out over there." She sashayed away and Sophie chuckled.

"I think you might have a fan. Imagine if she heard you sing." She slipped into her blazer. "I'm going to use the washroom real quick. It's past the dungeon, but I'm sure it's not as ominous as it sounds. Meet you at the entrance?"

Miles stood. "Dungeon? Be careful." He winked and let her pass before making his way to the bar. While he waited for his receipt and the two servers chattered about the storm, he took several deep breaths and rotated his neck. His appointment couldn't come soon enough. Hopefully, he was masking his current pain in front of Sophie with as much conviction as he did on stage.

Sophie managed to navigate her way to the washroom and back

again by way of a tiny open courtyard, without getting too wet. The rain was coming down in sheets now. Raining cats and dogs, as her late grandparents would always say. The thought of driving Georgia's small car on unfamiliar wet roads with thunder booming and lightning striking the surrounding countryside was less than appealing. *Should I wait it out?* She hurried along the corridor filled with lingering smells of gravy and sausages.

"Hey." Miles glanced up from his phone as he leaned against the stone wall of the hallway near the entrance door. "Checking my weather app. It seems our server was pretty accurate about the storm warning."

"Great." Sophie slowed her steps until she stood in front of him. He was almost a foot taller than her, even with mid-sized heels on her boots. She looked up into his gorgeous gray eyes. "I was wondering if I should hang out here for the afternoon. Worst case scenario, I could stay in one of their rooms and head back home first thing tomorrow."

A crease appeared between his brows. "I'm not leaving you here stranded." He slid his phone into his jeans pocket. "I'm no weather expert, but I've been in England enough times to know it can stay socked in like this all day if it chooses to. My appointment is at four but—"

"I'll be fine. You should call your taxi and I'll give Georgia a shout and see what she thinks. It's her car. I don't mind grabbing another coffee and waiting for a few hours if necessary. I have a book in the vehicle." She flicked her hair. "I always come prepared."

Miles ran his fingers over his stubbly chin. "I don't like it. Especially after what you just told me about potential danger." His face was paler than before. He seemed to be taking this harder than she was.

Sophie stood tall. "I'm perfectly capable of looking after myself. This is a cute pub in the middle of nowhere with a bunch of friendly locals."

He took both her hands in his. "Stubborn, aren't you?"

"Strong. When I want to be. Thanks for lunch, by the way."

He squeezed one hand and then the other. "You're welcome. So, how about we compromise? Bath is literally fifteen minutes away. I can be back here by 5:30PM at the latest. If you're still here, you either let me drive you home, or I'll be the silent passenger if you prefer to drive, or we'll taxi back to Bath. I can check to see if my hotel has a free room."

Sophie tucked her chin. "This is rather forward for a first date, don't you think?"

His cheeks reddened and he released her hands. "No. No, that's not what I meant. Oh, my word. Please…"

Sophie laughed. "I'm teasing, Miles. I believe you're a perfect gentleman. If I didn't know better, I'd accuse you of being a solid Christian guy. I've had my fill of those, thank you. A perfect gentleman is a better fit."

Miles joined in her laughter, but he wasn't convincing. The light in his eyes had dimmed. Had she insulted him? She reached up and touched his warm cheek. "I'm kidding. I like your plan. Let's make our calls. I'll run out quick and grab my book so I can hunker down here for a while." This was turning out to be quite the adventure. She opened the door and spotted the red Mini. The car was close enough, yet she'd get drenched running over there without an umbrella, which she left in the car. *Brilliant.*

Miles rubbed her arm. "Stay here and I'll get it. I'm going to get wet going to my appointment anyway and there's no point in us both catching cold. Can you unlock it from here?"

This man was a catch. "Sure. Thanks. The book is on the

front passenger seat." She dug in her bag and pressed the key fob. The beep sounded and Miles pulled the collar of his jacket up and sprinted across the gravel. Rain bounced up from the ground and Sophie cringed as she watched him getting more soaked by the second. He made quick work of getting into the car and stuffed her book beneath his jacket. He stopped for an extra beat and jogged around the circumference of the car before running back.

Strange. What is he doing?

Sophie stood back and gave him space to come inside. "You're an angel. Thanks so much. Is everything all right?"

Miles stomped his shoes on the doormat and retrieved her protected book. "You're welcome, and at least your book is dry." He shook his head and droplets of water dispersed in every direction.

How did this man manage to look fantastic soaking wet? Sophie forced her mind not to wander…

"But I'm afraid I have bad news." His eyes narrowed. "You're not going anywhere this afternoon."

Sophie blinked, her focus recovered. "What do you mean?"

Miles put an arm around her and led her back toward the bar. "I'm so sorry. I don't know what's going on, but it appears someone has punctured both your front tires."

Chapter Nine

"GEORGIA, YOU'RE NOT GOING TO BELIEVE this." Sophie flopped onto her hotel bed, put her phone on speaker mode, and covered her face with her hands. A headache was brewing.

"Sophie? What's happening? I got your text but it was very cryptic. Where are you?" Georgia's voice quivered. She'd had more than her own fair share of drama last year. Sophie had to downplay this as much as possible.

"Don't freak out. I'm at a lovely little hotel in Bath."

"What?"

"It's a long story but I'm perfectly fine. I was worried about driving home in the storm."

"No kidding. It's horrific out there. So, you're staying overnight? In Bath?" The creak of the staircase indicated she was walking to the living room. "Wait, you're with Miles. Should I be… concerned?"

Sophie sat up and kicked off her boots. "No. For goodness' sake, I'm a grown woman and old enough to make smart choices, if that's what you're inferring. Besides, Miles is a perfect gentleman. He made it very clear to the hotel receptionist that we didn't need adjoining rooms." She smiled at the memory of him blushing. "I think you're going to like him, you know."

"Ah, lunch went well, I take it. That's good news, at least."

"Yeah." Other than discovering someone attacked the Mini's tires. "I ended up doing most of the talking though because Miles is such a great listener."

"That's refreshing. Tell me more."

"Not much to tell yet. I'm hoping to dig for details about him this evening at dinner. He had the appointment here in Bath, so I'm waiting for him to swing by for me once he's finished. There's a little Italian place next door to the hotel, so we won't even have to get wet."

The sound of water gushed from a tap on Georgia's end. "Will you drive home in the morning then? The forecast says it's supposed to clear up. Although weren't you meeting with Dorothy tomorrow at the tearoom?"

"I've already texted her and changed to Thursday, so that's not the problem."

"Sounds reasonable. So, what *is* the problem? I'm working from home again tomorrow. No need to stress about me having the car."

Sophie winced. "Yes, about the Mini."

"So-phie?" Georgia drew out both syllables.

"There are two flat tires. I'm really sorry. I already called a guy who's heading out there first thing in the morning. I'll pay if you don't have the coverage—"

"Two flat tires? How on earth? Did it happen while you were driving? That would have been so scary. You could have been killed…"

"No, I didn't notice it until later. Actually, I think someone did it in the parking lot at the inn while I was having lunch with Miles."

Georgia let out a gasp. "On purpose? You could have had an accident if you'd tried to drive home. Or been stranded on the road in the storm. Wait, is there any chance someone was targeting your guy if he's some famous singer?" Her words tumbled out in a torrent.

"Miles? No." Should she tell her about Troy now? Maybe the news could wait until she was home and could explain face-to-face. "I don't think so. It could have been a prank or some bored local kids. For the record, Miles is not exactly Pavarotti-famous, and I'm fairly sure regular opera singers don't get harassed like that."

"Promise me you'll do some investigation over dinner tonight and find out some background info on this guy?" The kettle whistled in the background. "I don't like the idea of you being stranded there with him one bit."

Sophie groaned. "I don't want you thinking badly about Miles. The truth is…" Her mouth went dry.

"Soph? Hello? What's the truth?" Georgia's tone was tender and Sophie could picture her kind brown eyes round with concern.

"Well, the truth is I'm not entirely sure what's going on, but I don't think Miles is at fault." Her skin prickled at the memory of Troy, and she peered across the room to make sure she'd locked the door. "I'll explain everything when I see you. I'm safe here with Miles. He said he'd travel with me tomorrow as he's on his way to the south coast anyway. He's a good guy, Georgia. You can meet him. See for yourself. Give him a big sister grilling."

Silence stretched out for several beats until Georgia sighed into her phone. "I know you already have Mom nagging you about checking in, but will you text me when you set off tomorrow? I don't care about my car, but I do care about you. I guess I feel responsible for you now that you're here. Harriet and I have been so excited to have you in Bramble Downs."

"Where you can keep an eye on me?" Sophie pouted.

"No. I mean where it's nice and safe."

Sophie let out a joyless laugh. "Umm, do I need to point out how deathly dangerous Bramble Downs was for you when you first arrived?"

"Fair point. That's history now. We've been worried about you. You… you haven't seemed yourself in ages."

Sophie bit her bottom lip. Did she think she could hide everything from her own sisters? Maybe from a distance, but now things would be different. "Thanks for caring, I appreciate it, I really do. We'll talk about it. Okay? I'll text you in the morning. Have a good night."

"You, too. Stay safe."

Sophie walked over to the curtains and shut out the dark and gloomy evening. If only she could shut out the dark and gloomy memories stirred up by Troy Sanders.

With no change of clothes and only the emergency travel kit of basic toiletries provided by the hotel, Sophie made her best efforts to freshen up, grateful she at least had lipstick and a comb in her bag. She inspected her reflection in the full-length mirror, somewhat amazed she'd managed to keep her white skinny jeans clean all day thus far. She stepped into her boots, pulled her blazer back over the green silk blouse, and decided to leave her scarf in the room, as they were only going next door to the restaurant.

A quick rummage in the side pocket of her leather bag, and she found a random sample of perfume she'd been given on her way through a Paris department store. Perfect. Two spritzes and then a knock sounded on her door.

She checked the peephole. Miles.

Sophie slid her bag over one shoulder, grabbed the plastic key card, and opened the door wide. "Hi." Was he ever a sight for sore eyes?

"Hi, there. You look lovely." His grin radiated everything that was good and kind. "Are you ready to go?"

"Yes, and I'm craving Italian food like you wouldn't believe."

"Great. Me, too." He made sure her door closed properly behind them. "Mmm. You smell nice." Miles sniffed the air.

"Thanks. A lucky perfume sample I discovered in my purse." Sophie hit the button on the elevator and stood next to him while they watched the numbers on the display ascend.

Miles cleared his throat. "Sorry my appointment took longer than I'd hoped. The traffic was the pits. Maybe everyone's driving a bit slower—which is not a bad thing." His voice sounded softer than earlier. Perhaps he'd been singing.

"No problem at all. I quite enjoyed a little reading time in my room. I filled my sister, Georgia, in on the situation, too… I've got some explaining to do when I see her."

They entered the empty elevator and descended to the lobby.

"About her car?"

"About my ex."

The doors opened and Miles followed Sophie across the marble lobby floor. "I see."

They stood together under the overhang and watched the never-ending downpour ricochet off the road before them.

"Shall we make a run for it?" Miles pointed to the left. "It's literally ten steps in that direction."

"I'm right behind you." Sophie pulled up her collar and stayed close to Miles as they dodged another couple walking along with a huge umbrella.

Miles held the restaurant door open and Sophie darted inside.

She stamped her wet boots on the doormat and chuckled.

"I'm glad we didn't have to venture any farther." Would this rain ever stop? The restaurant was almost empty. "I guess the good news is the lousy weather means we get a table without booking."

"True. Every cloud…"

The young hostess approached them with a warm welcome and Miles put a hand on Sophie's lower back as they were shown to an available spot by the window. The table-for-two was covered in a white linen tablecloth and a red candle flickered in the center.

"Perfect." Sophie shrugged out of her blazer and glanced through the rain-splattered window next to them. "What a day this turned out to be."

"Crazy." Miles had changed into a black V-neck sweater that looked oh-so-soft to the touch, and it was all Sophie could do to not reach over and check if the wool was cashmere or merino. His eyes sparkled in the glow of the candlelight, and he winked as he caught her staring.

Flustered, Sophie studied the list of food in front of her as her stomach rumbled. Earlier, thoughts of Troy dampened her appetite, and she'd worried she wouldn't be able to manage a meal. Now, here in this cute and cozy restaurant on a rainy evening with Miles Morgan for company, she was ravenous. "This all seems so delicious. What do you think you'll have?"

A server nodded at them both and filled their water glasses. "Would anyone like wine this evening?"

Sophie realized she didn't even know if Miles drank wine. What *did* she know about him?

"Not for me, thanks." He gestured to Sophie. "But please, go ahead."

"I'll pass, thanks. Water is great."

The server moved on and left them to peruse the menus.

"So, did the appointment go well?" Sophie decided to start digging. She couldn't quite put her finger on it, but Miles seemed a tad distracted. Although the fact that she could have someone stalking her—namely Troy—would be enough to distract anyone. Miles didn't even know the half of what her ex was capable of...

He looked up from his menu. "Not bad. Could have been better and could have been worse." He shrugged. "I've got some decisions to make with my career. Things have come to a bit of a head, you could say. Most of it's out of my hands." Something in his eyes—pain or maybe fear—flashed for the briefest of seconds before he blinked it away. "It's nothing to put me off my dinner though. For now, I hear the lasagna calling my name." A wide grin split his face. "I think Italian food might be my favorite. You?"

"Well, Italian comes a close second after French cuisine, of course," she batted her lashes, "and I think I'll go for the butternut squash ravioli."

The server took the cue and came back for their orders. Sophie resumed her interrogation.

"Although you know quite a chunk about me, my family, my issues, and my insecurities already—do you realize I know next to nothing about you? How did you manage that?"

A smirk. "I didn't like to interrupt..."

She gasped and set her hands on her hips. "The cheek of the man."

His booming laughter made her insides warm. "You know I was joking. I guess I do enjoy listening to others. In my business, there are few who listen and many who like the sound of their own voice, or so it seems. I find people's lives fascinating. We're all so uniquely created."

Interesting. "So, why singing? I mean, when did you know

you wanted to do it as a career?"

Miles leaned back in his chair and gazed through the window as if searching for an answer. "I think I always knew it was what I was supposed to do. I come from a musical family. My mom's a music teacher. Elementary school. She had lofty dreams of being a professional pianist once upon a time, but got pregnant with me as soon as she married my dad and decided teaching was a better fit." A hint of sorrow turned his irises a darker shade of gray. "I think she's always regretted it, though she never actually said so."

"How sad. Is she from England originally? I know you said you have family here, and I couldn't place your accent if I tried."

"She is. Although she only has one sister here now, my Aunt Joyce. She lives in Poole, down on the south coast. That's who I'm going to stay with for a while. My aunt is like my second mom." A muscle in his cheek twitched and he paused for several seconds.

There was clearly more to be said about his mother, but Sophie had no intention of rushing him. "Aunt Joyce sounds lovely."

"She's a lot of fun. I'm closer to her than anyone else in my family, to be quite honest. My uncle was an amazing guy, too. He died maybe five years ago now. He's the one who left me the sports car."

"Wow." Curious. "Well, I'm glad you have Aunt Joyce in your life." She sipped her water. "And your dad?"

The server placed a small basket of bread on the table, its yeasty freshness promising warm, scrumptious carbs.

Miles let out a long sigh. "We have a complicated relationship. He's always lived in New York. Finance world. Disappointed that I didn't follow in his footsteps."

"Really?" Sophie tilted her head. "He wasn't keen on you going into music then?"

"You could say that. Cut me off financially and emotionally when I insisted on pursuing singing as a career."

Brutal. "Ouch. I guess that goes to show how badly you wanted it, though. You pursued it anyway." Sophie offered him the bread. "How did your mom feel about you choosing music?"

Miles took a slice, which he then set on his plate. "She was elated that I was strong and determined enough to follow my passion. Unfortunately, it was the nail in the coffin of their marriage."

"Miles, I'm so sorry. They aren't together then?" Sophie swallowed. Finding out about each other's lives was both delightful and devastating.

Miles shook his head and inspected his plate as if the bread were some fascinating object he'd never seen before. "Dad and I have a strained relationship. I try to reach out when I can, but he's... difficult. Looking back, he and Mom had trouble for as long as I can remember. I know now that Mom always wore long sleeves, even in summer, to cover her bruises."

Sophie's mouth went dry. This was sounding horribly familiar.

"She always said it was because she didn't like her arms, and I never questioned it. She'd sometimes take me, and we'd go and stay with her best friend for a few days while Dad had a 'busy time' with work. He drank when he was stressed. Never let it affect his business, though." He ran a hand through his wavy hair, still a little damp from the rain. "Anyway, I ended up studying in Canada because it was way cheaper than the States."

Sophie's heart ached. No wonder he was keen to make sure she was safe from Troy. He didn't know the details, but he must suspect her ex was abusive. "What about your mom? Did she stay in New York?"

"She did. They got divorced as soon as I left for college, but she loved her job and had good friends, so got a nice apartment and stayed in the city. She never reported Dad for his abuse, and as far as I know, only her closest friends have any idea it went on all those years."

"Your poor mom." Sophie rubbed her arm, memories of her own threatening to resurface. "She never considered coming back to England?"

"I think she was always too ashamed to come back. She knew I was close to my aunt and uncle and was happy to let them be my parent-figures for the most part. I see her occasionally, whenever I'm in New York. We always have a good time together and she's fine now Dad isn't in her life anymore."

Sophie reached across the table and squeezed his hand. "I didn't mean to pry. I'm sorry it's still hard for you all."

He looked up and sighed. "No family is perfect. I imagine you approve that I ended up doing a stint in Canada."

She shrugged a shoulder. "I knew there was something I liked about you. Canada clearly rubbed off. Whereabouts did you study?"

They paused while their plates of steaming pasta were served. The aromatic smell of garlic wafted between them.

Sophie inhaled deeply. "Now this reminds me of Paris."

"Ah, garlic. You either love it or hate it. I'm a fan, and I'm guessing you are, too."

"Love it. What were you saying about Canada?"

Miles nodded. "Right. I was in Toronto. It was an amazing experience. Changed my life..." He shook out his linen napkin and placed it on his lap. Took a sip of water. Touched his fork.

Winced. Put his hands in his lap. Peered out the window.

What was going on in this man's head? Sophie squinted. "Are you okay?" He was beyond awkward, and she couldn't figure out what had changed between them all of a sudden.

Miles dipped his chin. "I'm sorry."

"What is it?" Was he breaking up with her before they'd even started anything? "Is it about Canada? Was I being too nosey?"

"Not at all." He folded his arms and met her gaze. "I can't pretend to be someone I'm not. Even if it means you want nothing more to do with me."

Sophie's stomach knotted. *What on earth?* "O-kay. Could you let me decide?"

"Of course. The thing is, Sophie… I'm a Christian."

Chapter Ten

Miles cringed. He'd spoken his confession so quietly, he wasn't sure if Sophie heard. *Since when have I been ashamed of my faith?*

"I'm sorry, did you say you're a *Christian*?" Her eyes mirrored the round plate before her. "Not like a murderer or cheat or thief or anything?"

"Definitely none of those. No."

"Well, that's a relief." She exhaled. "You had me worried for a minute there."

Miles fidgeted in his chair. "The thing is, talking about Toronto reminded me of when I became a Christian in university. It was such an awesome time in my life. Usually, I say grace before I eat dinner, and then suddenly I felt self-conscious because I told God I wasn't going to mention my faith to you for a while… after what you said about what happened before with…Troy and God and all."

Sophie reached across the table and squeezed his hand. "Miles, whatever are you rambling about?"

He bit the inside of his cheek. "Do you mind if I pray a sec? I'm really, really hungry."

She giggled. "Knock yourself out."

Miles clasped her hand a little tighter. "Thanks, God, for this delicious food, and for this lovely lady. Keep her safe and watch over us, I pray. Amen."

He released her hand and cut into his lasagna "Was I being

ridiculous? I mean, are you completely turned off now you know I'm a man of faith?" He chanced a glance at her face to gauge her reaction.

She stared back with a glint in her eye. "No. I kind of had my suspicions, I'm not gonna lie."

"You did?"

"There's something about you. Even to people who don't believe in God, they must see you have a special peace and a joy that radiates from your killer smile."

He couldn't help but break into a *killer smile* at that compliment. "Thanks." His shoulders relaxed. So, this woman wasn't leaving anytime soon. "My faith is important to me. God got me through some rough patches over the years."

Sophie picked up a fork and stabbed her ravioli in the puddle of creamy sauce. "I have my issues with God. I shared a bit with you already."

"The feeling of betrayal?"

"Yeah. Betrayed by the man I thought loved me as much as I loved him and betrayed by my Heavenly Father to whom I'd prayed and prayed for a partner. I trusted Troy to treat me with kindness, respect, and selflessness, and I'd trusted God to protect my heart."

Miles shook his head. "I don't know what to say. I have friends who have been upset or derailed by the church. Some found their way back. Others are still floundering. I don't want to give you platitudes, I know that much."

"I appreciate that. Don't get me wrong, I still went to church for the social aspect after Troy and I finished, but my personal relationship with God shifted. I was having trust issues with pretty much everyone, Him included."

"I think I understand that better now. The trusting God

thing." Better than Sophie knew, in fact. Trusting God with his questionable future yet again was proving to be more of a challenge than he had ever imagined.

"I don't know how to explain it well. It's as if I created an outer shell for myself, like…" Sophie studied the ceiling for a moment, "like the solid, caramelized sugar crust on a creme brûlée."

"Cream brûlée is one of my favorites."

"Perhaps I'll make one for you sometime."

"That would be awesome. Do you think… do you think your *shell* will ever get cracked open?" He held his breath waiting for her to answer. They were going deep. He needed her to know she could trust him.

She took a few seconds to answer. "Maybe eventually. For now, it's protecting my heart."

"I get it."

"But I still love God and eventually I'll find my way back to where I used to be, I'm sure of it. Hopefully, an even better place. I have some work to do. I know that."

"You have no idea how happy that makes me. I always said I'd need to find someone who shared my faith, you know, when it was time to settle down and think about marriage." Did he just say the marriage word on their first date?

"Marriage, hey? My, you are forward." She raised a brow.

"Oh, man." His cheeks burned. "I can't believe I said that out loud. Put it down to me needing food. Hypoglycemic or something." He spoke around his first forkful of lasagna, which was every bit as delicious as it looked. "This is amazing, by the way." The rich Bolognese combined with fresh pasta and excess of oozing cheese melted in his mouth, but it was nothing compared to the comfort he felt in hearing she wasn't washing her hands of him. Or God.

"Italian food always hits the spot when you're super hungry." Sophie bit into a pillow of pasta and closed her eyes. "This. Is. Incredible."

Miles watched her open her eyes and rejoin real life. She loved food. Of course, she did—she was a baker. He nodded at her plate. "I'm glad you like it."

Sophie sank her fork into the next piece. "It's phenomenal. I'm going to remember this place when I'm next in Bath."

"Did you decide what time you want to head home tomorrow? My schedule is wide open." He munched on a thick slice of warm bread infused with garlic butter. At this rate, garlic would be seeping from his pores. Good thing she was partaking too, because he might have to kiss her this evening. Now where did that thought come from? Heat flooded into his cheeks for the second time in minutes.

"Mmm." She wiped her mouth with a cloth napkin. "I was thinking maybe lunchtime? That gives the tire guy a chance to get the Mini up and running, plus I'll be able to hit a couple of my favorite bookstores."

"I've heard Bath is a literary city, but I've never hung around long enough to explore. Have you spent much time here?"

"I try to visit when I can talk one of my sisters into coming for a shopping day. They usually leave me to do the bookstore tour while they hit the bougie boutiques and cute shops. Then we always meet up for Sally Lunn's buns." She tore a piece of bread and held it in the air. "There are certain food traditions that should not be messed with."

Miles nodded and swallowed. "I agree. Like being on the streets of New York and grabbing a slice of pizza or a hot dog with all the fixings."

"Exactly. Do you miss living in New York? I have to say, you don't have much of an accent."

"It was a fun city to live in and I miss my parents in spite of the past—I do have some sweet childhood memories, for sure. I miss some of the friends I grew up with, too, but give me the quiet suburbs any day of the week. My work takes me to major cities mostly, so I find myself craving the serenity of the countryside these days."

"Fair enough. I'll admit I enjoy both, but now I'm giving the countryside a whirl and I'm excited about this new adventure."

"I love that." He devoured another mouthful of lasagna and continued. "As for my accent, my mom never fully lost her English one, so it kinda rubbed off on me, and then she sent me to elocution lessons when I was little." He cringed at the memory. "I hated them at the time, but I think it helped with diction and my singing later on. Some say I have a generic American accent, but it depends where I am and who I'm talking to."

"Cool. Well, you're talking to a Canadian who lived in Paris and now is in England, so we make quite the pair."

They both looked up at the same time and her cheeks glowed the prettiest shade of pink.

Miles nodded. "We do, don't we?" What had Annabelle said in the Parisian bakery? Something like they would be so, so beautiful together. He'd tucked that little nugget away and now he had to disguise a grin as the words replayed in his mind.

They finished their main course, and then over a shared tiramisu, discovered a little more about their respective childhoods. Sophie shared how she lost her father in a house fire when she was only two years old. How her mom said goodbye to each of her girls as they all ended up far from their home in Vancouver. He still didn't know much about her writing, but there would be time for that. Conversation with Sophie was like plucking velvet petals from an exquisite rose and required the utmost care and attention.

Back in the lobby of their hotel, Sophie shook off a coating of raindrops from their brief sprint from the restaurant. "Do you fancy doing a quick bookstore hop with me in the morning?" She stomped her boots on the mat. "No pressure if it's not your jam." She led the way to the elevator.

How could he possibly say no to spending more time with this woman? "For sure. What time shall I come and knock on your door?"

"Nine? We can find some breakfast en-route." She pressed the elevator button to the second floor and folded her arms across her chest. "By the way, I'm not usually this... I want to say *confident,* but I think I mean *bossy.*"

The doors swooshed open and they stepped inside. Miles stood next to her, his arm brushing hers as some generic big band tune filled the space. "Not bossy. I can see there are certain things that bring you to life. Books. Food. Paris."

"Don't get me started on writing..."

"I'm waiting until you're ready to tell me all about it. I'm intrigued."

"By me?"

He looked down and her cheeks blushed again. "Yes, you." His heart skipped a beat.

The doors opened and they strolled down the deserted carpeted hallway in silence until they reached their adjacent rooms.

"This is me." Sophie pulled her plastic key card from her jacket pocket. "Miles, I'm sorry about the trouble with my ex and the tires and everything, although I'm not sorry I got to spend more time with you today as a result. I…I…" She studied her boots. "I feel inexplicably at peace when I'm with you… like I've known you forever. I don't want to… mess things up…"

"Hey." He lifted her chin and stared into her eyes that were like deep pools of melted chocolate. "I feel the same way about you. I know we're still getting to know one another, but there's nothing you can do to mess things up." He tucked a strand of her long, dark hair behind one of her ears and savored the moment.

"But I don't want to drag you into…"

"You're not dragging me anywhere." He leaned down and kissed her lips so gently they barely touched as he held back the one full of passion he longed to give her. There was no denying the erratic thud of his heartbeat right now. Could she feel the attraction, too? "I promise. You're safe here. I'm next door if you have any worries at all. Bang on the wall or text me."

Sophie lifted her hand to her mouth and cleared her throat. "Yes. Good. Thanks."

Was she as mesmerized by their chemistry as he was? No, this wasn't mere chemistry. He felt more alive than he had in a long time. Akin to the heart-bursting exuberance he felt performing on stage—yet this was real.

Lord, please let this be real.

"Sleep well, Miles. I'll see you at nine."

"Good night. Sweet dreams." Miles waited until she had gone into her room and twisted the lock into place before turning to the next door. He stood for a few seconds and massaged his neck. How long until he shared his reality with Sophie? Should he wait to see if she was serious about him? Was there a world in which they could have a future together? Their relationship was developing so fast, as if he'd been struck with love at first sight— was that possible? He'd never entertained the notion before now. Before Sophie.

In the silence of the hallway, he leaned his forehead against the door to his room and closed his eyes.

God, if this is what You want, would You give me the courage... and the words?

Chapter Eleven

SOPHIE STROLLED OUT OF MR. B'S BOOKSTORE into the spring sunshine and swung her canvas tote, enjoying the weight of her purchases. "Thanks for humoring me in there."

Miles followed close behind. "Are you kidding? Watching your face light up when you were chatting books to the staff was priceless."

"They were all so helpful. Bookstores and libraries have been special to me since I was little, way before I had dreams of being a writer. I've always been a bookworm. That was the main difference between me and Harriet when we were kids. She danced and I read." Harriet experienced life on the stage while Sophie studied life on the page.

"I think I would have liked you even back then." Miles crinkled his paper bag. "I'm rather bookish myself, you know. I've been meaning to pick up a copy of this WWII novel for ages."

Sophie smiled. *Imagine the two of us curled up reading on the couch together in front of a cozy fire. Or swinging on a giant hammock on a beach with the ocean breeze tickling the pages...*

He nudged her elbow with his. "How happy are you on a scale of one to ten right now?"

"Eleven." Not a single thought about Troy invaded her thoughts while in the bookstore. She peeked at her gleanings. "I'm delighted with my purchases. A picture book about ballerinas for Lucy, a romantic mystery set in Paris for me, and a gorgeous edition of *Little Women* for Bramble Cottage."

"For the cottage?"

They walked in synchronized steps along the cobbled street, and Sophie looked up at the handsome man she was falling for. "Mom calls us her *little women* and it's always been my favorite book. I thought it would be a nice touch to set this pretty edition on the coffee table in the cottage. Let anyone read it when they get the urge."

"That's adorable." Miles pulled her into a side-hug as they strolled. "You're adorable." He checked his watch. "I guess we should make our way to The George Inn. Ready to head back to the hotel first to grab my stuff?"

Sophie's shoulders sagged. "I suppose we should. Although it's such a glorious day after yesterday's storm. I wish we could stay here being tourists in the sunshine without a care in the world." The thought of Troy being out there somewhere made her stomach clench, and facing her sisters' interrogation was less than appealing. Georgia might be gracious enough, but Harriet would want to know everything. *I don't know if I want to share the heaviness of it all with them quite yet. Ignorance is bliss...*

The mellow chimes of church bells from the exquisite Bath Abbey hung in the air as they walked in the direction of the hotel. "Reminds me of Notre Dame." Her eyes welled with tears at the loss of living in her beloved city. She *had* made the right decision to move, hadn't she?

"It's beautiful. They're both beautiful. I love visiting cathedrals and churches when I travel." Miles took her hand, and they crossed a road packed with traffic. His gaze darted in all directions, even once they were on the pavement. "Almost there."

Sophie squeezed his hand. "Hey, are you worried? About Troy, I mean?" She'd lost herself in the world of books this morning, but now that they were back in the real world...

"Should I be? I mean, how far do you think he would go? Is he trying to scare you off or would he actually hurt you physically? The tires weren't a good sign, if that was him." They turned the corner and their hotel came into view. "I don't want to overstep, but I think I'll feel more comfortable once you're safely home."

"Me, too." Except Troy could have the address of Bramble Cottage. Details wouldn't be hard to track down, and the white SUV had followed her from somewhere, presumably the cottage, even though she hadn't noticed. "Wait." She stopped and pulled Miles to a standstill. "There has to be a way to check this out."

"Check what out?"

They both stood to one side of the pavement and allowed a young woman with a double-stroller to pass by. "I don't know why I didn't think of this before." Sophie pulled out her phone. "I know Troy was still in Paris on Saturday because Annabelle spoke to him in the bakery."

"She did?" His eyes widened.

"Sorry. Thought I'd mentioned that. Yes, she let me know he was looking for me."

"Wow. Our paths could have literally crossed in Paris without me knowing."

"True. Anyway, he could feasibly be in England by now, but I happen to know he's a social media junkie. Or at least he used to be. Total narcissist. I haven't been on there much lately, but let's have a look." She searched for him on Instagram. He had a decent following back when they were dating—although she hadn't been tempted to check since their break-up.

Miles stood behind Sophie and peered over her shoulder while she pulled up his account. "Impressive. He really does have a following." He pointed. "She must be his fiancée."

Sophie's hands trembled as she swiped from post to post, a stunning model-esque blonde draped on Troy's arm. Sophie pointed at the most recent photo. "Interesting. According to this, he's still in Paris, or he was yesterday. That's literally the Eiffel Tower behind them, and he's talking about Monday afternoon traffic. He can't have been in two places at once. I'd say there's a good chance he's not in England."

"So, the white SUV may not have been him, after all."

"No. Unless he has someone else stalking me." She dropped her phone back inside her bag and they continued walking. "Or it could have been some legit guy wanting me to pull over—but why?"

Miles rubbed his chin. "And then there's the tires."

"Weird coincidence? Could some kid have laid out a bunch of nails as a prank and I happened to drive over them?" Wishful thinking. She chewed on her lip. Neither one of them believed that scenario for a single minute.

Sophie squinted even with her sunglasses on as she drove the Mini into Bramble Downs. The drive back to the village was nothing like the harrowing experience from yesterday. No crazy rainstorm to navigate, instead there was sparse traffic, blue skies with a few marshmallow clouds high in the sky, and her opera singer in the passenger seat. Surreal.

"Are you ready to meet the sisters? You know they'll be waiting to interview you." Sophie chuckled. Their banter in the car had been easy and relaxed since they discovered Troy was in Paris, and the Mini was back in perfect working order.

"I think I can handle it. How do you feel? I mean, when was the last time you brought a guy here to meet them?" Miles closed his window as the breeze blew in the foul, pungent smell of manure from the surrounding fields.

When *was* the last time? "Let me think. Well, Georgia's only been living here for eight months or so and before that, I usually visited Harriet and her family on my own. Come to think of it, I've never brought a guy here. To England."

"Not even…" Miles let Troy's name hang in the foul air.

She shook her head. "Nope. Harriet met him once when she was visiting me in Paris. Made it very clear she didn't trust him. Turns out she was right, as usual. That was three years ago."

"Three years?" He shifted in his seat to face her as she drove. "Don't take this the wrong way, but how does a beautiful woman like you manage to stay single?"

"I could shoot that back at you, you know. How come you haven't been snapped up by now?"

Sophie studied his face and saw a flicker of regret.

He licked his lips. "I was snapped up once. Only once. Thought it would be forever, but she had other plans."

"I'm sorry. Was it recent?"

He shook his head. "We broke up two years ago, but we were together through most of my twenties. Met when I was at school in Toronto. It's ancient history now. Back to my question—how are *you* still single?"

Whoa. Long-term relationship gone bad. Miles obviously didn't want to elaborate, but Sophie tucked away that information for later. "When I came to Paris all starry-eyed, I wanted to do things the proper way. As a Christian, I mean. I didn't want to play the field, and parties were never my scene as an introvert, so I prayed God would bring the right guy along for me in His perfect timing." She jutted her chin. "I trusted Him and He gave me Troy."

"That's rough." Miles's voice was soft. "There's been no

one special since him?"

Sophie flicked on the indicator and meandered down the narrow country road that led to Bramble Cottage. "No. I stopped praying and stopped dating. Much to the frustration of my mom and sisters." She pulled to the side of the road, turned off the engine, and clutched the steering wheel in both hands. "I think I fooled them into believing I was simply unlucky in love. I would ask if they knew any perfect, eligible bachelors in Paris—which they didn't, so I was safe on that score. In reality, I kept any and all romantic notions to the pages of my stories."

"Until you met me?" He covered one of her hands with his. She noticed his strong, sinewy forearms now that his sleeves were rolled up.

"Yeah, actually. Until I met you." She turned to him and stared at his lips. Full and perfect. Lips that released the most tender-yet-powerful singing voice she had ever heard. She touched the side of his face. Her pulse was a percussive beat in her ears, almost like music…

"Hello there." Her older sister's voice calling from the driveway drowned out the melodic thrum.

Sophie whipped her head around. "Georgia. Hi." She looked back at Miles. "Sorry about that. Don't forget, all you need to do is be your charming self—they're going to adore you."

Miles hopped out of the car and raced around to hold Sophie's door open for her.

She gave him a wink. "Nice start."

Georgia met them at the Mini and hugged Sophie before addressing Miles. "Hi, I'm Georgia."

"Lovely to meet you. I'm Miles Morgan."

He went to shake her hand, but Georgia pulled him into a quick hug. "Welcome. How was the drive, guys?"

"Beautiful. Unlike yesterday." Sophie leaned into the back of the car and grabbed her bags, jacket, and umbrella. "Is Harriet here?"

"Of course. Lucy has a playdate, so Harriet's putting the kettle on as we speak. Come on in, both of you."

"Is it okay if I leave my jacket and bags in the trunk for now?" Miles stuffed his hands in his pockets. "I can grab them when my taxi comes later."

"Sure. Or I can give you a ride to the station. If Georgia trusts me with her car again." Sophie grimaced.

"No problem." Georgia slipped her arm through Sophie's. "The tires weren't your fault. If you don't fancy going out again in the Mini, Harriet might be able to drop Miles if she's leaving to pick up Lucy around the same time."

Sophie ground her teeth. Why did that bother her so much? Harriet was a happily married woman and since when had she become the jealous, possessive type? Perhaps since she'd snagged her own Prince Charming... he was indeed someone to be possessive about.

She glanced over at Miles as he entered the cottage and slid off his shoes. He appeared calm and comfortable as Georgia introduced Harriet. He was great with people, that much she knew already. Plus, when the sisters discovered he was a Christian— well, they'd probably start planning the wedding. Only she had some serious faith issues to work through before she could think about commitment and trust. Not to mention how Miles might feel if he knew the depth of her struggles and what was really going on between her and God. Miles seemed to have the perfect relationship with his Heavenly Father, if not his earthly one.

"You good, Soph?" Harriet came over and gave her a hug. "We were scared for you in the storm. I haven't seen one that bad in forever."

"Yeah, it was brutal, but I got to spend the morning in Bath, so that was a bonus." Sophie kicked off her boots and hung her jacket on the coatrack. "I also found a cute book for my favorite niece. I'll give it to her later."

"You're so sweet, thank you." Harriet eyed the tote on the floor. "You buy the best books."

"Book buying is Sophie's superpower. She always finds the perfect read for me." Georgia walked toward the kitchen. "Miles, can I get you some tea?"

"Yes, please. A little milk would be great."

"Come, sit." Sophie led him to the loveseat. She needed to change into some fresh clothes, but dare she leave him alone with her sisters?

Miles settled next to her, their thighs touching. Her heart rate escalated.

Sophie caught Harriet's eye as she brought in a tray of iced lemon pound cake.

Harriet raised a brow when she saw Miles's arm resting behind Sophie's head.

"Have you been baking, sis? This looks amazing." Sophie leaned forward and detected the hint of citrus.

"It's nowhere near as good as yours, but I'm getting better." Harriet perched on the edge of the opposite sofa and addressed Miles. "You do know she's the most fantastic baker and Parisian pastry chef ever, don't you?"

"Harriet..."

"And she's making my wedding cake." Georgia came in with small plates and dessert forks. "I can't wait. She's got a side-hustle going and everything."

Sophie's face heated. "Thanks, fan club, but Miles doesn't

want to hear all about me."

He laughed in that rich, deep way of his. "I think I do, actually."

Sophie's phone rang out from the entry where she'd dumped her bag. "Ah, saved by the bell. I better check and see if it's something important. Excuse me."

She hurried over to her bag and left the others chuckling about scones. A quick peek at the screen and she clenched her jaw tight. An unknown number again. *It's fine.* Could be nothing. A wrong number.

"I'll only be a minute. I'll change real quick while I take this." She jogged up the stairs to her bedroom and stared at the phone. Should she answer the call or let a message go to voicemail? If it was important, someone would leave a message, right?

Laughter carried up the stairs as Sophie stared at her screen, willing the call to be a wrong number. The ringing stopped. She licked her lips and waited to see if a message popped into her voicemail. It did. She hit the button to listen and held the phone tight to her ear.

"Bonjour, hello. This is Officer Dubois from the police station in Paris for Miss Sophie Brooks. This is the new number we have on file—I hope it is correct. There has been a further development after the attack you reported last Thursday night, Miss Brooks. A woman has been missing since then and unfortunately, the body has now been found. We have reason to believe it was the woman you witnessed being attacked. Please, call me back on this number as soon as possible. Merci."

Sophie dropped the phone and clutched her hands over her heart.

Troy. What have you done?

Chapter Twelve

MILES GLANCED AT THE STAIRCASE. WHAT was Sophie doing up there? She'd gone to answer her phone but that was—he checked his watch—almost ten minutes ago. The call must have been important for her to leave him with the sisters, although they were both charming and had been nothing but warm and polite so far.

"Should I go up and check on Sophie?" Harriet set down her mug. "She's been ages."

"Give her a couple of minutes. Maybe she can't decide what to wear. Besides, we get to chat longer with Miles." Georgia curled up on the couch.

Miles crossed one leg over his knee and attempted to go for a relaxed posture. "Have you lived in this cottage long, Georgia? Sophie mentioned this place has been in the family for many years."

"I've only been living here since last August, actually. I moved from Vancouver—but I bought the cottage from our grandma several years ago. We all wanted it to stay in the family, so I got it for a steal and intend to keep it available for any of us who might need it in the future. We've got so many great memories here from our childhood vacations, I didn't have the heart to let it go."

"Smart idea. It's gorgeous." He surveyed the room. "Cozy but contemporary."

"I'm afraid I can't take all the credit for that. I came up with the ideas and poor Harriet was the project manager and made sure it all got done properly." Georgia patted her sister's arm. "She was my feet on the ground in charge of the renos while I was still in Canada."

"I thoroughly enjoyed it, I'm not going to lie. I love all things design and decor." Harriet turned toward Miles and leaned in. "Talking about home, I know you're from the States, but where's home for you?"

"Good question." He let out a chuckle. "I have a small apartment in New York City. When I say small, I mean a glorified closet. Most of the time I'm traveling for work, or I stay with my aunt here in England."

"Interesting." Georgia's smile was kind. "Sophie hasn't told us much about you as it sounds like you've had quite the whirlwind encounter. Forgive the protective big sister in me, but what's next for you? I mean, she seems smitten, and you seem a decent guy. Thing is, we don't want to see her heart broken."

"Again." Harriet winced. "I hoped she'd meet someone local and settle down here, if I'm honest. If this is casual and you're passing through on your opera tour or whatever, that's fine and fun…" She lowered her voice. "But please be up front with Sophie. It feels like she's wanting a fresh start here and we desperately want her to be happy."

Miles glanced from one sister to the other. Harriet was the spitting image of Sophie, other than a shorter hairstyle. Georgia was a classic beauty and judging from a family photograph he noticed on a side table, looked much like their mother. Great genes in this family. Also, super protective. He rubbed the side of his face while he deciphered how much he should share with them.

Georgia waved her hands in front of her. "Goodness, I'm sorry, Miles. That was heavy-handed of us both." She gave Harriet the side-eye. "We have no right to intrude, and Sophie would kill us if she knew we'd been giving you a hard time."

"Hey, I get it. You love her. You want what's best for her." Miles leaned forward. "This may put your mind at ease a little. I know you guys are Christians, Sophie mentioned it. I need to assure you that I am, too."

"I knew it." Harriet squealed. "I could tell. You have a real sense of peace about you."

Miles's cheeks warmed. "Thanks for that. Listen, I have no intentions of breaking Sophie's heart, and I know it's all happening quickly, but I'm captivated by her. I'm praying about it. I think that's probably all I can say for now."

Georgia hugged a cushion on her lap. "Thanks. Forgive us for coming on strong?"

He picked up his mug. "Nothing to forgive."

"Who's forgiving who down here?" Sophie trotted down the staircase in a navy T-shirt and short navy skirt, then sank down next to Miles. She looked stunning, but her eyes were a little red and the edges of her hair seemed damp, as if she'd washed her face. "What have I missed? Wait, do I even want to know?"

"I'll get you some fresh tea." Georgia scurried to the kitchen.

"I'll help." Harriet followed.

Sophie swiveled in her seat to face Miles. "Oh no. That's suspicious. What did they say exactly?"

Miles drained his tea. "Nothing you need to worry about. They're great sisters and they love you very much."

"Hmm." She pulled an elastic from her wrist and expertly

pulled her long hair into some kind of elaborate topknot. "As long as they didn't grill you too badly."

"Not hardly at all." He set down his mug. "Is everything all right?" He smoothed a strand of her damp hair between his fingers.

"Honestly, I'm not sure. I did get some disturbing news. I'll give you a ride to the train station when you're ready to leave and explain it all then. I don't want to worry the girls yet so…" She mimed zipping her lips.

Miles nodded. "I've got your back."

"I know you do and I'm grateful. More than you know." She looked up at him, a sheen of tears in her big brown eyes.

A couple of hours later, Sophie pulled into the train station with Miles. She had explained her phone message from the Paris police to him, and now her heart ached at the thought of saying goodbye. What was with this instant head-over-heels attraction?

"Thanks for keeping me in the loop." He took off his seat belt. "How much are you going to tell the police in Paris?"

She killed the engine, pushed her sunglasses on top of her head, and stared through the windshield at the red brick building. "This is serious. I'll call them as soon as I get back to the cottage, but I'm not sure what I'll say. I want so badly to pour everything out to them. Turn Troy in and let them deal with him, but you have to understand it's not that simple."

"Why not? Surely, this will be the answer to your problems with him."

"There's a slight, slim chance it wasn't him. If I had any actual proof that it was Troy in the Paris alley, I wouldn't hesitate. It was dark. I'm ninety-nine percent certain. Especially with his sudden appearance after the opera last week."

Miles inclined his head. "If the attack wasn't him, why would he have told you to stay quiet after the opera and then sent those texts to you? The *final word* thing. Why would he go to such lengths if he had nothing to hide?" He reached over and took her hand in his.

Sophie chewed her lip. She hadn't told Miles the whole story with Troy, but now wasn't the time. He was about to jump on a train. "Our break-up was really bad and perhaps he wants to make sure I don't spread rumors about him that may interfere with his new, rich fiancée and the Clement family."

"Was it bad enough to affect his upcoming marriage?" He squeezed her fingers. "I don't expect you to share details, but I'm wondering if there's even the faintest possibility that the guy in the alley was not Troy. In which case, you would need to tread carefully with the police."

"It's not only that." She wrinkled her nose. "I've tried to report things to the Paris police before. When I was with Troy." Tears blurred her vision as devastating memories resurfaced. "He was pretty physical with me sometimes and they didn't believe me when I reported it. He has…contacts. I don't know how, but he managed to make me look like the deranged one. Like I blew things out of proportion." She took a deep breath. "Now, it sounds like he's got even more power as he's marrying into this wealthy family. He's been out of France for a while, at least I think he has, but he could have anyone in authority deep in his back pocket. The alley incident is my word against his."

Miles's face paled. "I don't know what to say. There's clearly a lot I don't know about your past, but I'm sorry you've been through a traumatic time, and I'm sorry you've had a less than positive experience with the authorities. I can't imagine. Add to that, accusing someone of actual murder is no small thing."

"I know."

Several seconds passed and pensive silence filled the Mini.

Miles cleared his throat. "Is it possible in any realm that he was merely telling you to keep quiet about your ugly past relationship with him?"

Could that even be possible? Sophie's gut told her the attacker—the murderer—was Troy. "Maybe. I could definitely cause a stir if I ever chose to go public with everything that happened between us before. Which I wouldn't, for the record. I think he knows I'm not that brave. I believed I was well and truly over him, but I guess he still has a hold on me somehow."

"Can you tell me how?"

Sophie rubbed her arm. "Threats. Major threats. He knows too much about me and he knows I'd be crazy to ever speak out against him."

A muscle popped in Miles's jaw. "Then he probably does have more to hide than your past relationship. Like maybe the attack in the alley."

"Exactly. Yet I can't be certain. I have no evidence. If it wasn't him and they go ahead and launch an investigation, the results would be damaging to him, to his fiancée, and to her rich and powerful family with the ability to sue anyone and everyone. Not to mention, he'd be furious with me, and a furious Troy is… bad."

"How bad?"

"Hmm?"

"Sophie, how bad was it with Troy?"

Not now. "I got over it. Thanks for listening. Again. I think I need to be careful with how much I report to the police. Hopefully, you can now see why."

"I get it. I'm happy to be your sounding board or listening

ear or bodyguard whenever you need it. Okay?"

"I appreciate that. Enough talking about Troy. I know this has all been super heavy." She checked her watch. "You need to hustle if you're going to catch this train to Poole. It leaves in ten minutes."

"True." He pushed open his door. "Thanks for the ride and for the last couple of days. It was a bit of a plot twist, but I got to spend more time with you than I'd even hoped."

Sophie smiled. "I'm glad you weren't disappointed with our first date that turned into a second full-day date."

"I enjoyed every minute." He leaned over and kissed her cheek. "I'll pray for you with this decision about what to tell the police."

"Thanks." Sophie didn't hold much weight in prayer these days, but the truth was she could benefit from a dose of holy wisdom about now.

"I'll call you once I'm at my aunt's house, and we can figure out our *next* date, if that's all right with you."

"Sounds lovely." She touched her cheek where his lips had been and sighed. "I'll speak to you later."

"Let me grab my bags from the trunk?" Miles closed the passenger door, and she watched in the rear-view mirror as he retrieved his gear and walked to the brick building. He turned back and blew a kiss her way.

Something inside her cracked wide open and her breath caught in her throat. This man was affecting her heart in the craziest ways. An air kiss wasn't going to cut it. "Wait." Sophie opened her door and hurried to where he stood squinting in bright sunshine.

"Did I forget something?"

"You did, actually." Sophie stood on tiptoes, took his

handsome face in her hands and gave him a kiss he would remember.

Miles dropped both bags to the ground and lifted her off her feet as he responded with a kiss so deep and true, for a moment nothing else mattered. His lips on hers. His fingers running through the length of her hair. Sophie forgot to breathe.

He eased her back down to earth and they came up for air. Her pulse raced faster than the train on the tracks behind them.

"Wow." That was all she could manage as she took a step backwards.

Miles's warm laugh touched her soul. "Wow, indeed." He picked up his bags.

No other words were necessary.

Sophie waited until he rounded the corner into the station, and then wandered back to the Mini. She sat in the driver's seat with a humungous grin plastered all over her face, started the engine, and searched the radio settings for something that sounded like opera. She had a sudden hankering to immerse herself in the melodic strains which always soothed her soul.

Her phone pinged. Was Miles texting her already? She licked her lips, which were now devoid of all lipstick, and checked her messages.

No, not Miles.

An unknown number. Her fingers froze.

"NO POLICE IN PARIS OR ENGLAND. OR YOUR DOUBLE WILL PAY."

What? Sophie's eyes blurred and she re-read the fresh threat in front of her. Troy. Who else could this possibly be? He must be using some kind of burner phone. Wasn't that what criminals used in order to not be traced? Her double will pay... Harriet. Would Troy hurt her twin?

Her chest ached at the thought of anything happening to Harriet. *God, if you're listening, what am I supposed to do?*

If God wasn't listening, if He'd given up on her like she'd given up on Him… where in the world could she turn? Was she even able to hear His voice anymore? A part of her longed for the relationship with her Heavenly Father she once enjoyed and treasured. He had more than made up for the loss of her earthly dad. Then Troy had messed with her heart and that triggered the downward spiral of everything else, her spiritual life included.

Sophie clenched her teeth. This trouble with Troy was bigger than an ex-lover's tiff. This was possible murder by a guy with a violent past and a family history of abusive men steeped in generational sickness. Troy had hinted at his father and grandfather demanding respect with no boundaries from their women. A shiver reverberated up Sophie's spine when she recalled the few memories he'd relayed in his more vulnerable moments. If she were honest, she'd silently questioned the vague details of his mother's death. An accident. Falling and breaking her neck…

I need to get home.

She had to tell her sisters what was going on. To be there to protect Harriet and make sure no harm came to her. Or little Lucy. Or any member of her beloved family. Snippets from her manuscript came to mind as she drove out onto the road. *What was I thinking?* She would speak with her agent. If she had a hope of rebuilding her close relationship with her twin, there were some major edits that needed to be made. The dreadful character she made the "wicked twin sister" out to be. There was nothing remotely wicked about Harriet. She didn't deserve that, and she certainly didn't deserve to be caught in the crossfire between Sophie and Troy Sanders.

She slid her sunglasses back on and put her foot down harder on the accelerator. The more she considered the elements of her fictitious story, the more she realized how the absurd details were somehow weaving their way through her real life. With a gulp she remembered her story's ending was far from happy. *That can't happen in real life. I won't let that story unfold.*

Sophie focused on the line of cars ahead. They'd slowed to a stop as three moth-eaten donkeys ambled across the road in no particular hurry.

Her erratic breathing slowed along with the donkeys' pace. She needed to take her next steps with caution. Not rush and make mistakes. If she couldn't talk to her sisters—and she would definitely not alarm her mom all the way over in Vancouver—should she tell everything to Miles? He already knew a big chunk of her predicament. He was level-headed, plus he had an actual relationship with God. Maybe he could be the go-between for her and God.

Jesus.

Whoa. That whisper was almost audible. So, God was listening. She turned off the opera music. Yes, her Christian upbringing cemented certain truths in her mind—and apparently her heart, too—but she'd never heard an actual voice before. Jesus. The One who makes a way to God. The only way. Her go-between or whatever.

Fine.

God, I know Miles is not my actual go-between for me and You. I know in the depths of my heart. For now, I'm going to have to lean on him and his faith because mine feels too weak. I'm not ready to give everything to You again. I'm sorry. Not yet.

Baby steps.

Miles already helped her to see there was a good chance

Troy was the attacker. She didn't trust the police back in Paris, not after her previous experience of trying to get a restraining order. She'd been humiliated and paid for her mistake later at Troy's hand. However, she couldn't, in all good conscience, ignore the authorities. Some poor woman was dead and had a family who were grieving her loss.

Could she speak to someone here in England about the attack? Miles mentioned his family's police connections. Perhaps she could get protection for Harriet and the family? The thought of little Lucy being in danger was unfathomable. Unless Troy had his fingers in the British police pie, too. *That's a possibility.* Plus, if Troy was arrested at first and then got out on bail or a technicality—he was obviously in with the wealthy crowd these days—then they would all be in trouble.

Sophie drummed her fingers on the steering wheel. *What to do*?

The donkeys moved on and the traffic picked up speed. A week ago, life was so exciting. She was moving to a new country in a new chapter with only good and lovely things in store. Since then, two men were in her life and now everything was complex. She'd barely had a chance to consider where her relationship with Miles might lead. He was everything she ever dreamed of, wasn't he?

A flash of light in Sophie's rear view mirror caused her to squint. She peered at the reflection to see who was riding her tail on a winding road and did a double-take. A white SUV. Coincidence? *Please let it be a coincidence.* She couldn't go anywhere with a minivan in front of her, so she tried to take in as much detail as possible, just in case. The windshield was darker at the top, but the driver was definitely male. Baseball cap and shades. Eerily familiar. No front number plate. Too close for comfort…

As the road widened for a stretch, the SUV flashed its lights and honked the horn before swerving around Sophie and the minivan in front of her and racing off beyond the next bend. The minivan beeped thorough indignation, but it was all Sophie could do to stay on the road and hurry back to her family at Bramble Cottage.

Before a white SUV arrived ahead of her.

Chapter Thirteen

"I'M SO SORRY TO DISTURB YOU AT your aunt's and dump all this on you, but I needed to talk to someone." Sophie paced the living room of Bramble Cottage as she poured out her news to Miles about the latest text and the SUV.

"You have nothing to be sorry about. I'm relieved there was no sign of the SUV when you got back to the cottage though. I can stay on the line with you until your sister gets home, if you like."

"That's kind of you. I'm hoping she'll be here soon. Weird about the SUV… I was wondering if Troy has someone else doing his dirty work for him." She shuddered. "Which makes it worse, in a way. I could walk past this individual on the street or serve them in the tearoom, and not even know."

Miles let out a heavy sigh. "I wish I could be there with you."

Me, too. "I'm safe. Not a white car in sight. I guess he wanted to spook me." Mission accomplished. Sophie glanced through the front window of Bramble Cottage, which opened out to a view of the road. The late afternoon sun threw shafts of light across the peaceful rose garden and no traffic passed through this particularly quiet area of the village. *I'm fine. We're all fine.*

"I guess in a way it's good that your sister is out. At least you'll have a chance to calm down and figure out how you're going to tell her everything."

Sophie padded over to the sofa, sank down into the soft cushions, and put her feet up on the coffee table. "I'm not keen to say anything to either of them yet. It'll freak them out for sure, and they might react and get our local police involved."

"Would that be so bad? I know you had a rough time with the Paris police before, but maybe there's someone you can find here. Someone you can trust."

Sophie rubbed her tired eyes. "Troy can be very persuasive. I know this is a different police force and everything, but if they did bungle it and something happened to Harriet, I'd never forgive myself."

"I get it, but didn't you say Georgia had a situation last year where someone threatened the family if she went to the police? Surely, she would understand your situation."

Sophie wound a strand of hair around her fingers. "True. I was grateful Georgia kept me in the loop, even though I was powerless to do anything. I guess my sisters have a right to know if Troy's watching the cottage. If you're in the praying mood, perhaps you might offer one up for a gentle way I can break the news to them."

"Of course."

"Thanks. This could be triggering for them both after last year." The sound of a car outside caused Sophie to jump up. "Someone's here."

"Sophie?" Miles voice was etched with concern.

She ran over to the side of the window and took a quick peek. A car was in the driveway. Sophie exhaled. "It's all good. Georgia's here with Will, her fiancé."

"The surgeon with the little boy?"

"You're catching on." Sophie returned to the sofa and rolled her tense shoulders.

The door squeaked open. "Sophie? Are you here?" Georgia came into view followed by Will.

"Hey. Harriet's not with you, is she?" Sophie tried to keep her tone casual.

"She's home with Leo and Lucy. You okay?"

"On the phone to Miles." Sophie held her cell in the air as the couple joined her in the living room.

"Perfect." Georgia beamed. "Can you put him on speakerphone for a sec?"

"O-kay." Sophie furrowed her brow. "What's up?"

"Why don't you go ahead and ask them?" Georgia nudged Will and he came closer to the phone.

"Hi, Miles. Will here. The lucky man engaged to Georgia." Will nodded at Sophie. "I hope this isn't too weird, but Georgia had what she thinks is a brilliant idea."

"It *is* brilliant." Georgia clutched his arm, a grin spreading across her face.

Will chuckled. "Well, Friday night it's our annual fundraiser ball for the kids' wing at the hospital where I work. It's a slap-up dinner, a couple of short speeches, and then a dance. People get pretty excited about it and to be honest, it's a posh evening at a great venue. Georgia thought you might like to come."

"Seeing as how Sophie's already coming." Georgia winked at her sister. "Without a date."

The fundraiser was this Friday? Sophie winced.

"Did you forget, Soph?" Georgia planted her hands on her hips. "Seriously?"

"I'm sorry. It's been a busy week…" To say the least. "But I'll come. No pressure though, Miles. This is rather last-minute and it's fine if you have Friday night plans."

Will nodded. "Yes, absolutely. No pressure."

A few seconds of silence passed until Miles responded.

"Looks like my calendar is clear that evening and Sophie

now has a date.”

Georgia cheered and Sophie couldn't help but chuckle. She was incorrigible.

Sophie stood. “If it's good with you two, I'm finishing my phone call upstairs.”

“Of course.” Will let Sophie pass by. “It'll be great to meet you on Friday, Miles. I promise we won't make you sing at this short notice.”

“I appreciate it.”

Sophie took him off speakerphone and plodded up the stairs to the privacy of her bedroom. “Sorry about that. I hope you didn't feel railroaded there. I'd honestly forgotten all about the ball.”

“I'm not entirely sure what a slap-up dinner is, but if it means I get to spend an evening with you, I'm all for it. Lucky I always travel with my tux.”

“The life of an opera singer?” She recalled how debonair he looked in his tux after the opera performance and her insides did a little flip.

“Something like that.”

“Well, don't worry about the slap-up dinner. It's nothing to do with slapping and the very best of English food.”

“Sure.” He let out a short laugh. “Makes no sense, but I love it. Do you think you should maybe go and talk with Georgia while Will's there? It might be good to have him around. He sounds like a logical sort of guy.”

Sophie shut her bedroom door. “He is. Typical surgeon-type. Doesn't stress easily.” She wandered over to the window and peered out across the quiet street and over to the patchwork of fields. Still no sign of a white SUV. The sunset painted a blurred tangerine glow across the horizon. Tranquil. Unlike her soul. “You're right. I'll speak with Georgia in a minute, but I'll let Harriet have a nice evening with her family. I don't think Leo's home very much these days. I can catch up with her tomorrow after I meet Dorothy at the Brambles and Berries tearoom. Come to think of it, I may have to borrow something from Harriet to wear to this ball."

"You looked stunning at the opera last week…"

Sophie opened the large wooden wardrobe and perused her options. "Thanks, that's awfully nice of you to say. I love my black dress, but I haven't had time to get it dry cleaned and I managed to get something sticky on the skirt. Probably from the taxi. Luckily, we're twins and Harriet's extra fancy so…"

"Sounds like you have a solution—and a busy day tomorrow." A voice called out in the background. "I think my aunt has dinner ready here, so I should go."

"Thanks for listening and for agreeing to be my date for the ball." She flopped onto the soft bed. "I'll text you the details."

"I'm here for you. Stay safe, okay?"

"I will. Have a lovely evening with your aunt. Goodnight."

Before Sophie did anything else, she needed to return the call to the Paris police. If she was unable to report her suspicions about Troy yet—and there was no way she would put her family's safety on the line—then she could at least see if they were willing to let her know any more details on what happened to the girl in the alley. She scrolled back to their incoming phone message and hit reply. Her call went through to a specific department.

"Bonjour. Hello, my name is Sophie Brooks. Officer Dubois called me from this number earlier this afternoon."

"Hello, yes, I'm Officer Dubois, thank you for calling back. We have you on file for reporting an attack on," he clicked on a keyboard, "the early hours around 1:00 AM of last Friday, April 26th, oui?"

"That's correct." Sophie clutched the phone with both hands. "You believe this woman has been found—dead, I presume?"

"I'm afraid so. If it is, in fact, the same woman. We are hoping you may be able to add more details to help in the investigation. You are not in Paris though, is that right?"

"I'm in England. I moved here, but I don't know what else I can tell you." She bit her lip. *God, forgive me, but I need to know who I can trust.* "It was very dark, and it all happened in a matter of a few seconds. I know her hair was long and blonde, my flashlight on my phone picked that up. I'm sure the attacker held a knife, I saw metal glint."

"Could it have been a gun?"

"My first thought was a knife, but like I said, it happened fast, and it was a dark alley." Sophie closed her eyes and tried to recall every detail. The smell of rain that fell earlier that evening. She'd been expecting to see a cat in the alley and shone her light at a low angle at first. "Wait, there's something else. I think she wore something shiny. Like leather maybe? It was shadowy, but I'm sure she wore either a leather skirt or pants, something that reflected the light just a little."

"Excellent. This is helpful, Miss Brooks. Our victim was wearing a leather skirt, so this fits with what we suspect. Nothing more about the attacker?"

Nausea rose from the pit of Sophie's stomach. For all she knew, Troy could have contacts at the top in the Paris police force. Besides, they had chosen not to believe her way back when Troy started his abusive behavior… her trust issues extended to those who were supposed to protect and serve. "I'm sorry." She was determined to get to the bottom of this and uncover the truth eventually. "Are you able to tell me anything about the woman?"

"Only what's in today's news—you can find details online. Her family has been notified. The investigation is ongoing. It appears to have been a random attack. This is all I can say."

"I understand." Sophie pulled her laptop from the bedside table and began typing in the familiar Paris local news channel. "I'm sorry I can't be more help. I'll let you know if I remember anything else though."

"Merci, Miss Brooks. Good evening."

Sophie ended the call, took a deep breath, and scoured the pages of news on her screen. There. A beautiful blonde. Madeline Moreau. Aged twenty-nine. Sophie gasped. Somehow, knowing her name and seeing her face made this even more excruciating. This woman's life had been snuffed out. Had Troy done this? He was violent and messed up, but why would he kill someone and how did he know her? Strange considering he was about to begin a new life with this Clement woman.

She continued reading the short paragraph, her heart aching for this family. Apparently, Madeline worked at the US Embassy in Paris…

No. Sophie's hand covered her mouth. That was where Troy worked when they were dating, before he took off and fled back to the States. Could this Madeline have been another of Troy's ex-girlfriends? Someone he needed to silence? She slammed the laptop shut and began pacing her bedroom. Surely not. When she met Troy, he'd recently arrived in Paris, and she was dating him the whole time he lived there, or so she assumed. Otherwise, perhaps he'd been back in France for a while and knew Madeline more recently.

Regardless, this connection was too much of a coincidence. Sophie perched on the end of her bed. What could she do? If Troy was capable of murdering one woman, what was to stop him from murdering more? From murdering her?

God, this is bigger than me. I'm going to go crazy if I have to keep all this bottled up for too long. Please, show me how I can say what I need to say without endangering the people I love.

Her phone lit up with another call. What now? Sophie retrieved her phone from the pillow and saw her literary agent's name. Her literary agent? She stood and paced toward the window to the soothing calm of the countryside.

"Gillian, hi. How are you?"

"Sophie, I'm on my way out, but I got an email and wanted to let you know. You now have *two* publishers interested in your manuscript for *The Paris Pumpkin*." A door slammed shut and another squeaked open. "How great is that?"

Sophie closed her gaping mouth. "Wow. Yes. That's amazing."

"Right? They both especially love your wicked twin character. I know you were unsure about her, but it's a hit with the bigwigs. Anyway, I'll email details to you, and we'll wait and see what they come back with. This is fab news. Brilliant. Have to fly." The call ended.

Sophie swallowed. How much more could she handle today? She should be ecstatic. This was her dream. *My poor sister.* The elephant currently sitting on her chest would be the elephant in the room tomorrow when she spoke to Harriet. She should have told her about this months ago. Cleared the air. Now she had to unload everything all at once onto the shoulders of her sweet, unassuming twin.

Of course, the manuscript was nothing compared to the personal safety of her family. Sophie flicked back to the latest text from Troy. Her skin prickled as she recalled the fear and frustration she'd lived with as his girlfriend. The pain he'd caused. Potentially, the grief he had caused another entire family.

Georgia needed to know what danger Sophie brought to Bramble Downs and into Bramble Cottage. Then she owed Harriet an explanation about Troy, and an apology for the manuscript. She pocketed the phone and balled her fists. Let the conversations begin.

She had allowed Troy to hurt her once upon a time, but she promised herself, never again.

Chapter Fourteen

"THIS IS THE BEST SCONE I'VE *ever* had." The morning light shimmered through the window of Brambles and Berries as Dorothy wiped the edges of her mouth with a white linen napkin. "And I've devoured many scones over the years. The zest of lemon combined with the richness of clotted cream…" The older woman shook her head. "When can you start, dear?"

Sophie smiled at the kind owner of the village tearoom and sat back in her seat. "I'm glad you like it. I can't tell you how grateful I am for this part-time position. I can start next week if that suits you."

"Perfect." Dorothy smoothed her gray hair from her face. "Your sisters are so excited to have you here. You come highly recommended—and they are like my nieces, so now you are like family, too."

"That means a lot. Thank you."

Dorothy brushed away the compliment. "Feel free to use my kitchen when you need it. I tend to do most of the baking from my home kitchen these days, as I live so close by. The other part-time baker is here in the mornings for a couple of hours, but I'm sure you can work around each other if necessary."

"Thank you. You said I could work on my wedding cakes here some evenings?"

"Of course, dear." Dorothy pulled a key from her pocket. "We close at five so it's all yours after that. I used to bake up a storm here at night, but I'm getting a little long in the tooth and lacking in energy these days."

"I find that hard to believe from what my sisters tell me." Sophie took the key and stood. "Don't forget, I'm more than happy to help out serving in the tearoom when you get busy."

Dorothy walked her to the door. "Ah yes, until you get your book deal and become a full-time author."

"You've been talking to Harriet?" Sophie attached the key onto her keyring.

"She's very proud of you. How lovely to have a twin. I'll have to look twice to see which one's which, you know. Even with your different hairstyles."

"We get that a lot. I'm going to see her now actually." Her gut clenched at the mere thought of upsetting Harriet.

"Say hello from me." Dorothy checked her watch. "Time to open up. Have a lovely day, dear."

"Thanks. You, too." Sophie gave the older woman a quick hug and hurried out to the Mini a few yards down the road, scanning the area for any suspicious onlookers, white SUV's in particular. No, this was just an ordinary quiet morning in the village. Her heart rate steadied as she walked past the familiar landmarks of the ancient library, charming florist, and traditional lawyers' offices. In spite of her current anxiety, Bramble Downs was starting to feel like home.

Sophie sat in the car and checked her phone. Nothing alarming. A text from Miles confirming arrangements for the ball tomorrow evening. Her insides warmed at the thought of spending more time with him. Maybe they would even get to dance together. The notion of being close to him caused her pulse to race. She scrolled down her emails, but there was nothing from her agent yet. *Good.*

Things were not all bad in her life right now. There was

Miles, and the possibility of a beautiful relationship. Bramble Cottage, where the rent Georgia charged was a pittance. A nice little job at the tearoom, which was not quite the Pretty Patisserie, but at least working there would allow her kitchen creativity to have wings. *I need to focus on the positive and count my blessings.*

Sophie pulled out of the tight parking spot with several maneuvers and made her way to Harriet's house. The conversation with Georgia and Will last night had been calm, in spite of the danger involved. They were concerned but understood her dilemma and promised to be extra vigilant. She hadn't told them all the details about her past with Troy, but did share about the threatening texts, the white SUV, and the possibility of him being the attacker in the Paris alley. They agreed she needed to proceed with care. Sophie had a plan in mind, but first she needed to talk with Harriet.

The Duval's picture-perfect, detached home came into view and Sophie pulled up outside. Harriet's life was so… together. The beautiful country house, the ballerina career in her repertoire, a gorgeous daughter and handsome French husband, even a vibrant faith—and then there was Sophie.

The complete opposite, but a work in progress.

"Soph, come on in." Harriet waved from the open door wearing a stylish black jumpsuit and a huge smile. She tipped a green watering can into her prolific hanging basket, all pinks and purples. "I put the kettle on for us."

"Thanks, but I already had two cups of Earl Grey."

"With Dorothy?" Harriet chuckled.

"How did you guess?" Sophie locked the Mini and handed her sister a plastic container. "But I did save you a couple of lemon scones."

Harriet gave her a hug. "You're the best, thanks. Lucy will love one of these after school."

"She seems so tiny for school."

"Tell me about it. Although she's definitely four going on twenty-four. Can I get you a glass of water instead?"

"Sure. That would be great." Sophie kicked off her shoes in the entrance. "Smells good in here."

"Lavender candle. Make yourself at home."

Sophie inhaled the comforting scent. Perhaps the calming effect would kick in. "Harriet, can we talk? I mean, really talk for a minute?" She sat on a leather barstool at the kitchen island.

"Sounds serious. Is this about borrowing an outfit for tomorrow night? Because I'm totally ticked about not being able to go after buying a fabulous dress. Leo's work is killing me at the moment."

"Wait, you're not going to the ball? I thought this was a thing we *all* had to attend." Plus, the thought of Harriet being home alone did not sit well given the circumstances with Troy.

"Leo's back in France tomorrow. It's fine. The sitter cancelled anyway, and it would have been a nightmare trying to find another on short notice. I pivoted, and now I've got some friends coming over for a girls' movie night instead."

"I'm sorry you'll miss it. Especially after buying a dress." But relief flowed through Sophie knowing her sister wouldn't be on her own for the evening.

"It's all good. You should totally wear my dress to the ball, Cinderella. I can't have you going in those ripped jeans. Even if they are Parisian chic." Harriet winked. "Seriously. You're more than welcome to wear it and you know it'll be a perfect fit." She poured boiling water into a mug and filled a glass with water from the stainless fridge. "I think you'll love it."

Sophie fidgeted in her seat. "That's ever so kind of you. You may not want to lend me anything after this conversation though."

Harriet handed her the full glass and joined her on an adjacent stool. "Don't be silly. What's this about? You look like you're about to confess to murder or something."

Sophie's mouth felt like the Sahara. She took a swig of water and set the glass on the island. "I have a few confessions, actually. Want to get your tea first?"

"No. Not really. I'd like you to spill whatever's eating you." Wide-eyed, Harriet clasped her hands on her knees. "I've known for ages something's been off with you. Please, will you tell me?"

Where to begin… the cruel character in her manuscript, which she in some warped and inaccurate way based on Harriet, currently garnishing attention from publishers? Or her ex-boyfriend, who may or may not have killed someone and was now stalking them and threatening to hurt Harriet if he was reported to the police?

Sophie took a deep, shaky breath. "You remember Troy?"

Sophie left Harriet's house with a marginally clearer conscience, no mascara left on her lashes, and a stunning red evening gown to wear the following night. Harriet had been hurt at first when she heard about the evil twin sister character in Sophie's manuscript, but gracious and understanding as Sophie poured out her confessions and her fears. The fiction story details paled in comparison to the current dangerous reality with Troy. By the end of their time together, they embraced and agreed to stick together always. Family was everything.

Drained, Sophie returned the Mini to Bramble Cottage, as Georgia needed to run some errands. Now she was finally alone in the cozy living room. This was her happy place, perhaps due to the countless childhood summers she spent here with their beloved grandparents. How many memorable books had she devoured in this room over the years, from picture books to chapter books to teen romances to today? She exhaled as she tapped out a text message to Miles to casually see how he was doing without sounding overbearing or desperate. She wanted to give him space to enjoy some time with his aunt, but her heart ached a tiny bit that she wouldn't see him until the fundraiser ball. So much yet to discover.

I wonder what childhood memories he has.

Sophie knew the bare bones about his parents and his English aunt and late uncle, but there were gaping holes in her knowledge of this opera man. She suggested they meet up in the foyer at the fundraiser the next evening so they could at least walk in together and with any luck, have a chance to chat one-on-one and deepen their relationship. Both Harriet and Georgia approved of him so far, but Sophie didn't have a stellar track record with men. They all seemed great at the beginning.

Her phone trilled and she answered. "Harriet?"

"Hey, sis. I know you just got home, but I had to call."

Sophie sat up straight, the hairs on the back of her neck standing to attention. "What's wrong? What happened?"

"I'm fine. Relax. I found something out though, and I don't know what to do about it. I mean, after you told me about Troy and everything."

"But you're safe?"

"Yes. Sorry. I didn't mean to scare you. Are you on your own at the cottage?"

Sophie pinched the bridge of her nose and closed her eyes. "Yeah, I'm fine. Georgia headed out. She won't be long. What is it? You sound rattled."

"I am. After you left, I went online and did a little research."

"On Troy?" Sophie grabbed the throw pillow next to her and hugged it.

"Yes, but also on his fiancée, Camille. The Clement family is ridiculously wealthy—and I mean ridiculous."

"That's what my old boss, Annabelle, told me."

"The thing is, the Clement name rang a bell for some reason. I thought I'd heard Leo mentioning the name before but wasn't sure if it was the same family."

"Oh?" Something about Leo had changed over the past year or so. He worked crazy hours and seemed less involved with his family. Apparently, he rarely went to church anymore—not that Sophie was one to talk, but he used to be super committed. She couldn't quite put her finger on why, but for some reason she didn't feel like she could fully trust him anymore. Not that she could tell Harriet any of this. Not yet. "What's the connection?"

"You know Leo's mom quite well, don't you?" Harriet rustled some papers.

"Yes. I like Madame Duval, actually. She's given me a lot of writing and editing work over the years with her Parisian magazine. I know she's well off, but does she run in the same circles as the Clement clan?" Where was this going?

"I don't quite know what to think. I hate going through Leo's stuff, but he's horrible at keeping his desk tidy and I remembered seeing an invitation when I was dusting the other day. The stationery was particularly lavish with this padded card and fancy writing." She went quiet. "I have it here. Even the envelope feels expensive. It's for Leo and *his mom* to attend the wedding in Paris."

"Troy and what's-her-name's wedding?" Sophie swallowed.

"Camille. Yes. It's in three weeks, like you said."

"Wait, Leo and his mom? That's a bit bizarre, isn't it?"

"That's what I thought, too. The point is, I can't believe Leo hasn't said anything about the invitation to me. Doesn't he want *me* to go with him rather than his mom? I don't know, maybe he already declined and didn't think he needed to bother me with it. Or maybe he actually *is* going to attend with his mom. Madame Duval can be rather domineering when it comes to her boy."

"You mean your husband."

"Exactly." Harriet huffed. "I'm ticked he hasn't even told me about it though. I'll ask him about it this evening. Maybe he knows something useful about Troy."

"Wait, wouldn't he remember Troy from when I was dating him?"

Harriet was silent for a beat. "Not necessarily. Leo's hopeless at remembering names at the best of times. He never met Troy in-person when you were dating, did he?"

"No. I guess not. I never brought him back to England, and you only met him once when you came to stay with me in Paris on your own."

"That's right. That man gave me the chills back then. I came home and told Leo what I thought, but that must be three years ago."

"A little longer."

"Personally, I think this is all Leo's mom and could be nothing but a curious coincidence, but I had to tell you."

"I appreciate it." Sophie stood and wandered into the kitchen in search of a snack. "But you should fill Leo in on this messy business with me and Troy so he can stay closer to home. I don't want you feeling spooked every time you see your shadow." *Like I do.* Sophie ran her fingers over a cool, smooth pumpkin ornament on a shelf. *The Paris Pumpkin.* Harriet had been so kind about the manuscript. "I want you to feel safe, sis."

"I'll tell him everything tonight. I promise. Hopefully, he'll have something to share about the Clement family. His mom might even know Camille."

Sophie examined her pale pink nails and made a mental note to dig out her red polish for tomorrow. "Camille doesn't know what she's letting herself in for with Troy. I realize people can change, but I don't believe he has. Not for the better, at least."

"I agree. Listen, I should go and collect Lucy from school. Take care. Try to have some fun with Miles at the ball tomorrow. You're going to look amazing."

Sophie picked at the rip in her jeans. "Thanks to your dress. You be careful. Keep me posted. Love you."

"Love you, too."

Sophie rummaged in the fridge and found a bag of carrot sticks and some hummus. Harriet's evening dress was not forgiving, and she wanted to be able to breathe at the event. Fruit and vegetables would be on the menu until she could indulge in that "slap-up" fancy dinner at the ball.

The ball.

Something felt off about this event. Uncomfortable, like an ill-fitting, itchy sweater. Understandable, given the events of the past week. Yet Miles had swept in with his rich laugh and kind heart… this had the potential to be an unforgettable, magical evening if she allowed herself to be in the moment and forget about Troy.

Growing up, Cinderella had always been Sophie's favorite fairy tale story, and she dreamed of going to a real ball one day with her own Prince Charming. Was Miles the one? Too soon to know. She thought she'd found her one true love before, and that turned out to be the biggest mistake of her life.

As Sophie crunched on her veggies and stared through the window at the cows dotting the emerald hills in the distance, the memory of Troy with the blonde woman in the Paris alley popped into her mind. The idyllic vista before her was a stark contrast to that damp, dark evening in the city. A chill swept over her. She glanced down at her bare arms and saw the covering of goosebumps.

Could she trust her judgment when it came to men? Sophie glanced back at the white ceramic pumpkin on the shelf and then down at her ripped jeans. Her novel manuscript and thoughts of Cinderella were messing with her mind. She was not living out the story she had written, and she'd moved on from the nightmare of her past. Right?

Time would tell. She set down her plate and wrapped her arms around her middle. Hopefully, her potentially dreamy evening tomorrow would not go pumpkin-shaped by the stroke of midnight.

Chapter Fifteen

MILES PARKED HIS PORSCHE IN THE well-lit grounds of the fundraiser ball venue and followed the smattering of well-dressed fellow attendees toward the entrance. He'd been to some swanky events in the past decade, and this was high end, for sure. He chose to decline the valet service due to his over-protective relationship with his sports car, and now his heart hammered in his chest at the thought of seeing Sophie again. Even his aunt picked up on his sappy face every time he mentioned Sophie's name. *I've got it bad.*

He took brisk strides to the front of the luxurious hotel. Less than forty-eight hours had passed since their kiss at the train station, but the time dragged for him, and he got the impression from her texts today that she was anxious for them to be together again, too.

"Miles?"

He lifted his gaze to the top of the steps and there stood a spectacular vision in red. Sophie. He took the steps two at a time without taking his eyes off her, and then held both her hands in his.

"Sophie." He couldn't manage a full sentence with the impact her appearance had on his stuttering heart. He noticed everything at once—her dark brown hair was swept up into an elaborate style showcasing her long, elegant neck. The dress was a deep scarlet that seemed to make her skin glow and accentuated her slight curves. She wore a little more make-up than usual. Even her fingernails were the exact shade of her gown. He'd seen his fair share of impressive garments and beautiful women on and off stage in his industry, but nothing compared to the one standing in front of him in this moment.

"Are you all right?" Her lips glistened with a glossy sheen.

Miles made plans to kiss that away later. "A little dumbstruck by your beauty. Don't mind me." He lifted one hand and twirled her around in a circle. "Wow. You are absolutely gorgeous."

Her cheeks turned pinker. "Thanks. You're rather dapper yourself." She ran her fingers down the length of his tux lapel. "Not bad at all. Although you probably wear this little get-up at least once a week in your glamorous line of work."

His grin dropped. *Maybe not for much longer…*

"Look at the pair of you." Georgia joined them and put a hand to her throat. "You guys are fabulous together."

Miles laughed and put an arm around Sophie's trim waist. "It's all this young lady, but thanks. You look very lovely, too, Georgia."

"Aww, thank you." Georgia smoothed her long, black dress. "I suppose the next time I wear a full-length gown will be on my wedding day. Now that *really* freaks me out. Talking of which, I should go in and find Will. I think I'm supposed to be welcoming people with him. See you both later?"

"Sure. Go do your thing." Sophie rubbed her sister's arm. "Will's going to be so proud of you."

Georgia smiled her appreciation and threaded her way through the throng of guests who were making their way inside.

Miles squeezed Sophie's hand. "Shall we?"

"We should, as much as I'd like to hang around out here for a while. You have no idea how much I'm pushing myself out of my comfort zone for this." She squeezed his hand tighter.

"Is a fundraiser ball a bit much for your slightly introverted self?"

"It is. I'm going to rely on you to cover for me when we encounter all the superficial small-talk and horribly awkward conversations playing out in my mind."

He leaned over and brushed a kiss on top of her head. "You're going to be fine. Be yourself, that's what drew me to you right away."

"Here's me thinking it was my cakes…"

"Well, that gave you a few extra *brownie* points. No pun intended."

Sophie chuckled. "Keep the levity coming and I think I'll survive the evening." They walked into the huge foyer. "Seating's allocated, so there will probably be a plan somewhere." She gave a smirk. "Let's hope we're sitting together."

"We better be." He put a hand on the small of her back and led her between two clusters of guests. "You are literally the reason I'm here. Other than giving to a great cause."

They both accepted a glass of something light and fizzy from a server carrying a silver tray.

"I brought my car so I should tell you I *can* make a quick escape if necessary…"

Sophie's face lit up. "Perfect. I was hoping you'd bring it. In that case, I may escape with you."

He rubbed his chin. "You want to go and meet her before this party begins?"

"Your car? Sure. The less small talk I have to do here, the better. We should hurry though."

Miles deposited both their glasses on an empty tray as they rushed back outside and down the steps. "I don't know how you walk in those." He nodded at her black satin stilettos with heels that had to be four inches high. "Let alone navigate steps in them."

"Please, don't speak too soon." She giggled. "Just tell me your car is close by."

"It is." He took her hand and nodded at several guests on his way to the parking lot.

"Oh my, that has to be yours." Sophie spotted his vehicle straight away. The girl knew her cars. "Cream is my favorite. It's stunning. Immaculate." She walked all the way around. "Right hand drive. Nice. Can I take a quick peek inside?"

"Of course." Miles opened the driver's door and she leaned in.

"Red leather with white piping. This might actually be my dream car, you know. Can you start her up for a sec? We have time." Sophie stood back.

"Sure." He didn't need to be asked twice. Miles jumped inside and started the engine, which purred like a satisfied cat. "This never gets old. Like I said, she was a special gift from my late uncle, and I don't get to drive her very often. Only when I happen to be in the UK."

"Fantastic." Sophie checked her watch. "I suppose we should go back inside before we're missed. Thanks, though."

"My pleasure." Miles locked the car. "Maybe I can give you a ride home later."

"Maybe."

He suppressed a whoop of joy.

She led the way back to the steps and they joined the last of the guests arriving in the foyer. The general hubbub inside made conversation difficult, so they sauntered over to a large chart and found their names—next to one another.

The air was thick with perfume as Miles followed Sophie

into the opulent dining hall dripping with crystal chandeliers and bejeweled by huge, cut-glass vases of fresh flowers on every surface. There was a small stage at one end of the space with a microphone set up, where the obligatory speeches would be made, no doubt. This wasn't Miles's first rodeo.

Sophie spotted the mic, too, and turned back toward him. "What will you do if they beg you to sing for charity tonight?" She raised a brow.

Miles blanched. A year ago, he would have been more than happy to oblige. "I'll have to give my apologies, I'm afraid." He concentrated on finding their seats.

"How come?"

"Vocal rest, at least from singing. Doctor's orders." He pointed to a round table several feet away. "I think that's us. Shall we settle in?"

She tilted her head. "Sure. Are you sick?"

"Nothing contagious, don't worry. It's a singing thing." Miles held a chair out for her to sit, and then sank into the one next to hers. A swift change of subject was in order. "So, tell me what you decided to do about your story. You said earlier that Harriet was cool with you keeping the manuscript as it is now, but have you had a chance to think more about it?"

Sophie set a tiny, sparkly clutch bag on the table and interlaced her fingers. "Harriet was amazingly kind about the whole thing. I ate a huge helping of humble pie when I described the character of the twin—I felt awful, even though I explained it was purely fiction and no harm was intended. I think she was putting on a brave face knowing I have publishers interested. She said she doesn't want me to miss this opportunity, which shows how completely opposite she is to the character in my story."

"Harriet knows you're a fiction writer."

"She does, and she's well aware of my overactive imagination. Besides, anyone who knows Harriet would realize I didn't base the character on her. For the general readership though, if they discovered I had a twin sister, they would surely think there's something more to it. I made a dreadful error, but I wrote during a dark time in my personal life. I wasn't thinking straight."

"Perhaps you needed to vent your frustration and anger at Troy, and then it happened to reveal itself mostly in your fictitious twin's character." Miles lifted a shoulder.

Sophie shook her head. "It was a rookie mistake. I had one of my writer friends critique the manuscript for me, and she asked if I'd based that character on my own sister. I said I hadn't, and I think I should have made changes right then. I guess I felt comfortable writing about a twin because…"

"You're a twin."

"They say *write what you know*, and so I did. Now, I can't imagine how Harriet might feel if anyone read the book and then believed she was anything like the wicked twin I've written. I went dark and deep with this one." Sophie pressed her lips together. "I'm going to chat with my agent. I think I've found a compromise that will keep the publishers happy and help me sleep better at night."

"Nice. What do you have in mind?" Miles leaned in to listen above the classical music playing in the background.

"I hope it'll work. Instead of having the character be an identical twin, she's going to be a jealous cousin, to keep the familial complexities. Then there can be no comparison if anyone decides to go digging into my private family life." Sophie was quiet for a few seconds. "I feel horrible about the whole thing. Harriet only ever wants the best for me."

"She had no clue you felt so insecure about your relationship with her?"

The surrounding tables were filling up.

"She thought she'd upset me somehow, but never knew I compared myself with her constantly or that I felt like I lived in her shadow." She shrugged her bare shoulders. "She apologized. I apologized again. She cried. I cried. It was lovely."

Miles shook his head. "I don't pretend to understand the relationship, but I'm happy you cleared things up."

Sophie spoke close enough to his ear that only he could hear. "To be honest, compared to the news about Troy threatening her safety, a fictitious storyline about an evil twin wasn't as big a deal as it could have been."

Fair enough. Sophie had to be concerned about Harriet's safety. "You think she'll be okay this evening? I know you said she was having a girls' night, but what about when they all leave?"

Sophie took a sip of sparkling water. "Her next-door neighbor is her best friend and she's sleeping over so her little girl can stay with Lucy. The husband will be mere feet away. I think Leo is due home sometime tomorrow."

"We can check on Harriet after this, if you like. I don't mind swinging by her house so you can be sure all is well."

"Thank you. You're a good man." She peered up through long dark lashes. "In your Porsche?"

Miles's lips twitched. "You know it. I hoped you wouldn't be able to resist…"

"Got that right."

He grinned and took a sip from his full glass. "You mentioned Leo didn't have much to offer in the way of info about the Clement family?"

"Nothing helpful." Sophie shrugged. "Harriet said he brushed off the wedding invitation saying it was a friend of his mother and he had no intention of going. Never heard of Troy Sanders." She narrowed her eyes. "Might be worth me trying to get in touch with Leo's mom myself though. See what she knows about the Clements."

Sophie smiled at the party of four joining them around the table and pivoted in her chair to see the stage, where an elderly man was making his way toward the mic stand. "Looks like things are about to begin."

The background music drew to a close and the hum of conversation stilled. The gentleman went to speak into the mic and winced at a squeal of feedback.

"My apologies. Good evening, ladies and gentlemen, and welcome to our annual Children's Hospital Wing Fundraising Ball. As always, we are most grateful for your generous donations, and you will be rewarded by a fantastic meal and an evening of live music and dancing." A round of applause rippled through the room. "I'm not going to keep you much longer, but I do want to introduce you to our generous guest of honor for this event. I won't make her come up here, but perhaps I could ask her to stand while we express our gratitude." He lifted his hand toward the table nearest the stage. "All the way from France, we would like to welcome Miss Camille Clement."

Miles clenched his jaw as he turned to Sophie.

She put a hand over her mouth.

The room erupted in applause and a blonde-haired woman in a sparkly blue dress stood with her chin held high, nodding and smiling at the surrounding guests.

Miles watched as Sophie strained to see past the tall man on her right who blocked her view of Camille. He reached over and clutched her hand. "You need to get out of here?"

"Is he with her? Troy?" Her voice wobbled. "I can't see."

"I'm not sure." Miles had only seen a few posts of him on social media, but there was a dark-haired man in a black suit next to Camille.

Sophie retrieved her hand from his and grabbed her bag. "I'm sorry. I don't feel so good. I'll be back in a minute." Her face contorted.

"Want me to come with you?" He stood and pulled Sophie's chair out to help her.

"No. You stay here. Please. I don't want to make a fuss. I won't be long." She slipped away while the applause died down.

Sophie reached the door to the lobby and looked back at the front tables. Miles had to force himself to stay seated as he watched her face crumple when she spotted Camille Clement's fiancé.

Chapter Sixteen

Sophie blinked back tears and ran to the ladies' room as fast as her high heels permitted. She avoided making eye contact with anyone en route and locked herself in a bathroom stall, grateful no one else was around. She caught her breath and leaned against the smooth, wooden door. Troy. She'd recognize those dark brown curls anywhere, even from the back.

The next second, she was folded over the toilet bowl, retching. The ladies' room door opened, and footsteps clicked across the floor. "Sophie? You in here?"

"Georgia?" Sophie wiped her mouth with some toilet paper and flushed.

"Hon, you okay?"

Sophie unlatched the stall and fell into her sister's arms. "No. Not really. He's here. Troy."

Georgia stroked her hair. "I'm so sorry. Will had no idea who the sponsor was this year. I didn't meet Troy when you were dating, but I'm guessing he's the dark-haired guy sitting next to Camille?"

Sophie nodded and pulled back. "It was a shock to see him, it caught me off guard." She rubbed her churning stomach.

"Did you throw up?"

"Yeah." She checked the front of her dress. "Lucky I got here in time."

Georgia dug in her purse. "You poor girl. I always carry travel-size toothbrush and toothpaste. Here."

"You do?" Sophie tucked a strand of hair behind her ear. "Thanks. Please, go back inside so you don't miss anything. Will needs you there with him tonight."

"What about you? I'm guessing you lost your appetite." She squeezed Sophie's shoulder. "Want me to arrange a taxi to take you home? I don't expect you to be in the same room as that man. I can't believe he has the nerve to be here."

Georgia didn't even know everything about him yet.

"I can't leave Miles here."

"Can he drive you home, do you think? I'm sure he'd rather hang out with you than stay at a stuffy event where he doesn't know anyone. I can go get him."

"I hate to bail." Sophie shivered. "But I think I'm going to have to. I can't face Troy. Especially here."

"Stay and freshen up. Take your time. I'll tell Miles to meet you in the foyer in a couple of minutes. I'll be subtle. Promise me you'll be careful and call if there's any problem. I'll leave my phone on vibrate all night."

"Promise. Thanks. Apologize to Will for me?"

"Sweetie, there's nothing to apologize for." Georgia smoothed her sister's cheek. "Trust me, Will is going to feel dreadful about this. An unfortunate coincidence, I suppose."

"I'll be fine. Please, go and make the most of the evening."

"If you're sure."

"I am."

"Okay then. Please call if you need anything at all." Georgia blew her a kiss and hurried back to the main room, leaving Sophie to brush her teeth with trembling fingers.

Oh Lord, why did Troy have to be here tonight? What's going on? I don't see him for three years and now suddenly he's everywhere?

As Sophie rinsed her mouth and slid the tiny toothbrush and paste into her clutch, she had a flash of realization. *No matter how distant I'm feeling from God, I always call on Him when I'm in trouble.* Muscle memory or the Holy Spirit? She studied her reflection in the mirror and wiped traces of mascara from beneath her eyes. God was as close as her reflection. As her shadow. No matter how much she protested, He was and always would be with her.

The ladies' room door swung open. Sophie jumped back.

"Sophie." Troy took four long strides toward her, checking the doors of each stall as he went.

She froze. Her mouth was filled with fear that felt like cotton balls. Why was he in here? This man was audacious.

Troy stopped inches in front of her and squinted. "We have to stop meeting like this." He looked her up and down with a leer. "I'm about to marry into one of the wealthiest families in Europe, so I'm only going to tell you this once. Don't interfere. Whatever you thought you saw—amnesia better be your plan. If you do anything to ruin my chances, I *will* ruin you. Your twin. Your new boyfriend." His bite over the word boyfriend held a sardonic tone. "Got it?" He grabbed her upper arm, and she flinched. "No police. No nothing. I have people everywhere. Or those bad memories I left you with will be child's play compared to what will happen next."

Rage simmered beneath her skin, but before she could say a single word, Troy dropped her arm, stalked away, and left her a shaking wreck. Déjà vu. She stumbled to the sink and rubbed her arm. Wafts of his sickly-sweet cologne permeated the air and a claustrophobic urge to run welled up within her. Grabbing her clutch from the counter, she trotted into the foyer where several servers fussed with trays of drinks. The soothing music did nothing to calm her nerves. Her gaze darted toward the two sets of double doors that led into the dining area and the silhouette of Miles appeared in one of them.

She hurried over and tugged on his arm. "Can we go, please? Now?"

"Of course. Whatever you need. Georgia explained." He put a protective arm around her shoulder and led her outside. The air seemed cooler, and she relished the warmth of Miles's torso as he pulled her closer to him. "Want my jacket? It's a little chilly." He led her to the parking lot.

"I'm fine. Thanks." Her teeth chattered but not from the cool air. "Could you take me home?"

"Whatever you prefer. Although I'm not keen on leaving you there alone. I could take you to Harriet's, if you like. Or should we go for a drive to clear your mind a bit? Then I'll hang out at the cottage until Georgia gets back. We can talk or not talk. Your choice."

"I-I don't know." Could she even make a decision after that unnerving encounter?

Miles took a key from his pocket. "In that case, let's just go." He opened the passenger door and helped Sophie ease into the low seat.

She couldn't help gasp when he took her upper arm, the exact place Troy had squeezed.

Miles squatted down next to her and frowned. "I'm sorry. Did I hurt you?"

She shook her head and fastened the seat belt. "Troy found me in the washroom."

His face changed in a flash. "What? You were with him alone? What did he do?" He stood and turned back toward the lit building, both fists clenched.

"I'm all right. We had words and he squeezed my arm." She reached out and tugged the edge of his jacket. "Can we leave now? Please?"

Miles looked down at her in his car and then back at the place where Troy and his fiancée were schmoozing with doctors and influential people from the area. "Of course."

He closed her door, jogged around to the driver's side, slid behind the wheel, and pulled out of the grounds onto a narrow road. "Can you give me directions? I don't mind where we go, but I guess we should eventually get to Bramble Downs."

"Sure." Sophie took several deep breaths. The trembling was subsiding, at least. She dug her phone from her clutch bag and figured out where they were heading. "I'm not too bad at finding my way around, but I don't quite trust myself without GPS yet. We're fairly close to the coast here. Want to drive there? Not much of a sunset but the sea air calms me."

"Sounds like a plan. You know I'll stay outside your cottage in my car all night if it helps you feel safer. I'm serious. I don't mind."

"That's sweet of you, but I think we'll find a better solution. I can ask Will if you could crash at his place tonight, so you don't have to drive all the way back to your aunt's. His house is huge and there's only him and his little son there. Jack may even be staying with Will's parents tonight. I know they like to babysit whenever they can."

"Do you think Will would mind? That would be ideal as I'd like to stay with you until Georgia gets home. That could be pretty late."

"I'll text Georgia now and see what she thinks." Sophie tapped out a message, and within seconds Georgia responded. "That was quick. Will says he's totally fine with you staying at his place."

"Great." Miles turned down the volume on a classical radio station. "So… are you able to tell me what happened with Troy tonight? You said he came into the ladies' room…"

She rubbed her arm. There was going to be a heck of a bruise by tomorrow. "He took me by surprise. Told me not to interfere with his future in the Clement family. He said not to involve the police and then threatened Harriet again and… you."

"Me?" Miles's eyebrows shot up. "He knows about me?"

"I don't know how much. Or if he even knows your name."

"I don't care about that. I care about you." Miles reached over and took her hand.

They didn't speak for a couple of minutes.

"Did he hurt your arm badly? Something tells me it wasn't the first time."

Sophie stared through the passenger window at the various shades of green blurring together. She blinked moisture from her eyes and cleared her throat. If Miles was going to get involved, he needed to know what he was walking into.

"Sophie? I'm not going to judge you."

"I know. It's… it's so messed up. I hoped I'd put it behind me. Put *him* behind me." She groaned.

Miles pulled into an empty parking area on a cliff top and chose a perfect spot overlooking the sea. "This work for you?"

"Perfect." She went to open her door and Miles was already there to help her out. "We're not really dressed for a beach walk. Can we sit on a bench for a while?" She nodded at a bench in front of his car.

"Sounds good. I have a blanket in the backseat in case the bench is dirty. I don't think Harriet would appreciate you getting her gown in a mess." He grabbed a red plaid blanket and set it over the wooden slats.

Could this guy be any more considerate? Her shoulders relaxed as she watched him take care of her. How refreshing.

"You okay, Sophie? Want my jacket?"

She shook her head and perched on the bench. Surveying the horizon as dusk descended, she took in a deep breath of salty air and patted the space next to her.

"Miles, I'm going to tell you something I've never told anyone else before."

He lowered himself next to Sophie and took her hand in his. *Please don't think less of me.*

Chapter Seventeen

"It happened three years ago." Sophie looked out over the expanse of water before them. The sea was gunmetal gray, the exact color of Miles's eyes. If she was going to be able to get through this, she would have to focus on the sea rather than the pain—or pity—in this man's face.

"Take your time." Miles squeezed her hand and followed her lead by averting his gaze from her flushed cheeks. "We've got all night. I'm not going anywhere."

"I appreciate that." Where to begin? "When I moved to Paris after university in Vancouver, I had some grandiose ideals and plans for my life. My writing career would take off and I would learn to bake as a side hustle. I always loved experimenting with baking growing up." Images of her mom's warm and welcoming kitchen welled up from childhood memories and spilled over like chocolate from her molten lava cakes. Sophie's heart squeezed. "Of course, I would fall madly in love while living in one of the most romantic cities in the world. I mentioned before that I was a good Christian girl and prayed that God would provide me with my perfect man when the time was right." She chanced a quick glance at Miles's handsome profile. "When I say perfect, I'm not so naive to think there is such a thing as a perfect man. I mean someone who is a perfect fit for me."

He nodded and cracked a smile.

"I was picky. Mom always told us our man would be worth waiting for and that we should never settle. In fact, I only went on a handful of dates in the first few years and was pretty content to wait for *the one*. Then, when I was beginning to wonder if my Mr. Right would ever turn up and that my happily-ever-after would purely be fictional in my stories, I met Troy Sanders." Her stomach roiled at the mere mention of his name.

"Where did you meet?" Miles's voice was soft. Gentle. Kind. Everything Troy was not.

"We met at church. The English-speaking service. I always sat in the same area with friends at the front near the stage and got to know familiar faces. I shook Troy's hand in the greeting part at the beginning of one service and was delighted to hear an American accent. In France, you gravitate toward anyone from North America. There's this connection, a wash of homesickness and camaraderie. You probably understand what I mean?"

"Totally. Hearing a familiar accent is like a taste of home."

"Exactly. So, we got talking and I told him I was from Vancouver, which he'd visited once from his home near Seattle when he was in his teens. He spoke excellent French and had been to Paris before, but now he was pursuing his dream of living there with an entry job at the US Embassy. He was delightful. I was delighted."

Sophie took a beat and licked her dry lips. Explaining this to Miles was more awkward than she'd imagined, but she needed to press on.

"I missed the next week at church as I was sick with the flu but saw him again the following service. My small group always sat together, and we invited Troy and the two guys he was with to come for brunch afterwards. I found out a little more—Troy was renting an apartment near mine in Paris, his dad was a businessman back in Seattle, and his mom, who was born in France, died in an accident when he was twelve years old."

Miles winced. "That's rough."

"I know. He didn't ever speak much about the accident, but obviously his mother's death affected him. To be honest, we bonded on several levels—losing a parent as a child, moving from North America to Paris, and our shared faith. He asked me out for coffee that Wednesday evening, and again, we hit it off. He'd been in church all his life and was happy to banter about theological subjects and discuss our experiences and faith journeys." She shrugged. "I felt comfortable around Troy. I prayed about him, asked God if this was a good idea—and there didn't seem to be any red flags. Or in hindsight, maybe I was determined not to look too closely."

The sound of seagulls screeched overhead and they both watched the feathered air show.

Miles spoke first. "How could a creature so graceful make such a wretched noise?"

"Appearances can be deceiving." She waited until they disappeared. "Our next date was dinner in a fancy restaurant. It was romantic and everything felt… perfect. It was happening fast, but I was twenty-seven years old and yet to have a serious relationship. I felt ready. Maybe a tad impatient, too. We went all in and started spending every possible moment together." Her body felt antsy. She needed to move. "Want to walk for a while? I can go a little way in these shoes."

Miles stood and pointed to a paved path that ran along the top of the cliff. The area was deserted. Private. "This way?"

"Sure." Sophie stood and took his hand. She strolled in silence and studied the ground. "I should have listened to my friends. To my boss, Annabelle. Within a few weeks, Troy's possessive nature was obvious to everyone except me. I was flattered that he wanted to spend so much time with me. He'd pick me up from work at the patisserie whenever it fit his schedule, and he showered me with attention. Bought me a gold necklace for our three-month dating anniversary. The only thing we didn't have in common was the opera."

At this, Miles peered down at her face. "Interesting."

Of course, that hit a nerve for Miles. "I told you I'd been brought up listening to opera music at home, and I remember loving the annual tradition of going to the opera in Vancouver with Mom and my sisters. I'd close my eyes and dream Daddy was alive and we were a complete family again. He enjoyed the opera, too."

"That's a precious memory." Miles let the moment linger. "Troy wasn't a fan?"

"He hated it with a passion. Refused to ever go with me, not that I went to the Paris Opera House often. Only on the rare occasion when I'd treat myself or Mom would send me a ticket for my birthday or Christmas. I stopped going when I dated Troy, and it was a sacrifice I was willing to make. His obsession was running. He was a fitness fanatic and ran around the city like it was his job. He'd run marathons back in the States. He was in good shape, to say the least."

"Did you go with him?"

She let out a humorless laugh. "I took up running for him, after not doing any at all since high school. You can imagine what that was like for me. Troy bought me some great running shoes and we started running together through the city, when our work schedules allowed. He thought I could maybe lose a few pounds, as I worked in the patisserie, and he was worried I might be tempted to indulge too often."

"Seriously?"

"I know, but I figured the exercise would be good for me

regardless. Harriet was always the super fit and healthy twin, being a pro ballerina and all."

"You said Harriet met Troy?"

Sophie nodded. "Harriet came to stay with me for a weekend as I wanted her to meet him, and she got creepy vibes. Tried to talk sense into me. She knew I was having difficulty with my writing—I'd never encountered writer's block before my relationship with Troy, but I was suddenly lacking any kind of creativity and could barely string two sentences together. I put it down to being in love. Harriet had her doubts. She said I was unhealthily skinny, and that Troy shouldn't be so demanding and possessive. She didn't get it…"

"Because she was happily married?"

"Yes. With a baby at home. How could she understand? I'd prayed and prayed, certain Troy was the real deal. Now I see how gradually Troy became my everything. Other than work at the patisserie and Sundays at church, where he clutched my hand like I was on a leash, I saw nobody else socially. He cleared his schedule for me, and we had fun at first. I saw Paris through fresh eyes as we went up the Eiffel Tower and visited Notre Dame Cathedral. Other than the running, which I honestly hated, I was happy… until I was not."

She glanced to her right as a sliver of tangerine sun dipped behind a bank of charcoal clouds. A splash of yellow highlighted the horizon and she inhaled the crisp, tangy sea air. This would've been so beautiful if she didn't have to share her ugly story. A shiver ran through her.

"Please, let me give you this?" Miles took off his jacket and draped it over her shoulders. Sophie didn't argue. The weight of it felt comforting and warm. Troy started off as a polite gentleman, too…

"Thanks. That's better. I don't know if it's the evening air getting chillier or the fact that I'm remembering life with Troy."

Miles took her hand again. "You want to stop? We can carry on another time if this is too much."

She shook her head. "I need to get this out. It might help if we both know where he's coming from."

"Whatever you think is best."

Sophie took a deep breath and continued. "In church, when my friends invited us out for brunch, Troy would squeeze my arm a little too tightly until I declined. When my small group asked why I stopped attending, Troy answered for me and said we were studying the Bible as a couple. That was an actual lie. If Annabelle asked me to work a little later when the line-up was through the door, Troy would come in and practically drag me out—charming with his words to Annabelle, but downright rude in his actions. She didn't like him one bit, but I made feeble excuses for his behavior every single time."

"That's awful." Miles's voice was hoarse.

"Mom sent me a ticket to the opera for Christmas, and I planned to go with a writing friend as I knew Troy would have no interest in attending. Actually, I checked if it was okay with Troy like I was six years old or something, and he begrudgingly permitted it, as the ticket was a gift from my mom."

Miles grunted. "How decent of him."

"I know. It should have sounded alarm bells for me, but I was so desperate to keep him happy."

"Can I ask, had he been violent with you up to now, other than the forceful controlling, I mean?"

Here we go. "Yes." She blinked back tears. "Like I said, it started with being a little too forceful with his actions, and then he started getting physical in my apartment. Really physical. I made the mistake of going to the police and attempted to get a restraining order at one point, but Troy had contacts there. Made me out to be a hysterical fool. The police did nothing, Troy begged my forgiveness, and he was a gentleman again—until this particular night at the opera."

"It's no wonder you have trouble trusting the police. I'm so sorry." Miles squeezed her hand.

"This all sounds ridiculous, and I can't believe I stayed with him, but in the moment, I guess I didn't realize how horrific things were… until this happened." She swallowed a sob. *I need to tell someone. I need to tell Miles.* A deep breath.

"Troy had to work late that night, and I was thrilled to finally be going to the opera again. Unfortunately, my friend had to cancel last minute as she was sick with food poisoning, and she gave her ticket to her younger brother. I'd met him before, so it wasn't uncomfortable at all. We were both there to see the performance. He was kind enough to drive me home afterwards. It was a freezing night, so I was grateful. When I got to my apartment, Troy was waiting at the entrance. He took one look at my friend's brother in the driver's seat, and I knew I was in trouble."

"Oh, Sophie."

"His face was like thunder as he put an arm around me and I dug out my keys. The guy waved and drove away oblivious, and Troy was silent. I babbled about how great the opera was and how it was a shame my friend was sick and gave her ticket to her brother. Still silent, Troy joined me in the elevator, and we went up to the fourth floor, where my apartment was." Sophie's mouth was dry as she recalled her terror. "He didn't answer any of my questions and I knew he was seething. Biding his time."

A tear escaped and ran down her cheek. She could almost

smell Troy's sickly cologne. "We walked along the deserted hallway. Outside my door, he finally spoke. He asked if I thought he was stupid. His face was red and a vein in his forehead throbbed, like when he ran too fast. Before I had a chance to reply, he grabbed both my shoulders and marched me backwards toward the narrow staircase. At the top, he pulled my face up to his and he hissed *you're mine* and pushed me hard. I grabbed handfuls of air and fell backwards down a flight of stairs."

Miles clenched the fist that wasn't holding Sophie's hand and attempted to mask his rage. He'd guessed this guy was a jerk, but hearing the details? Memories of his own mother filled his mind. Bruises. Bloodied lip. Black eye. The excuses she made for his father. At least Sophie wasn't candy-coating this…

He stopped walking and pulled her into a gentle hug. "I'm so, so sorry." He whispered the words into her hair. "I know this must be excruciating for you to relive."

Sophie pulled back and sniffed. "I want to tell you, Miles. I need to tell you. You need to know what Troy is like."

Several choice descriptors came to mind, none of which he wanted to say in front of Sophie. "I get the picture." He lifted her chin and looked into those chocolate eyes. "Were you badly hurt?"

She pursed her lips and stared right past him. "I remember I covered my face with my arms as I banged against the wall and the iron railings and the unforgiving floor. I must have blacked out when I reached the bottom because when I dared to open my eyes, I was alone. Troy had disappeared."

"He left you there? You could have been seriously injured."

This guy was a piece of work.

"I guess I should be grateful I didn't get a major head injury or something. I eventually sat up, found my phone on the stairs, and called a taxi to take me to the hospital." She touched her arm, the one she was rubbing earlier. "I knew for sure I'd broken my left arm because I'd broken it falling out of a tree when I was eight years old and it felt the same. I was shocked, in agony, and utterly alone." She wiped tears from her cheeks.

"You didn't call a friend? Annabelle?"

She shook her head. "I couldn't. I was… ashamed? Embarrassed? I don't know. In the taxi, I decided I would stay silent. I wasn't going back to the police, for sure. When anyone asked about my arm, I would say I tripped on my long dress and fell down the stairs. Aggravated an old injury. I'd become proficient in making excuses for my bruises in the name of clumsiness."

Miles pulled her close and felt her heart beating wildly against his torso. No woman should have to endure violence. No man had a right to do this. After seeing such horrors in his own home, he vowed he would do whatever he could for anyone else going through such a nightmare. "I'll help you. I promise."

"Thank you."

An older couple ambled toward them from farther along the path, so Miles put an arm around Sophie, and they turned back in the direction of his car. "Did you see him again after that?"

"No. That was literally the last I saw of Troy until a week ago. I don't know if there was guilt or shame on his part—somehow, I doubt it—or whether he was done with me and knew I'd never take him back. I heard he got a transfer home to the

States, and he told everyone in Paris that we made a mutual decision to break up. I told no one the truth, not even my twin, although I'm pretty sure she suspected there was more to the story."

"That's so much for you to carry on your own."

Sophie tucked a wayward strand of hair behind her ear. "I wanted to share it with my family, but I think pride got in the way. I was adept at hiding my true feelings by then, and I wanted them to think I was living my best life. After the break-up, I put on a brave face, my arm healed, and I kept up the charade."

Miles concentrated on the tiny yellow flowers at the edge of the path as they strolled along, when all he wanted to do was take her in his arms and never let go. Keep her safe. Love her. Love…where did that come from? He cleared his throat. "Too bad you didn't feel you could lean on your sisters. After meeting them both, I'm pretty sure they would have been there for you."

"They would. Georgia and Mom were in Canada, of course, but Harriet would have been at my side like a shot."

"Georgia wouldn't have been far behind, distance or not."

Sophie let out a short sigh. "True. I know Mom would drop everything if she knew something was remotely wrong, too. In hindsight, I should have reached out. Maybe I was in denial myself. Hiding the truth from them was hard at first, but it got easier as time went on. I told them I was giving men a wide berth after having my heart broken, which was true. I also threw out the expensive running shoes Troy bought me and declared myself a non-runner—a huge relief—and then I poured myself into writing, work at the bakery, and resumed hanging out with my friends. I survived." She chewed on a thumbnail. "I'll share all the details about the break-up with my family… when the time is right."

Miles's heart squeezed at the thought of all she'd been through. He surveyed the last glimpse of the sun. "Troy has to be nervous about Camille finding out about any of this with his upcoming wedding. I can't imagine his future in-laws would be impressed with him being remotely linked with an attack of any woman."

They reached the bench by the parking area and Sophie spun around to face him. "I agree. I need to report him, but please understand, I can't do anything rash. We don't know what he's capable of and we've got to be smart. He wants to be part of this Clement family and is power-hungry enough to hurt or even kill for it."

"Now he's hopping in and out of England, too." Miles stroked Sophie's cheek. "Thanks for sharing all this with me. It can't have been easy, but know that I'm not going to let this slide. This man needs to be stopped before he's in a position of power where he could hurt more people."

"More women."

"Precisely. I'll bet his fiancée doesn't know the half of what he's capable of."

Sophie groaned. "She needs to know. I've no idea how, but I've got to step in and do something about Troy Sanders before it's too late."

Miles tilted his head and stared at the rigid set of her chin. She was strong and determined, in spite of the fear that must be coursing through her body at the thought of this disgusting man she had once loved. "What did you have in mind?"

She turned toward the sea. "I'm not entirely sure."

He gave her space as he picked up his blanket from the bench and then led her back to the car. "You don't have to do any of this alone anymore, Sophie."

"I appreciate that. So much. I've felt alone for a long time." She looked up and fresh tears coursed down her cheeks. "Have I told you you're a great listener?"

"You have." He touched her quivering chin. "I'd like to be so much more than that, if you'll let me."

Sophie wiped her wet face, reached up on tiptoes, and kissed him with a passion that left his lips tingling and his heart hammering, before sliding her petite frame into the car.

Miles ran a hand through his hair. "I'll take that as a yes."

Chapter Eighteen

Back at Bramble Cottage, Sophie rushed to her bedroom, hung Harriet's red gown on a padded hanger, and changed into jeans and a black T-shirt while Miles poured them both a glass of water downstairs. He'd had a coughing fit on his way in from the car and offered to fetch drinks while she changed. On their drive from the sea, they both realized how hungry they were, and now the aroma of the fish and chips they picked up on their way through the village permeated the home.

Miles turned when he heard her scurrying down the stairs. "You really think it's better eaten straight out of the paper?" He frowned from his seat on the couch, their meal covering the large coffee table.

"Absolutely. I can't believe you've never had fish and chips this way before in all your years visiting England. Back in the day it was actual newspaper. Now the paper's plain but still has the same effect. I made sure they added plenty of malt vinegar and salt. I'll get the ketchup."

Sophie retrieved a full bottle from the pantry and peeled off the lid. When she went to discard the plastic in the garbage can, she hesitated. A scrunched piece of kitchen towel was stuffed down at the bottom, covered with what appeared to be a splotch of blood. A fair amount. Or ketchup? No. She knew they ran out of ketchup because Georgia picked up this new bottle today. Had her sister cut herself this evening before the ball? Unless Miles…

An uneasy knot formed in her stomach. She called into the

living room. "Hey, Miles, are you feeling okay?"

He didn't answer straight away. "Umm other than starving to death here, yes. Why do you ask?"

"Just checking. Sounded like a nasty cough when we came in." She'd talk to Georgia later. The splotchy kitchen towel was most likely something silly. She passed Miles the ketchup. "It goes without saying that this particular condiment is a must."

He coughed again and drained the rest of his water. Now that she studied his face in the lamplight, he seemed a little pale.

"Let me grab you a refill before I get settled." Sophie collected his glass and returned to the water dispenser in the fridge door. She stared at the garbage bin again and chewed her thumbnail for several seconds.

"You're right. This is the best." Miles had already started his feast when Sophie returned to the room, and as she studied him again, his face already a healthier color. Perhaps he was simply in need of food.

She popped a greasy fry into her mouth. "Didn't wait for me to say grace this time?"

Miles stopped chewing. "Oh man, I said my own. I'm so sorry. Guess I'm a little too used to eating by myself."

Sophie chuckled. "I'm kidding. You're clearly famished." She wiped a speck of ketchup from her jeans. "I hope you don't get any food on your nice clothes. Sorry we don't have any guy stuff here." Although she wasn't about to complain—he looked fantastic. He'd undone the top button and rolled up the sleeves of his white shirt, but the black tux pants were in danger of suffering grease stains from a chippie dinner.

Miles held his fork in the air. "Do you mind if I sit on the floor?" His voice sounded hoarse.

"Of course not. I'll join you. Is your throat sore or something?"

"I'm fine." He chugged more water and nodded to a framed photo on a side table. "That must be your grandparents."

Sophie stretched over and brought the frame closer to show him. "It is. They were the absolute best. Lived in this cottage for as long as I can remember." She stared at the white-haired couple with ruddy cheeks and matching jackets. They radiated love and kindness. "We had the best summers here. Grandma was the one who first ignited my passion for baking."

"In that case, we are all very grateful to her. What a wonderful legacy she left." Miles pointed at her grandfather. "He seems a jolly fellow."

"He was. Loved Jesus and his family so much. He would have adored your car. He was always tinkering with an engine or restoring some old jalopy."

"Sounds like you inherited a lot from your grandparents. It's cool that you get to live in their home now."

"So cool." She set down the photo and picked up a fork. "I would never have imagined all three sisters living in Bramble Downs, but I know Grandma and Grandad would be thrilled."

They sat side-by-side on the rug leaning their backs against the couch. This was comfortable and cozy. A far cry from earlier in the evening. She let out a contented sigh. A load had lifted from her shoulders in sharing her story with Miles, and their bond seemed to be strengthening at a rapid rate.

"Everything all right?" Miles nudged her with his elbow.

"It is now." Sophie dug into her piece of battered cod and groaned. "This is perfect. Better than a stuffy slap-up meal on actual chairs in a fancy venue."

"Agreed." Miles turned to her with a huge grin and used his thumb to wipe her lip. "Ketchup."

She grabbed a paper napkin from the table and patted her mouth. "I'm hungrier than I thought." After her interaction with Troy, and then explaining everything to Miles, she was surprised her stomach could hold any food at all. "Thanks."

"For the fish and chips? You're welcome. I promise I'll upgrade next time." He winked.

"I mean thanks for being there for me tonight. For being my escape plan and then letting me share the burden. I'm sure you had no idea what you were walking into when you decided I might be worth pursuing." She studied her red fingernails. "I want you to know that I'm here for you, too. I'm actually a good listener if you ever want to share anything." Would he trust her with whatever he was carrying or dealing with in his own life? "You implied before that you have your own stuff to work through…"

Miles finished his mouthful and shifted to face her fully. "Can I be honest?"

"Please."

"Even if it comes dangerously close to cheesy?"

Sophie took a sip of water. "I'm fond of cheese."

He stared into her eyes, his gray irises closer to blue than she'd seen before. "I may not have known what I was walking into, but I knew it would be a risk worth taking. I don't know if you're one to believe in love at first sight—I've always been a skeptic—but the second I saw you holding that pink box of cakes with a smudge of flour on your cheek, I was captivated."

Sophie felt her face heat up and knew she was blushing. This was like a dream. Like some kind of fairy tale. Like her actual manuscript. She took his hands in hers. He wasn't going to open up quite yet, but this was a beautiful start. "I felt the same. It was like a God thing—even though I'm not *officially* close to God at the moment." Who was she trying to fool?

"I am." His gaze fell to her mouth. "For the record, I've been praying about and for you, and intend to continue…" He closed the space between them, his lips found hers, and Sophie sank into their kiss. Her hands travelled around from his face to his thick hair, and she allowed her fingers to run through its waves. He held her with such tenderness, such care, she didn't want the moment to end—but he pulled back, their foreheads touching as they both caught their breath.

"I guess we should finish our food before it gets cold." Sophie's words sounded lame, but she knew they needed to slow things down.

"I think we generated enough heat to keep it warm for a while." Miles let her go. "But you're probably right." He took another gulp of water and Sophie did the same.

"Changing the subject completely, can I ask you more about your novel manuscript?" Miles stabbed a chip with his fork. "The original version. If you're willing to tell me, that is."

Sophie nodded as she finished a mouthful of flaky cod. This would be interesting. "Of course, I'd love to. The working title is *The Paris Pumpkin,* and it's loosely based on the Cinderella story. Sort of. I always adored the original and wanted to write a contemporary adaptation set in the city I loved."

"Nice. How long ago did you write it?"

She tilted her head. "I finished it maybe two years ago? I never intended for it to be published initially."

Miles frowned. "How come?"

"Writing is how I process everything. After what happened with Troy, I started this story, and before I knew what was happening, my frustration seeped into the pages and I allowed my heart to spill out. It was cathartic. Want more ketchup?"

"Thanks." Miles took the bottle and squeezed a blob onto his paper. "So, were you Cinderella?"

"Cindy. How did you guess? I definitely channeled my feelings of being used and abused. Instead of having mean, ugly stepsisters, my protagonist was a mean, beautiful, perfect twin." Sophie set down her fork and wiped her hands on a napkin. "A horribly warped version of my own sweet sister. Major regrets on that decision, as you know. This is how the story started. I still can't believe how understanding Harriet was about the whole thing. We never used to have secrets from each other. Originally, we shared a womb, after all."

"Womb mates?" Miles chuckled at his own wise crack. "I'm glad you called her on the way home tonight."

"Me, too. I'm satisfied she's safe, but I needed to warn her that Troy's in the vicinity."

Miles reached over and held her hand. "She promised to let you know if she was worried. Back to the story though, what happens to Cindy? Please tell me she meets Prince Charming."

Here goes nothing. "She does. There's a pumpkin farm outside the city. After a nasty break-up, she meets Charlie. Although it's not the happily ever after you might imagine. It's pretty brutal and hits on much of what happened between Troy and me—plus, a beastly twin sister is in the mix. Charlie and Cindy do end up together—but they are both shot by the evil ex-boyfriend, no prizes for guessing who that's based on, and then the beastly twin has a change of heart and ends up shooting the ex."

"Wow. Definitely not what I expected."

"The beloved couple are hospitalized, stable but unconscious. The book concludes with the twin running down the hospital corridor as she hears the sustained beep from their monitors… only to find them side by side in their beds, holding hands, finally together. Gone. Dead."

Miles's eyes widened. "Dead?"

"I know, it's morbid but it's beautiful. More Romeo and Juliet than Prince Charming and Cinderella. I sent it to my literary agent about eight months ago and she loved it. Was sure she could send it to some of her contacts in a few publishing houses. One of them asked for the full manuscript, then another, so that's where we're at right now."

"You think your revisions on Harriet's character will be accepted?"

Sophie chewed her thumbnail. "They have to be. I can't do that to Harriet. Not now. Cousin replaces the twin, that's the deal. I'll make it even better."

"Are you worried about how Troy may react with the evil ex in your story?"

"Maybe. Yes, I guess I am. Although publication is still a dream. I'm more worried about you though." She focused on her food on the table.

"Me? What do you mean?"

"This is going to sound silly, but the couple in love? Their relationship mirrors ours so much it freaks me out when I think about it."

He dipped his chin. "Interesting. How so?"

"She's a poor baker in Paris. He's a successful wealthy businessman—hear me out—his physical description is you to a tee. When I saw you for the first time, it was as if I'd conjured you right out from my manuscript."

Miles swallowed. "O-kay."

"So, Cindy has to move to the country to be cook and

cleaner for her dreadful twin's family. Baking is her escape. She writes songs in her spare time, the little that she has. Charlie goes searching for her after she disappears and finds out from the bakery that she's moved to a rural area."

"Sounds… familiar."

"There's more. Charlie tracks her down and they fall desperately in love. He finds her songs and sings them—he has the most magnificent voice she has ever heard."

"Is that so?"

"I know. Uncanny. It's all glorious until her violent ex-boyfriend comes after her. I described him pretty accurately as Troy, too." Sophie cringed. "Then long story short, he starts stalking her, terrorizing her, and one day he hears Charlie singing one of Cindy's love songs—recognizes it. In a fit of rage and realizing he can never have Cindy for himself, the ex decides Charlie can't have her either and he shoots them both. Like I said, the twin finds them and shoots the ex, but in the end the lovers die, Miles. *They both die.* They're together for eternity, but I don't want our ending to be the same. I know I'm sounding hysterical and ridiculous, but can't you see how reality and my fictional story are intertwined?"

Miles looked into her imploring eyes. "This isn't our story, Sophie. I agree, the similarities are there, but it's fiction. Born of your imagination. We're not going to die—not yet—but I hope we're going to end up together. I truly do." He wrapped her in a hug.

"I bet you didn't expect that for a description of my manuscript." She spoke the words into his shoulder.

"Yeah, I didn't think you'd kill me off. I've heard it's never a good idea to get on the wrong side of a writer."

She giggled. "I'm sorry. We need a little levity, don't you think?"

Miles pulled back. "It's been rather a heavy evening. What did you have in mind?"

Sophie quirked an eyebrow, dipped a stodgy chip in the pool of ketchup, and dabbed Miles's nose. "That's better." The shock on his face was priceless.

Miles gasped… and reciprocated.

Wasn't expecting that.

After some more attempts in a ketchup exchange that morphed into a tickle fight, Sophie took charge and kissed Miles with a fervor that started in fun and soon fueled into fire.

She collapsed against the sofa. "I'm going to say it again, we really should finish our food." She was falling fast for this man, and he seemed too good to be true. "As much as I love having you around," she munched on a half-cold chip, "and trust me, I truly do, I'm dreading you're going to tell me you have to take off and go to sing in Italy or the States for six months or something. I understand it's your job, but I rather like having you around."

She avoided his gaze and he didn't reply. They ate in companionable silence.

He took another sip of water.

"Come to think of it, we haven't talked much at all about what's next for you." She rested her fork on the paper wrapping. "My issues seem to have taken up most of our time together."

This time the silence made her pulse pick up speed.

"Miles?" She tilted her head and stroked his hair. "You okay there?"

He wiped his hands on a napkin. "Sorry. I don't mean to be

aloof. You've had a heck of a lot going on, that's all. In answer to your question, I'm not sure what's next for me. I'm taking a bit of a… break."

"Not because of me and my mess, I hope?" She frowned. They were falling for each other more every day, yet how much could she ask of him this early on in their relationship? "I don't want you to feel the need to babysit me or anything." She lifted her chin. "I'm more than capable of taking care of myself. I lived alone in Paris for years and—"

"No." Miles put a finger over her lips. "You're not stopping me from doing anything, it's all good. I'm aware you are capable of looking after yourself, too. I'd planned on slowing down this summer, spend some time with my aunt, and I want to stick around and help you figure this stuff out, if that's all right with you."

His eyes widened and her heart melted.

"Please, Sophie? Let me help? I'll stay with my aunt and give you space, but I'm only an hour or so away if you need me for anything."

"But your career? I don't want you to resent me or pass up an opportunity."

"I couldn't possibly resent you. I have some stuff I need to work through. Some appointments. A rest of sorts. It's complicated…"

"You think I don't know how to do complicated? Have you not been paying attention here?" She sat back and huffed. "Why won't you tell me what's wrong?"

Miles didn't look her in the eyes. He stared at their entwined hands.

"Are you in trouble with the law? Is it your aunt? Finances?" She squeezed his hand. "I could keep guessing here…"

"No. It's none of the above. It's not you either. It's a…work thing. I appreciate you wanting to help, but I'm waiting to find out my next steps. Can you be patient with me? Please? I'll share as soon as I'm able."

"Of course." Sophie pulled him in for a hug and bit her tongue.

She didn't want to push things. He'd been kind and patient with her, she should give him the same grace.

If You're listening, God, I like this guy a lot and he seems like the real deal, but please don't let me fall for someone who's going to hurt me. I can't do this again.

Something—other than the late-night fish and chips—was not sitting well in Sophie's gut.

Chapter Nineteen

Sophie washed the muffin pan in soapy suds and stared through the kitchen window at the dark and dismal morning. Rain teemed from stormy clouds and showed no signs of easing up.

"Hey." Georgia's voice croaked behind her.

"Morning, sleepyhead." Sophie turned and chuckled as her sister stood in the doorway, more bedraggled than she'd ever seen her with crazy curls and shadows beneath her eyes. "Long night?"

"Please tell me there's coffee in the pot." Georgia stretched her arms out like a cat on a sunny windowsill. "I can't believe how late we got back home last night. Or I should say, this morning."

"Why don't you sit and let me take care of you for a change?" Sophie pulled out a chair at the kitchen table and fixed Georgia a mug of coffee with a splash of cream.

"Thanks. I literally drank sparkling water all night before you get all judge-y on me."

Sophie held up her hands in mock surrender. "I didn't say a word."

"You didn't need to. It's written all over that smirk on your face. I'm not used to late nights. I don't know how Will pulls those all-night shifts at the hospital. So much socializing… I'm drained." She took a sip of hot coffee. "Mmm. That's what I needed."

"I made lemon blueberry muffins. Interested?"

"I knew I could smell heaven down here. Yes, please.

You're a life saver." She accepted the warm muffin and patted the chair next to her. "Join me?"

"Don't mind if I do." Sophie set down her mug and plate with a half-eaten muffin. "Split a banana?"

"Sure, let's go crazy. Listen, I'm sorry you guys had to wait so long for Will and me to get home. He needed to stay until all the guests were on their way. Were you all right after seeing… you know, Troy and his fiancée there?"

Sophie's stomach curdled as she explained how Troy found her in the ladies' room and threatened her.

"I had no idea. I'm so sorry." Georgia paled. "I shouldn't have left you alone in there."

"Don't be silly. You had no way of knowing he'd have the nerve to barge into the ladies' washroom." Sophie traced the rim of her mug with her finger. "Did you or Will speak to Troy at all?"

"No, I managed to avoid him one-on-one. After what you told me about how potentially dangerous he is, I was in no hurry to even make eye contact with him. I still can't get over his audacity to attend anything in this neighborhood. Could he have known you would be there?"

"I wouldn't be surprised. He likes to intimidate. Even if he hadn't come and found me, he knew full well that if I saw him there, I would freak out." Sophie bit her trembling lip. "I wish I knew what he was up to. What his game plan is with marrying into that wealthy family. I don't trust him one bit. Clearly, his fiancée has no idea about his true character."

Georgia cleared her throat. "Actually, we were introduced to Camille. All the doctors were."

"What's she like?" Sophie was more than curious.

"Seemed nice enough." Georgia pulled her long hair into a

bun on top of her head. "Speaks good English with a thick French accent. It was obvious she's used to attending events like ours. My guess is her family does this kind of thing a lot. She was polite. Quite reserved really."

Sophie grunted. "Is it awful that I hoped she was horrid and rude? Then I could almost think she deserved Troy."

"No. I get it. I suppose she's fallen for his charm. You said he was all kinds of wonderful with you at the beginning."

"Yeah. He's a chameleon. The scary part is when you don't know which color he's going to embody at any given time. I don't want her to have to experience that." Sophie fiddled with her dangly earring. "She needs to know who she's dealing with." *There has to be a way for me to warn Camille.*

"You mean, who she's in love with and about to marry? You know what it's like when you're besotted with someone. You can't accept anything negative." Georgia bit into her muffin. "It's still warm? This is divine."

"Thanks. What about Will? Did he hear anything?"

Georgia finished her mouthful. "He told me on the way home that Camille was talking about their wedding in a couple of weeks, which seems fast seeing as how they only recently got engaged."

That can't happen. "For some reason, I'll bet Troy's in a hurry. Did they hint at how long they'd be in England?"

"Again, I didn't enter into any conversation, but I did happen to overhear at our table that the wedding is in Paris, and that the two of them were going to be back in England again before they get married. Something about him now working for the Clement family business."

Sophie leaned her elbow on the table and picked up her muffin. "That business could be anything. I looked them up and they have fingers in multiple pies. Finance, hospital charities, real estate, even perfume. I'm surprised he didn't come and speak with you or Will. He obviously knew who you were."

"Maybe he was on his best behavior in front of his fiancée." Georgia brushed crumbs from her fingers onto her plate. "So, what did you guys end up doing? Did you come straight back here?"

"No, I needed some fresh air, so we drove to the cliffs."

Georgia shuddered. "The cliffs? I know it's beautiful, but that's one place I avoid with Will."

Sophie cringed. She'd forgotten Will's late wife had died there. "Of course. That's bound to be painful for him. The sea air clears my head though. It seemed like a good place to talk last night. I opened up to Miles and explained more about Troy."

"I'm glad you put him in the picture. If he's interested in you—which he clearly is—he needs to know what you're dealing with and why." Georgia pulled the sleeves of her pajamas down over her hands. "Seeing as how you guys had a chance to chat, did Miles mention he bumped into us at the hospital yesterday afternoon?"

Strange. "No. He was at Will's hospital?"

"Actually, it was at the big hospital in Poole. Will had a meeting there and I met him for lunch afterwards. We literally bumped into Miles in a corridor."

The muffin lost its appeal, and Sophie dropped the remainder onto her plate. "Weird that he didn't say anything to me." She hadn't thought to ask how he'd spent his Friday. She'd assumed he was relaxing and hanging out with his aunt.

"He was probably visiting somebody in the hospital."

Georgia reached over and squeezed her arm. "Just thought I should check to make sure he was okay. I didn't mean to worry you."

"I'm sure everything's fine." Only his hospital visit did worry her. Sophie stared at the kitchen garbage bin. "Funny question, but did you cut yourself yesterday, by any chance?"

"Cut myself? What are you talking about?"

Sophie lifted the mug in both hands in an attempt to warm the chill that ran through her body. "Last night. In the garbage, there was a balled-up bunch of paper towel with blood on it."

"Eww. Sure it was blood?" Georgia padded over to the bin and pressed the pedal with her foot.

Sophie joined her and they both peered inside.

The fish and chip papers were smeared with grease and ketchup, the stale aroma wafted up and assaulted Sophie's senses. "Ugh. I'll take that outside to the garbage after breakfast."

"Good plan. Is this what you saw?" Georgia put a hand on her hip. "Because that's definitely ketchup."

"No. I saw it before we ate." Sophie set her mug on the counter, bent down, and took out the scrunched papers. "There." She swallowed and nodded at the paper towel she'd seen before.

"Oh." Georgia squatted down next to the bin. "That does look rather ominous. It definitely wasn't me. Do you think it's blood?"

"What else could it be?" Tears sprung to Sophie's eyes. "Miles was the only other person in this kitchen. I should have asked him in the moment."

"Maybe he cut himself and didn't want to make a fuss?" Georgia took the greasy papers from Sophie and shoved them back in the bin. "Try not to worry."

"I know." Sophie collapsed onto the chair and drew her

knees up to her chest. "I'm overreacting. Troy got my head in a spin. I'll speak to Miles later."

Georgia went on to explain other details about the ball, but all Sophie could think about was Miles at the hospital, the blood on the paper towel, and how he needed to know as soon as possible that she was here for him, no matter what.

Miles was about to pull out of Will's driveway when his phone lit up with a call from Sophie. He killed the engine and answered straight away. After last night, he was in extra-protective mode. "Hey, everything all right?"

"Morning. Yes. I'm good, thanks. How was your brief stay at Will's place?"

His tense shoulders relaxed. She was fine. "Great. His son got dropped off already, so I met Will's parents, too. Nice couple. I'm on the driveway in the car now, in fact, after saying my goodbyes to Will and Jack. He's a cute little dude."

"Isn't he adorable? I'm glad you felt comfortable. Will's one of the nicest guys you could ever hope to meet."

"I agree. So, what are your plans for today?"

She let out a sigh. "I should work on my manuscript. I also need to grab some baking supplies for my cupboard in the tearoom kitchen."

"You start on Monday?"

"I do. I'm looking forward to it. Baking grounds me. Especially when life is stressful."

"You *are* under a crazy amount of stress. I know that now."

"Right? There's something comforting about the act of simply combining a bunch of ingredients and creating a delicious dessert that will bring people joy." Soft music started playing in the background. "I'm sure you have a thing that grounds you."

Miles leaned back in his seat and ran his fingers over the leather steering wheel. "Cleaning my car."

"Excuse me?"

"That's my thing. When I'm in England, I love meticulously cleaning this car, inside and out. It's therapeutic. No pressure. It's awesome."

Sophie giggled. "I can totally imagine you doing that. She's a beauty. Will you clean her today, do you think? Or are you going to take a rest day. You do sound tired."

He rubbed his eyes. "Do I? Yeah, I may take it easy today. Perhaps you should, too. I think we've both had a pretty full week. Although I can totally drive back and see you if you want…"

"Miles, are you feeling okay?" She huffed. "I mean, health wise? If you're … sick… I don't want you to push yourself and keep having to drive to see me. That's all."

He screwed up his face. She'd guessed something was wrong.

"Miles?" Her voice was a whisper.

How could he keep her in the dark after everything she'd shared with him? He didn't have all the details yet, but he owed her the truth. Especially at the rate their relationship was progressing.

"Are you still there?"

He cleared his throat. "Yes, sorry. Do you want to meet for a quick chat?"

"Now?"

"Yes." Before I have second thoughts. "As long as you don't mind me wearing last night's tux. I have showered. Promise."

"Sure. Why don't we walk in the park close to our cottage? You know the one I pointed out to you before? The rain's letting up and I could do with the fresh air. I'll bring an umbrella in case."

"Sounds good. I can be at Bramble Cottage in a few minutes."

"Miles, I'm worried."

"Don't be. See you soon." Miles wiped a hand down his face, started the engine, and pulled out onto the road. How come Sophie suddenly suspected he was sick? Maybe Georgia mentioned seeing him at the hospital yesterday. His conversation with Will this morning had been somewhat stilted when the subject of the hospital came up, but this doctor was the epitome of discretion and left the topic open if Miles wanted to talk with him about anything medical. He hadn't thought for a minute that he'd be entering into such a conversation with Sophie today.

What if Sophie reacted the same way his ex-girlfriend did last time he went through this? He could recall the devastation like it happened yesterday—the initial pity in her eyes, the promise to stay with him and help him through, then the painful parting when things got tough. He thought he'd never recover from the heartache, even after he recovered from his health issues. Would this be too much for Sophie? She was in the midst of so much turmoil in her own life.

Sophie is different.

Those three words reverberated deep in his chest. Was that God's whisper or his own wishful thinking?

Miles slid the windshield wipers to clear the drizzle. He would give Sophie the opportunity to decide for herself. She was special. There was something between them he didn't even have words for. Yes, the risk was worth taking.

Here goes nothing.

Miles hunched over the steering wheel. *Focus.* Driving his sports car on wet roads wasn't his idea of fun, especially when cars sped past and sprayed a deluge of road water across his line of vision. On a dry road, he'd take anyone on with this engine, but he refused to take chances on slippery surfaces. This car was his pride and joy. *No, not really. My pride perhaps, but my joy goes way deeper than a vehicle.*

He let out a long sigh. Up until this year, singing was his joy. Music was his world. Second only to his faith. To His relationship with God. Although now…

Miles coughed, his throat raw and inflamed. His nostrils flared as he tightened his grip on the steering wheel. His future threatened to be as bleak as this dreary day. How on earth would he navigate his life if he couldn't sing? Aunt Joyce always said he'd been gifted by God with the voice of an angel, and when he got sick last time, the experience had been terrifying for him—but their prayers for healing were answered.

Now this. Worse than before. As if his heart was being ripped from his body as his voice was being taken from him. He slammed his fist on the steering wheel.

Why, God? Why have you allowed this to happen to me again?

Sophie Brooks wasn't the only one who felt betrayed by the God she loved.

Chapter Twenty

Miles parked on the road right outside Bramble Cottage and Sophie appeared at the front door wearing a brown leather jacket, umbrella in hand. He pulled up the collar of his tux jacket and joined her on the path. She smiled, but her eyes were filled with concern.

"Hey." She looked down at her jeans with ankle boots and then at his black dress pants and shiny shoes. "Are you sure you want to walk? Georgia's inside but she'll give us some privacy."

He took her hand. "I'm fine. Honestly, being overdressed is nothing new for me. Remember when you first saw me in all my Prince finery?"

"True." She scanned the almost-deserted high street, a line appearing between her eyebrows.

"Unless you're nervous about… Troy?" He hadn't considered that she might be scared he would come and confront her again. He was in the area, after all.

"No. I refuse to stay hidden away. Let's go." She squeezed his hand, and they walked in silence for several seconds. "So, you wanted to talk?"

"Yes." Miles took a deep breath. "It's a confession, of sorts. I'm sorry. I know you have a lot on your plate these days, but I can't believe how fast I'm… well, I'm falling for you." He stared at the wet pavement ahead. "If there's one thing I've observed from mistakes others have made—my parents included—it's that communication is vital and secrets are venomous."

"Got it. Yes to communication and no to secrets. Are you sharing now because I spilled my guts to you last night? I know it was a lot."

He glanced at Sophie and she returned his gaze, her face suddenly stoic and eyes narrowed. She had put up a shield, a hard edge on her soft features. Was this the creme brûlée shell she spoke of that protected her heart?

"Partly. It's also because I saw Georgia and Will at the hospital yesterday and I don't want to put them in an awkward position."

She nodded but stayed quiet.

"Chances are, I could run into Will again. Or one of his colleagues. I don't want him to have to keep secrets from Georgia, or Georgia from you. Sorry, I'm rambling again."

She squeezed his hand. "No problem. It's my turn to tell *you* to take your time."

"Thanks. I already mentioned I was taking a break from singing for a while. It's because I'm… sick." He swallowed. "Not deathly sick, but it's bad enough that I may have to give up my career. My dream. My entire life, as I know it." He swallowed down the bitter taste of bile as he said the words out loud.

Sophie stopped and pulled him into a hug right there in the middle of the sidewalk. "I'm sorry, Miles. So, so sorry." She peered up at him. "What is it exactly?"

He blinked back tears of his own and took her hand again. Walking helped him keep his emotions in check. "Vocal cord polyps—and there are some complications. I've had trouble with hemorrhaging in the past and this time they believe I'll need surgery."

"The blood on the paper towel last night…"

Oh, no. "I'm sorry. You saw that? I was in such a hurry to eat, I guess I didn't do a very good job at hiding it."

She groaned. "Why would you want to hide being sick, Miles? I realize this is all going super-fast and we've gone deep way sooner than is probably the norm, but I'd just given you all the sordid details on my past and you thought I'd be freaked out by a little blood?"

He shrugged. "You're dealing with a heck of a lot. You don't need to worry about my issues on top of all that."

"W-will you still be able to sing?" She steered him around the corner and down a quiet, tree-lined road.

He didn't want to sound like a defeatist, but he needed to be realistic. "Honestly, not like I have been. I was warned not to push it before but when a role comes up and it feels so perfect…"

"You have to grab it. I understand." She let out a long sigh. "I can't begin to imagine what this is like for you. How long have you known?"

"I had my suspicions the polyps had returned when I took the role in *The Magic Flute* in Paris, but my appointment in Bath on Monday confirmed it. My specialist has referred me to a surgeon in Poole Hospital on Tuesday to explore if there are any less invasive options. I was in Poole yesterday to have a preliminary chat and that's when I bumped into Will and Georgia."

They slowed their pace as he let the news settle over Sophie.

"What happened last time? You said you'd had similar health issues before."

Miles cringed. Did he need to tell her about his ex? Yes, he knew in his gut he needed to spill everything. "Yeah, it happened when my career began to skyrocket. I told you before I had a serious girlfriend through most of my twenties—she was in music, too. Violinist, actually. She understood what a blow it was for me to have to stop performing for a season, and at the beginning she was supportive. Promised we'd get through it together, but when an opportunity came up for her in another city, she left me."

"No. After all those years together?" Sophie's brow furrowed.

"I guess as my star dimmed, hers got brighter. I was devastated, I'm not going to lie. My faith fell apart and my heart was broken."

"I don't know what to say. I guess you healed—your heart and your body, eventually. It seems like you came back singing stronger than ever."

"Eventually, yes, and I'm grateful." Miles stared up at thin rays of sunshine now filtering through the gnarly branches. "My Aunt Joyce helped me deal with a huge bout of depression after that."

"I can't imagine you depressed." She touched his arm. "You emanate joy."

"Guess I'm human." He lifted a shoulder.

"Of course, you are. Like all of us."

"My faith took a beating back then for a while, but in the end, it got me to a place where I learned to rely on God more. I was strengthened and grew through the process somehow. Now," he let out an exasperated huff, "here I am again. The injury is way worse than it ever was before."

"Miles, why wouldn't you tell me this earlier?" There was a thread of hurt in her question.

"The truth is I guess I didn't want to risk losing you. Last time, my relationship disintegrated when the going got tough, and I don't want to lose you after only just finding you." He couldn't look at her face for this, but he wanted to give her an out. "Sophie, if this is too much for you, if my unknown future is something that doesn't sit well with you or whatever—please, tell me now. I'll understand. I will. You thought you were entering into a relationship with a successful opera singer, and I can't guarantee anything."

Sophie stopped and turned to him, her jaw set. "Let's get a few things straight, shall we? You say you can't guarantee anything—what do you suppose I can guarantee for you? What can anyone guarantee for tomorrow? Secondly, I didn't fall for your singing voice." She touched his chest with the palm of her hand. "I fell for your heart. Thirdly, with all the drama and baggage I'm currently dragging behind me like a dragon's tail, who am I to demand perfection and plain-sailing?"

Miles quirked a brow. "A dragon's tail?"

"It's all I could muster in the moment." She reached up on tiptoes and kissed his cheek. "Thank you for sharing. I know that wasn't easy for you, but I'm not going anywhere." She picked up their pace again on the path. "What can I do to help?"

Her question caught him off guard. He took a few seconds to think. "Being able to talk this through is helpful, actually. My aunt knows the situation but she's always so optimistic, I feel like I'm letting her down if I tell her how I'm really feeling. She's been through this with me before and it wasn't pretty."

"I'm sure she'd understand."

"She would. I know she prays for me all the time. This will go to the top of her list, for certain." Miles sank his free hand into his pocket. "You said you feel betrayed by God on some level after trusting Him with your future. Well, that's pretty much what I'm feeling at the moment. I can't tell you how often I've prayed for my health so that I can sing—I believe God gave me this gift and I want to keep doing it forever. Yet now it seems He's led me up to this point only to drop my dreams in my lap."

Sophie nodded. "I feel for you. I truly do. Even though I'm taking baby steps in my faith, I don't think God's dropped your dreams. Maybe He's asking you to trust Him more. Trust that He has a plan for your story, and it may look different than the one you imagined." She held up a hand. "And yes, I realize I'm preaching to myself."

Was God talking to both of them through all this?

A breeze swept by and Sophie pulled up the collar of her jacket. "Okay, so I can listen to you and try to be as supportive as possible. My original question was more on a practical level though. Is there something I can *do* to help?"

He put an arm around her shoulder. "Don't you have enough to concern yourself with?"

"That works both ways, you know. You didn't hesitate to jump right in and be there for me with the Troy situation. Shouldn't you be resting or something?"

"Touché. I'm fine. Really. Although there is something you can help with if you want to, and it's totally in your wheelhouse— but only if you have time."

"Name it. I'll make time." She pointed to a bench beneath a huge oak tree, its leaves fresh and fluttering in the light wind. "Let's sit. This one was sheltered from the rain."

They sat side by side and swiveled to face each other. Shafts of sunlight illuminated copper streaks in Sophie's long, dark hair, and Miles had to suppress the urge to run his fingers through the thick tendrils.

She's stunning. How did I get so lucky?

"What are you grinning at?" She nudged him with her shoulder.

"Sometimes I get a little flustered at your beauty, that's all."

Her cheeks blushed pink. "You're making me very self-conscious here."

"Sorry." He tried to think straight. "Back to your question. When I was at Poole Hospital yesterday, I also met with an acquaintance who's putting on a fundraiser for the children's ward. Not like the ball we were supposed to be at last night. This one is geared toward kids in the community to have a fun time by donations, while raising funds for sick kids in the hospital. Some of the schools have arranged a proper field trip, as they have pupils who have been in the children's ward."

"Nice. Kids helping kids." She crossed her legs and leaned in. "When is it happening?"

He wrinkled his nose. "It's Tuesday afternoon. After my appointment. Too late notice?"

"Not at all. What did you have in mind for me to do? You want me to bake something?"

"You read my mind. That would be a bonus. They have kid food arranged for the most part and I volunteered to pick up a huge cake."

"I'll do it." Sophie rubbed her hands together. "I'm going shopping for baking supplies this afternoon with Georgia. How about a cupcake tower? Kids love cupcakes. Any particular colors or theme I should know about?"

Miles pulled her in for a quick kiss on the lips. "It's a car theme."

"Great." She tucked a strand of hair behind her ear. "And I'll take that kiss as your offer to help me out."

"Me? Help you bake? Are you sure?" Who was he kidding? He would do anything to spend one-on-one time with this woman.

"It'll be fun. Why don't you have an actual day of rest tomorrow—it's Sunday, after all—and then join me on Monday at the tearoom? I have an afternoon shift there anyway, and I'll check to see if Dorothy's happy for us to use the kitchen after we close. You and I will bake up a storm together."

"You'll teach me how to frost cupcakes and everything?" He pictured them working side-by-side for hours on end and his pulse sped up. "You'll have to be patient with me."

"I'm up for the challenge. Are you?"

Another kiss sealed the deal.

Chapter Twenty-One

Sophie stood at the headstone of her late grandparents and allowed a tear to trickle down her face. The muted strains of organ music started up as the congregation sang the final hymn of the morning service inside the beautiful, ancient church. She'd slipped out early, craving a little solitude and needing to process what was breaking open in her soul. She wiped the tear from her chin.

The vicar had spoken from the beginning of the fourth chapter of the book of James. How God lifts us up when we humble ourselves. *I feel like I've been well and truly humbled. Nothing is going to plan. Except Miles.* He'd been an unexpected ray of sunshine in her tumultuous storm. Now she knew his health concerns, even that was fragile. *I hope he's resting well today.* She slid her phone from her pocket and found her Bible app. One she used to frequent daily. Selecting the James 4:10 verse, she muttered the words from The Message translation—

"Get down on your knees before the Master; it's the only way you'll get on your feet."

Sophie's voice broke on the final word and she crouched down at the graveside and rested her knees on the damp grass.

"Get down on your knees." She'd come to this particular spot to pour out her heart to her grandparents. They were always so kind. So generous with their time. Grandma with baking and Grandad with his cars. She'd learned so much from them. Knowing they prayed for Sophie and her sisters every single day was a comfort. The loss of them hit her afresh.

"…before the Master"—yes, she needed to talk to her Heavenly Father even more. He was still present in her life. Still pursuing her. Still holding her hand as she stumbled and struggled.

"…it's the only way you'll get on your feet." *I know. I know, Lord. Surrendering to You is the only way forward. The only way I'll get through…*

A crunch of twigs sounded from the huge bushes behind her. Sophie stood and turned around in a circle. The organ was still playing in St. Pete's, but she was alone out here in the graveyard.

"Hello? Who's there?" She clutched her phone and eyed the church door.

More twigs snapped and a man-sized figure retreated within the prolific foliage and ran toward the road.

Sophie froze, half-wanting to follow him and half-wanting to sprint to the safety of the church.

A car engine started and a blur of white whizzed down the street toward the village.

A hand on her shoulder. "Sophie?"

Sophie let out a cry and spun around. "Georgia, you frightened the life out of me. Did you see that?"

"See what?"

Sophie pointed to the street. "The white car that doubled the speed limit there. I couldn't see it very well through the trees, but it could have been my phantom white SUV." She held up her phone. "Why didn't I think to take a photo?"

Georgia put an arm around her shoulder. "Hey, what's going on? Why are you even out here? I thought you were using the ladies' room and then got worried when you didn't come back in for the last hymn."

A general hum of conversation and laughter poured out from the ornate church doors as the service emptied.

Sophie tucked her long hair behind her ears. "I needed a little alone time. I think someone was watching me out here though."

"Really?" Georgia scanned the church grounds and beyond. "That explains you looking for a white car. Let's get out of here."

"Don't you have to meet Will after his shift?" Sophie trotted alongside her sister as they managed to avoid entering into conversation with the church folk and made their way to Georgia's Mini in the parking lot.

"Nope. Not until this evening. Harriet made reservations for her, Leo, and Lucy to have lunch and a little family time. So, it's you and me." Georgia unlocked the car doors. "What do you want to do?"

"Are you willing to humor me?" Sophie clasped her hands in front of her chin. "Even if it sounds crazy?"

Georgia climbed into the driver's side and Sophie sank into the passenger's seat. "I guess so…"

"Can we go for a little Sunday afternoon drive?"

"Like Grandma and Grandad used to do? That's not crazy. It's sweet." Georgia started the car. "Where shall we go?"

Sophie clicked her seat belt in place and looked straight ahead. "I was thinking the Clements' mansion."

"Are we getting close yet?" Georgia slid her shades up on top of her head as the sun hid behind a bank of white, cotton ball clouds. "I still can't believe we're doing this, by the way."

"The turn should be soon." Sophie held up her phone and studied the GPS. "Don't worry, it's not like I'm going to barge in there and demand answers or anything. I did my research on the family as soon as I heard Troy was engaged, and I'll admit I'm more than a little curious to see if it lives up to the photos of the family estate online."

"Who even lives here? I thought they were based in Paris?"

"They are. However, when you're as rich as the Clements, you get to have several homes in several countries. They probably only use this one occasionally. Like when they needed to go to the fundraiser ball."

"Right. I can't even imagine." Georgia shook her head. "So, how are you feeling about Camille Clement?"

"I'm petrified for her."

Georgia blinked. "Me, too. I know what it's like to be in a marriage where you don't know who your husband really is."

Sophie reached over and squeezed her hand. "I'm sorry you went through so much. Will is going to help you forget everything bad that ever happened, you know."

"You're right. I'm beyond grateful that I get to have a future with him." She paused for a moment. "And I'm praying you get your chance at happiness, too. Miles is a wonderful guy."

"You're not wrong there." Sophie leaned forward. "Next left. You might want to slow down as the road could be questionable and I've already given this Mini enough trouble."

"If this road's good enough for the Clement family…"

"True. Yes, look, they've actually had it paved." She snorted. "I guess when you have that sort of money."

Georgia took her foot off the gas. "How far along do we need to go?"

"According to my GPS, we're almost here." Sophie let out a slow whistle. "Good grief. Impressive home-away-from-home. Why don't you pull in by these double gates for a minute?"

"Sure." Georgia drove on the crunchy gravel in a sizable area in front of the grandiose gates and idled the car. "What exactly are we looking for here?"

Sophie rolled down her window. "I don't know. I have no intention of getting out. I guess I was hoping there would be a big ol' white SUV parked out front or something."

They surveyed the stunning mansion at the end of a long driveway with its triple garage and several other buildings dotted around the fields surrounding the home.

Georgia pointed. "I hate to burst your bubble but I'm thinking their vehicles are tucked away in one of the many garages."

"Probably." Sophie spotted a security camera on top of the gate post. "Perhaps we should leave. I'm sorry I dragged you out here."

"No problem at all. It's a gorgeous afternoon. Maybe we should grab some lunch. Unless you're still worried about that guy from the church grounds."

"No, you're right. We should make the most of this spring sunshine and maybe find somewhere to eat near the sea. It's not much farther to drive, is it?"

"Sounds good to me. I know the perfect place."

"Wait." Sophie grabbed Georgia's arm. "Look. Someone's coming out of the front door." She squinted. "That's Camille. I'm sure of it."

"The garage doors are going up, too. We should go, Soph."

"Let's just check out those vehicles… some black sporty thing. Oh, there's a white vehicle. See it? In the middle." Sophie's pulse raced. "I think Camille is heading toward the white one."

"I'm getting us out of here. The gates are opening." Georgia put her foot down and gravel spewed out from beneath the tires as she made a U-turn and sped back down the country road. "Hold tight."

"Nice getaway. Now I'm confused if Camille is the driver of the white SUV who's been following me around. Why would she do that? A woman of her means. It doesn't make any sense." Sophie bit her thumb nail. "Plus, I was certain it was a man behind the wheel on at least one occasion."

"You realize there are many white SUV's driving around these parts, don't you?"

"I guess. Yes, of course. I wonder where she's going."

Georgia turned onto the dual carriageway toward the coast. "Before you ask, no I am not going to follow her."

Sophie snorted. "I wouldn't dream of asking. Let's try to forget about all the stuff that's keeping me up at night and have ourselves a nice lunch overlooking the sea."

"Sounds like a plan." Georgia turned on some music—opera, of course—and they both opened their windows. "I can imagine Miles singing this one."

Sophie closed her eyes and leaned her head back against the head rest. "Mmm. Me, too." *Lord, please let him be able to sing again.*

Her phone pinged and she studied the screen. Could be him.

"Is it Miles?"

Sophie checked her texts and her stomach clenched. An unknown number. "No." Her voice wobbled.

"What's wrong?"

"I-it's Troy. He saw us outside the Clements' place. I'm sorry, Georgia. This was a dumb idea."

Georgia indicated and pulled over at a sweet little pub with a thatched roof and tables and chairs outside in the beer garden. She parked and turned off the engine. "What did he say?"

"Only that he saw me outside." Sophie blinked back tears. "I hate that he makes me feel so scared and so foolish."

Georgia drew her into a hug. "Don't you worry. He probably gets a kick out of watching who's coming and going through the camera at the gate. Maybe he even watches Camille's movements—that sounds like the sort of thing he would do, right?"

"Of course." He had been possessive and jealous to the extreme with Sophie. Kept tabs on who she was meeting and talking to and working with. Sophie sat back in her seat. "Poor Camille. She has no idea."

"Maybe you'll find a way to warn her, but you must be careful. Don't take any chances with your own safety. Promise me."

Sophie nodded and looked up at the quaint pub. "I know we're not at the seaside yet, but Troy's managed to put a dampener on things, yet again. Do you fancy grabbing some lunch here instead?"

Georgia's face brightened. "Yes. I'm famished and I happen to know they do the best bangers and mash here."

Sophie raised a brow.

"Trust me on this. You'll thank me later." Georgia picked up her purse and Sophie did likewise. "Why don't you grab us a table outside and I'll go and put in our order."

"Will do. Sounds like you've done this a time or two before."

Georgia hurried to the entrance and Sophie wandered over to the outdoor dining area with wooden tables and chairs beneath large yellow umbrellas acting as cheery sunshades or rain protection, depending on the moment. The British weather was another one of the unpredictable elements in her current life. She nodded at an elderly couple eating fish and chips and a young family attempting to wrangle a curious toddler.

Satisfied with her table of choice, Sophie settled on a cushioned chair and placed her purse on the ground, her phone buried within. She wouldn't let Troy's taunting texts ruin her day. This was sister time, something she had craved these past years. Then tomorrow, she would have some Miles time. Her heart pitter-pattered at the thought of him. Hopefully, he was making good on his promise to sleep today and rest as much as possible. He had his big appointment in a couple of days, and then—well, they would face the next step when they knew what that looked like.

Her ears pricked at the guttural purr of a sports car approaching—Sophie loved that sound. Reminded her of her grandad and his old cars, and now the sound reminded her of Miles, too. She leaned forward on the table to see what eye-candy was coming her way. A Porsche. Same color as Miles's. The top was down and… wait, Miles? That was actually him. What was he doing up and about when he was supposed to be at his aunt's place resting for the day?

More to the point, who was the woman in the passenger seat with sunglasses and long blonde hair blowing in the breeze?

Chapter Twenty-Two

"YOU DON'T SUPPOSE…? NO, THAT'S RIDICULOUS." Harriet was silent for several long seconds.

"What?" Sophie balanced the phone between her shoulder and ear as she sat cross-legged on her bed, an unread book strewn next to her and a plate of chocolate-chip cookie crumbs on her lap. "Say what you're thinking. Please? Georgia thinks I'm being ridiculous and reading too much into seeing Miles in his car with that woman, but I have a sick feeling in the pit of my stomach."

"Fine. You don't suppose there's any chance it was Camille Clement with him, do you?"

Sophie moved the plate to the nightstand, the cookies now sitting heavy in her belly. "No." She scrunched her eyes shut and attempted to recall the image as the car drove past the pub. "No, it wasn't Camille, I'm sure of it. We literally saw her minutes before at her mansion, and Miles's car was coming from the opposite direction. Plus, from what I remember, this woman's hair was long and blonde, but not waist-length like Camille's perfect locks."

"Well, that's a relief. Why didn't you call Miles and simply ask him?"

"You mean casually ask who on earth the woman was in his passenger seat? Or why he was out galivanting when he told me he was going to rest? I think not."

"Sweet girl, I think you're making this a lot harder than it needs to be. You guys are perfect together. Anyone can see that.

I'm sure Miles can explain this to you if you give him the chance. Don't overreact, okay?"

Sophie flopped against the padded headboard and groaned. "I'm becoming what I swore I'd never be after my relationship with Troy. Jealous and possessive. Oh, my word. We've only known each other a couple of weeks. Not even." She swiped a hand down her face. "What's happening to me?"

"Hey, you're fine." Harriet's soothing voice was the one she used on Lucy to calm her when she was upset. "You've fallen hard and fast for this guy. You don't want to lose him. Please, pray about it, sleep on it, and make sure you talk it through when you see him tomorrow. Sound good?"

Sophie picked up the last of the cookie crumbs and licked her fingers. Her heart had stopped racing, and she felt tired enough to actually sleep now. "Thanks, sis. You're right. I'm a bit of a disaster these days. Sorry for interrupting your evening."

"No problem at all. I'm here for you."

"How come you're so smart, anyway?"

"I'm a whole five minutes older and wiser than you. Goodnight. Sleep tight."

After a long, hot shower and a leisurely lunch with Aunt Joyce in her beautiful home, Miles was anxious to meet Sophie this afternoon. He'd missed her yesterday and was more than ready to hold her in his arms again. He sensed her independence was a big deal to her, yet he couldn't help longing to protect her. This business with Troy was serious—the man was dangerous, and she was vulnerable.

By the time he arrived in Bramble Downs, a rain shower had let up and the sun was struggling to peek through the clouds as he found an empty parking spot along from the Brambles and Berries tearoom. He checked his reflection in the rear-view mirror. Rough. A shade paler than normal and the shadows beneath his eyes did nothing to hide how exhausted he felt, in spite of resting as much as possible yesterday. He was not good at being still, that was for sure. He may have a lot of being still in his future if surgery was required…

Come on, dude. You're about to see the most gorgeous girl in the world.

He ran a hand through his wavy hair and slapped his cheeks. *Ready.*

As Miles made his way to the entrance, he checked the street for any signs of Troy, a white SUV, or any other suspicious individuals scouting the tearoom. The only white SUV within sight had a mom loading two children into the backseat. All was well in this sleepy village.

A bell above the door jangled as Miles stepped inside, his mouth watering at the medley of delicious aromas in the air. Cinnamon buns, chocolate, and wafts of vanilla.

"Hey." He was greeted by Sophie, a white apron tied around her waist and her hair in a high ponytail, making her look a decade younger.

She gave him a quick hug. A little bit stiff. Was she upset? Or was he being paranoid?

He stepped back. "Hi, how's your day going?"

"Good. I shouldn't be much longer. Want to take a seat here while I finish emptying the display case?"

"No problem. Been busy?" He gave her ponytail a tweak, observed a smattering of customers seated at tiny tables, and then sat at a booth next to the counter.

"Busier than I expected, actually. Dorothy, the owner, just nipped out. She'll be back soon to close up. Want something to snack on?"

"As delicious as everything smells," Miles patted his stomach, "I'm still recovering from the massive lunch my aunt made me eat."

"Fair. Let me know if you want me to box anything up for later."

Yes, she sounded a little formal, but her eyes sparkled as she picked up a variety of scones, profiteroles, and tiny cakes displayed on decorative cake plates. With the utmost care, she placed each item in a huge container.

"You look great, by the way."

"Thanks. Aprons are all the rage these days." Sophie wore an apron over a navy blouse and skinny jeans, yet she could even make an apron look stylish.

"I believe you. Someone is super organized, too. This place is immaculate."

"Dorothy's a neat freak, which makes my job a whole lot easier. Literally every drawer in the kitchen is labelled and you could eat your cinnamon bun off the floor, it's so squeaky clean."

Miles sniffed. Yes, cinnamon. "I'm going to have to come back another day for one of those."

"You totally should. I know it's not quite the Pretty Patisserie, but I think I'm going to enjoy working here part-time."

"When you're not writing?"

"Exactly." She checked her phone. "Sorry, my agent keeps texting. I have to call tomorrow afternoon at the latest with my final decision on where I want to take the story, so we can discuss what changes need to be made. She's doing me a favor giving me this long."

Maybe Sophie didn't have time for baking with him. He swallowed down his disappointment. "Do you need some time to work on your manuscript this evening? I can easily buy a cake for the kids' event…"

"No, it's not a problem. I'll look at my edits later. I'd like to hang out with you first."

Phew. Music to my ears.

The bell jangled from the front door and a spry woman with silver-gray hair marched into the tearoom. "Sorry, lovely. That Mr. Baxter at the bank could talk the hind legs off a donkey." She spotted Miles and stopped talking for a moment. "Well, good afternoon, young man." Her eyes darted from his face back to Sophie. "I see why our girl was so anxious to finish up here today."

Sophie cleared her throat. "Dorothy, this is Miles Morgan."

"Pleased to meet you." Miles stood and reached out to shake Dorothy's hand.

"Wait. I know that name. You're a tenor, are you not?" Her face lit up like she'd been given a puppy. "I saw you perform in London last year. *La Bohème*, I believe."

Miles felt his cheeks heat. "Correct. Thanks for remembering me."

"You're rather unforgettable."

Sophie closed her gaping mouth. "Wow. You clearly make an impression on *all* the ladies."

His loud laugh attracted the attention of several customers, and he grimaced. "Sorry about that."

Dorothy took her place behind the counter and patted Sophie's arm. "Why don't you two go for a nice walk and I'll finish off here. Come back in a half hour and you'll have the place to yourselves. I hear you have some serious cupcakes to bake."

"Thanks, Dorothy. If you're sure…"

"You've been cooped up in here all afternoon, go get some

fresh air. The sun's actually shining again. Might even see a rainbow."

"If you insist…" Sophie hung her apron on a hook. "Go ahead, Miles, I'll grab my bag and jacket from the back and be with you in a sec."

Miles walked out into the spring afternoon and pushed up the sleeves of his crewneck cream sweater. He recognized the muted sound of a jazz tune being played on a saxophone from somewhere and looked across the street. Sure enough, a young man was silhouetted in the window of the house opposite, completely engrossed in his music practice.

Sophie joined Miles and fiddled with the collar of her jacket. "Music and sunshine. You never know what you're going to get in this village." She scanned the street up and down, a frown on her pretty face.

"Sure you want to go for a walk? We can stay if you're feeling nervous."

"No. Let's head to the park. The benches might still be wet, but we can take a stroll through the grounds. It's right around the corner." She eyed his Porsche. "Unless you want to go for a spin?"

Before he had a chance to reply, she forced out a laugh. "No, of course not. You're probably exhausted after taking some other girl for a spin yesterday. When you were *resting*."

Whoa. Miles stopped mid-stride.

Sophie arched a brow.

"Umm, what are we talking about exactly?" He stuffed his hands into his pockets.

She was ticked.

"I'm sorry, but I can't pretend like I'm not upset. Yesterday, I thought you were resting. You told me you were hanging out at your aunt's and I saw you driving in this car with some girl…" Sophie pulled him to the side of the pavement and leaned against the brick wall next to the florist, her arms folded across her chest. "I hate sounding jealous, but I also hate being lied to."

Miles tapped his chin. "Where were you when you saw me and this… girl?"

"Having lunch outside a little pub with Georgia. Somewhere near Poole."

He leaned a shoulder against the wall. "I'm sorry. I'm horrible at resting. I stayed in bed for as long as I could and read for a while, but then I needed some fresh air and had a ridiculous idea. When my aunt got back from church, I offered to take her out for a Sunday afternoon drive—she used to do that with my uncle—and I confess that I researched the place the Clement family own…"

"Are you telling me the blonde in your car was—Aunt Joyce?" Sophie's eyes rounded.

He attempted to suppress a laugh. "Yes. She'll be delighted you were jealous of her, by the way."

Sophie blushed and then broke into a giggle. "She has great hair. Wait, so you went to the Clements' property, too?"

"What do you mean, *too*?"

Sophie's mood changed for the better as they continued on down the street. She explained what happened at the graveyard and how she and Georgia went on their own afternoon drive, and then how she received another text from Troy.

Miles's gut clenched when he imagined Sophie at the Clements' property. Why would she do that? Her compassion and concern for Camille could land her in a whole heap of trouble. He decided not to press the issue. "I suppose Troy saw my Porsche through his security camera, too, unless he'd finished watching his fiancée by that point."

"Please, be careful. He's unpredictable."

"Let's both take extra care. Talking of my Porsche, I do have another favor I have to ask. How do you feel about driving it to the event tomorrow?"

"Are you teasing me? Because you really shouldn't lead a girl on with offers like that if you don't mean it."

He laughed and put an arm around her shoulder as they walked. "I mean it. Here's the plan. A bunch of us are bringing our classic cars to a private area at the hospital, where the kids are allowed to take photos with the cars, sit in the driving seats, that kind of thing. Then there's an outdoor movie screen where they get to watch some car movies and cartoons. Hence, the car theme."

Sophie tilted her head. "Everything sounds fabulous, but you want me to *drive* your car?"

Miles nodded. "I have my appointment with the surgeon before the event starts. I may miss the beginning, but I'd love my car to be set up for the kids. You're way prettier than me to look at anyway…"

"That's debatable."

"Not even close. So… if you're game, I can catch the train home this evening and you can drive the Porsche to Poole tomorrow with the cakes. Do you think that might work?"

Sophie squinted and nodded. "I'll make it work. This may mean I need to bake you something special one of these days, in return." She tapped her chin. "Are you familiar with opera cake?"

"No. Tell me all the delicious details." Miles's mouth literally watered when she'd given him in-depth descriptions of scones and profiteroles, but opera cake was a new one for him—and he, of all people, should experience this treat at some point.

"Sure." Sophie let go of his hand in readiness. She had an adorable habit of using her hands to gesticulate when she was talking about food or books. "Opera cake is totally perfect for you, of course, and it's as decadent as you might imagine. I already know you're a fan of coffee and chocolate, so this is going to blow your mind. Think rectangular layers of almond sponge brushed with homemade coffee syrup, French coffee buttercream, and dark chocolate ganache."

Miles groaned. "Sounds like perfection—and you'll make it for me one day?"

"I'd love to. I'm hoping to introduce it into the Brambles and Berries tearoom eventually as a special French addition."

"You're pretty amazing, you know."

She shrugged. "It's just cake. Although I'm looking forward to us baking together this evening."

"You are?" He ran his fingers down the side of her face, her silky skin soft to the touch. "Me, too."

"As long as you promise to tell me when you're not feeling good or if you get tired." She wagged her finger at him. "You're going to be busy tomorrow with the doctor and then this fundraiser."

"Promise." Miles kissed her cheek. "And while we're mixing and frosting, you can use me as a sounding board with your story ideas for the agent, if you like. You can talk into your voice memo app and show me how your writer brain works."

"Sounds like a perfect date to me. Baking and writing with my handsome man."

Miles's heart swelled. "So… now you've had a chance to think about my health issues and the fact that I have no clue what my future holds, am I right in hoping I haven't scared you off yet?"

Sophie stopped, reached up, and cupped his face in her hands. "In case you haven't noticed, Miles Morgan, I don't scare easily."

Chapter Twenty-Three

"He's too good for me." Sophie put a hand on her hip. "Miles not only has a voice that swoons an entire opera house, he can also frost a cupcake like a pro pastry chef." She held up one of his masterpieces and examined the swirls of pale-yellow icing topped with a tiny car ornament. "He was here with me for hours making these last night."

Harriet closed up one large cake box, which she then tied with a shiny white ribbon. "Don't sell yourself short, sis. He sees what a gem you are." She picked up the second box. "Although it sounds like he has a heart of gold doing this fundraiser for the children's ward."

"He's the whole enchilada." Sophie had agreed not to share his health issues with anyone until after his appointment this afternoon, when he knew what the next course of action would be. "He's been really understanding about my problems with Troy, too." She kept her voice low in the tearoom kitchen. Classical music played in the dining area, but she didn't want anyone to overhear their conversation.

"Still crickets from that lowlife since the ball?" Harriet's forehead wrinkled. "I guess that's good news."

"Other than the text after I was at the Clement mansion, nothing at all." Sophie placed the last of the cupcakes in the box. "I don't trust him for one minute though. Whether he's here or back in France, I don't think I've heard the last of him, which makes my skin crawl."

"Mine, too."

Sophie studied her sister. "I hate that you may be in danger. Troy is a nasty piece of work. He knows I'll never put you at risk by going to the authorities."

"Let's hope and pray he's back in France then, convinced you'll keep quiet so he can get on with his plan to marry a Clement and be set for life."

"I feel like that's wishful thinking. Is Leo home for a while?" She'd feel better knowing Harriet at least had the protection of her husband.

"He's home with us for a few days. I talked to him a bit more about Troy last night, but he didn't have much in the way of helpful information to offer. He didn't even remember his name from when you dated, and insists they've never actually met."

"Do you believe him?"

"I have no reason not to believe him. He's the absolute worst with names and was super nonchalant about the wedding invitation." She struggled with folding the next cake box. "Apparently, Leo's mom knows Camille's mother. That's the family connection."

"Makes sense, I guess. She knows a lot of people in high places over there." The thought popped into Sophie's head that perhaps Leo's mom would have contacts in the Paris police. If Troy was using his connections, maybe two could play at that game.

"What's that look?" Harriet narrowed her eyes. "What are you thinking?"

"I don't know. I must be desperate but now I'm considering the possibility of Leo's mom having her own connections in the Paris police and whether they'd be willing to hear me out regarding Troy. I'm frustrated that I don't feel able to report him for what he's done."

"The woman in the alley?"

Sophie's chest ached. "I think about her every day. Her family. The questions they must have. I want to find a way to give them closure and to let Camille Clement know what she's letting herself in for with Troy."

"I hate that he's got his people in high places. I feel like even if Leo's mom did know someone in the police force there, it would be hard to keep your story quiet. She's… how can I put this… better at sharing news than keeping secrets. Plus, she might be afraid to go up against the Clement family. If this all backfired and they decided to start suing anyone involved, she could be in a tight spot."

"I get it. I do." Sophie finished loading the next box with cupcakes. "I don't want to put you in an awkward position with her. Do we know how she got to know the Clements?"

Harriet licked a blob of frosting from her fingers. "Mmm. This is delicious. Yeah, Leo's mom did a magazine piece on the family several years ago and has been an acquaintance ever since. A good enough friend to be invited to their daughter's wedding, apparently. Although I would imagine this is going to be a huge event and they've probably invited everyone and their dog to celebrate with a splash."

"You mean every magazine owner and their son?"

Harriet scrunched her nose. "That's still weird. Maybe with Leo's dad being gone and him being the only child, it's not as crazy as it seems to us. Anyway, Leo never intended to go to the wedding. How could he possibly attend now that he knows all this stuff about Troy?"

"Not to mention the fact Troy's threatening *your* safety."

"Exactly."

"Think Leo will tell his mom?" That had the potential to be dangerous.

"He wanted to at first, but I thought it best to stay quiet for now. His mom isn't what you would call discreet. He made some excuse for not going to the wedding and will have to deal with her wrath like a man. Serves him right for keeping me out of the loop." Harriet's phone pinged and she pulled it from her back pocket. "I'm sorry, I have to go. I'm volunteering at Lucy's school for the afternoon reading session." She grabbed her jacket from a stool. "I wish I could come with you and ride in that sports car parked outside though."

Sophie chuckled. "I can't believe Miles trusted me with his baby. Dorothy promised to watch it like a hawk through the front windows this morning. Apparently, it's had several admirers. You go ahead, thanks for stopping by to chat. Hug Lucy for me and give her this…" She produced an individual cupcake box. "I set one aside for my favorite niece."

Harriet took the box and hugged her sister. "She'll be thrilled. Drive carefully—for goodness' sake."

"Absolutely. Take care and I'll give you a shout later and let you know how the kids' fundraiser went."

"Sounds good." Harriet left through the kitchen door just as Sophie's phone rang out. A quick glance. Her mom. *This could be a long one.* She pressed speaker as she finished tying another bow.

"Hey, Mom."

"Sophie, sweetheart. Have I caught you at a bad time?"

"No, I'm here doing my thing in the kitchen at the tearoom. Cupcakes and more cupcakes."

"I'm sure they're amazing. How are you doing?"

Sophie took a swig from her water bottle. "I'm good." She

checked her watch. "Shouldn't you be sleeping?"

"Probably. I had a huge bridal shower event last night that ran late, and I'm still buzzing."

"Good grief, Mom. Ever the party animal."

"Hardly."

Sophie chuckled. Her mom was the furthest thing from a party animal that she could imagine. If she wasn't hosting an event for clients, she was either at church or at home. "You should be taking it easy."

"I'm not that old, you know." A huff. "Besides, I was worried about you. Georgia messaged and told me about your ex from Paris showing up at the fundraiser ball. I'm so sorry, sweetheart."

"How much did she tell you?"

"Georgia didn't go into detail. Only that it upset you. I'm glad you had your opera singer man there to look after you."

Sophie pulled a fresh tray of cupcakes from the other counter. "I don't need anyone to do that. I'm a grown woman. Seeing Troy there was a shock. No big deal." *Liar.*

"You know I can fly out there if you need me. I have an event tomorrow and then there's a big lull in my calendar. I'd love to meet this new man in your life."

"No. Please..." How could she put yet another family member in danger? "I'm trying to settle in here and find my feet."

"And the opera singer?"

"You're incorrigible. I've known him for all of ten days." A pivot was in order. "How about *your* new man?"

Silence.

"Mom?"

"I don't know what you're talking about."

Sophie grinned as she packed away the mess she'd made with Miles's cupcakes. As much as the idea of her mom in a serious relationship was a little uncomfortable, her dad died so long ago, and he would want her to find love again. "You're allowed to date, you know. You're beautiful and healthy and successful—you're a catch for those Vancouver guys. Your little girls are all in their thirties now. We're not going to throw hissy fits or get grossed out."

Her mom cleared her throat. "Thanks, sweetheart. I'm here for you if you need me, okay? Call me. I should try to get some sleep. Love you—and I'm praying for you."

Mom's not so chatty about her own love life. Interesting. "Love you, too. Bye." As soon as the call ended, a text notification pinged. Sophie swiped to see an unknown contact. A knot formed in her stomach as she perched on the stool and studied her screen.

"Bonjour Sophie, this is Camille Clement."

Chapter Twenty-Four

CAMILLE? SOPHIE'S BREATH CAUGHT IN her throat.

"I'm sure you were not expecting to hear from me, but this is urgent. As you know, I'm about to marry Troy, but I fear he is keeping something from me. I know you dated him and am hoping we can talk woman-to-woman. I'm at my family home in Dorset and am heading back to France this afternoon but have time to meet at 1:00PM. Please, say you will come? I will not keep you long. My address is below."

Sophie's pulse raced as she reread the message. Camille Clement? This could be her chance to share the truth with a woman wielding a great deal of influence. Troy said not to tell the police… why should she not tell his fiancée what kind of man he was? Camille may even go to the police in Paris and further investigate the attack of the woman in the alley. This was her one chance.

Unless the meeting was a trap. She wouldn't put it past Troy to have Camille pretend to be the nervous bride-to-be in order to get Sophie's attention and agree to meet. Was this a risk worth taking?

Her thumbs hovered over the keys of her phone. The cupcakes needed to be at the hospital before 1:00PM but the event didn't start until 2:00PM. She needed to make a decision. Fast. She would have time to meet with Camille in between. Not at her mansion though. Somewhere neutral. Close to the hospital. The timing could be tight, but doable…

"Camille—I have an appointment, but I can meet briefly at 1pm. Poole Hospital. The outside parking lot. We can walk and talk or go to a coffee shop nearby."

Sophie hit send and held her breath. A reply came within seconds.

"Thank you, Sophie. See you at 1:00PM. I'll be there."

Oh, my goodness. This was the chance she'd been hoping for. Sophie checked the time, and slid her phone into her purse so she could complete the tearoom tasks she needed to do for Dorothy. What about Miles? She should call and let him know about Camille. No. He had enough on his mind today with that specialist appointment. She'd use her usual method of verbal processing by spilling the details in a voice memo on her phone, and then drop Miles a quick text saying she needed to run an errand, so as not to cause alarm in case he tried to reach her. Email him with all the details as a safeguard, just in case.

Miles wouldn't check his email until that evening—he'd explained that he usually caught up with his messages then. Besides, he promised to rest this morning before his appointment and then the fundraiser. What if his doctor had bad news? Her chest ached for what his treatment might entail. Poor guy. If only he didn't have to give up his singing.

I can't imagine not being able to write anymore or being told I could never bake again.

Sophie tried to focus on the fondant flowers she had to create for the top of the blackberry cupcakes on today's menu. The cupcakes were never ending this morning. While she flattened each tiny ball of malleable lilac icing and molded them to make a perfect rosebud, a Bible verse sprung to mind. Isaiah somewhere-or-other? About God being the Potter and people being the clay. How in His skillful hands, we could be molded into something beautiful and purposeful.

Not that I've given Him much to work with recently.

Sophie pursed her lips as she thought back to what Miles said last night working on his cupcakes at this very countertop. He admitted he was struggling in his faith as he didn't know what God planned for him if he was forced to end his singing career, but he also said he was working on surrendering to God. Giving over everything.

That sounds terrifying.

She pressed the final petals around the rosebud. Once upon a time, she'd trusted God with her hope of finding someone to do life with, and she'd ended up with Troy. That had been an absolute disaster. Yet had she completely surrendered the relationship to God? Or had she clung to her own ideals deep down and maybe only heard what she wanted to hear from her loving Father?

Shaking her head, she set the flower atop a prepared cupcake and placed the sweet treat on a glass cake plate. Only eleven more and then she could go and meet with the woman who had captured the cruel heart of Troy Sanders. A shudder ran through her.

Okay, God, I may not be ready to trust You with everything in my life quite yet, but I could do with a hefty dose of Your wisdom as I speak to Camille Clement...

Windows down and fresh spring air billowing through her hair, Sophie couldn't hide the huge smile on her face. She'd already turned several heads driving this stunning vehicle. Did Miles attract this kind of attention every time he took the Porsche out for a spin? Probably. With his good looks and a classic sports car in such mint condition, he was sure to draw the attention of admirers.

She stopped at an intersection and checked that the two rectangular cake boxes were secure on the passenger seat. She'd buckled them in to be safe. Too much work had gone into making these treats for them to get mushed or squished if she needed to brake without warning. The radio was set to an opera station, and she enjoyed familiar strains of Maria Callas singing one of her mom's favorites. Puccini perhaps? She'd have to ask Miles.

The sun glared through the windshield and Sophie slid her shades down from the top of her head. She needed to pay extra attention while driving this baby. Miles assured her that he trusted her implicitly, but she was taking no chances.

She'd texted him about her quick errand after the cakes were dropped off and promised to be back for the fundraiser in plenty of time. A slither of guilt stuck in her conscience, but she couldn't burden him this afternoon with the worry of her meeting Camille. She'd blocked off the rest of her day to be with him, especially if his doctor's news wasn't great and she could be helpful in some way or attempt to cheer him up. *He's been so good to me.*

The car behind honked and Sophie surveyed the clear road ahead. Her phone gave directions to the hospital in Poole while she pondered her best angle talking to Camille. How much did the woman already suspect and how much should Sophie share? She squared her shoulders. Camille had reached out and wanted Sophie's opinion, so she wouldn't hold back. She felt nauseous at the mere thought of having to relay Troy's actions and behaviors to someone who presumably loved him. This would come as a massive shock. Troy would go ballistic if he found out she was doing this and was putting his grand plans in jeopardy.

Too bad.

Her phone rang out with the classical tune she'd set for Miles's calls. Sophie winced. She couldn't take the call while she was driving. He would understand as he knew the one downfall of his classic car was the lack of modern technology. She'd call him back as soon as possible.

Sophie checked the rear-view mirror to overtake a particularly slow red compact car driven by an elderly lady, and noted the same black vehicle had been behind her for ages. Of course, he could be on his way to Poole, too, that wouldn't be unusual. Why did he have to drive so close? Surely, he knew this was dangerous driving.

Come on, Porsche. Let's see what you've got. Sophie saw the outside lane was clear and in one swift motion, maneuvered the steering wheel and floored the accelerator, leaving the old woman in her dust. The rear view told her she'd also lost the black car. She patted the dashboard and exhaled. *Nice work.*

Traffic started to build as she neared the hospital area and saw signs for the multi-story parking. Miles said it was nightmarish trying to find somewhere to stop here, so there was a spot reserved on the top floor near the elevator. She would take the elevator all the way down to reception to drop off the cakes. The receptionist would then give her details on where to take the car for the event… although that would have to wait until after her meeting with Camille.

She followed several other vehicles to the parkade entrance and leaned out through her open window to grab a ticket from the booth, careful not to get too close in Miles's car. She would never forgive herself if she got a single scratch on the paint.

I hate these parkades.

She'd seen one too many crime shows where the girl gets attacked in a multi-story or someone follows with echoing footsteps and hides behind cars. *Calm yourself.* She was doing a cupcake drop-off—not a drug deal.

After winding up and up, and rather enjoying the throaty

purr of the Porsche engine reverberating back at her, Sophie located the elevator and saw several vacant parking spots nearby. She pulled into the biggest and cut the engine. Slinging her bag over one shoulder, she tucked her phone into the back pocket of her skinny jeans and went around to the passenger side, surveying the deserted area for any creepy-looking individual.

Satisfied she was alone, Sophie gathered the two large cake boxes in her arms, thankful a cupcake tower was already here from a previous event and she didn't have to balance that, too. Careful to keep the boxes horizontal, she managed to lock the car door and made her way over to the elevator, the familiar sound of squealing tires protesting as they circled within the parkade floors below.

Miles. She forgot to check and see if he'd left a message. Better make sure his message wasn't anything to do with her drop-off before she arrived down at reception. Facing the elevator and leaning her knee against the wall, she balanced the boxes with one arm around them both and snagged the phone from her jeans pocket.

Heavy footsteps sounded and before she had a chance to turn around, someone pressed her up against the wall, her boxes and phone flying in every direction. Sophie's breath caught in her throat as her cheek grazed the brick wall and she struggled to stand upright. A hand snapped her head back and gripped her mouth from behind, a pinprick jabbed her neck like a bee sting, and her knees buckled.

Help. He-lp. Her mouth moved but no words came out. Her limbs grew heavier by the second until she sensed strong arms lifting her from her feet and carrying her away. She couldn't hold her eyelids open, and all sounds blurred into the muffle of a car engine.

Darkness took over and Sophie sank into its depths.

Chapter Twenty-Five

Miles checked his phone. Again. Still no response from Sophie. He paced the waiting area. 1:10PM—five minutes before his appointment—and she still hadn't shown up with the cakes at reception. They were getting restless downstairs and so was he. Had she been in a fender-bender with his car and was nervous to tell him?

As if I'd care about the car if she was hurt or even shaken up.

The more concerning fear was that Troy could be harassing her again, and Miles would not stand by and let that happen. He tried her one last time and the call went straight through to voicemail.

"Miles Morgan?" The black-haired woman at the desk stood with a chart in her hands. "Doctor will see you now. He's running a little early."

Miles froze. Should he go in and get his consultation over with? Who knew when this specialist would be able to fit him in again. Yet if Sophie was in trouble…

"Could you give me five minutes, please? I'm having a bit of an emergency here and need to quickly check on someone. My appointment wasn't until 1:15PM." He finished with a smile, which he hoped effused more charm than grimace.

The receptionist adjusted her red glasses and checked her watch. "I'm sure we can work with that. We'll see you in five."

"Thank you." Miles clasped his hands in front of him in

gratitude and hurried out of the office, calling reception downstairs as he located the elevator.

The woman he'd spoken to earlier greeted him on the first ring.

"Hello, this is Miles Morgan again about the cupcakes. I don't suppose my friend has arrived since we last spoke?"

"No. No, I'm afraid not and we are setting everything up now. Should we duck out to find another cake or something? The kids will be expecting cake and we hate to disappoint them."

Miles hit the elevator button for the top level in case Sophie was running late or needed help. Maybe she couldn't get the elevator to work or was having trouble locking his car. "Can you stay on the line for a minute? I'm checking the parkade now to see if she's arrived." He pulled at the collar of his button-down shirt as he rose to the top floor.

"No problem."

"Great. Bear with me…" One crisp ping and the doors swooshed open. Miles stepped out onto the cement floor of the parkade and his stomach dropped. *No.*

He took in the scene before him. White cardboard boxes half-empty with smooshed familiar cupcakes littered the area. His car was parked in a stall close by. Georgia's purse and phone were on the floor next to his back tire. His head spun and he let out a groan.

"Mr. Morgan?"

"Um, hello. I'm so sorry. You're going to need to get that replacement cake. I'll cover the cost." He finished the call before she could ask anything more and ran around the circumference of his car, desperate to find Sophie.

Lord, where is she? Let her be safe. Please.

"Sophie?"

He scanned the area. Not a soul in sight.

"Sophie?" His throat burned as he cried out her name.

What was he supposed to do first? Everything in him wanted to call the police. He picked up her purse and checked her phone for the latest calls. A list of his incoming attempts. She hadn't made a call recently so had someone jumped her? Surprised her and taken her somewhere? The attack could have been random, especially if they saw her with his fancy car—but why would they not take the car? Or steal her purse and leave her here? Troy. He stared at the strewn cupcakes and ran a hand through his hair. Think. Think.

Georgia or Harriet. They knew the situation with Troy. He scrolled to her latest calls and found Harriet's number. There was no way of doing this without freaking her out. She picked up on the third ring.

"Hello? Hello?" Her voice cut in and out.

"Harriet? Can you hear me?" A multistory was the worst place for cell reception. Miles growled and dug in his pocket for his car key, thankful he'd at least thought to bring the spare as he'd given Sophie his regular one. "Harriet, it's Miles, please stay on the line if you can hear me."

"Miles? Miles, what's wrong?"

He put her on speaker and kept calling her name as he started the car and spiraled all the way down to ground level, the tires screaming all the way. "Can you hear me?" He pulled out his wallet and flashed his credit card at the ticket machine and waited for the barricade to rise.

"Yes, that's way better. Are you okay?" Harriet's voice was loud and clear.

Miles pulled into an empty reserved space outside and cut the engine so he could concentrate. "Something's wrong and I need your help."

"Of course. Anything."

"Sophie's missing."

"What?" Her voice was shrill. "Is it Troy? Does he have her? I knew I should have come with her this afternoon. I had an uneasy feeling."

"I don't know. I'm guessing it's him. She came to the hospital early to deliver the cakes. Texted me beforehand to say she had an appointment at 1:00PM but she'd be back for the fundraiser. I just checked up in the multistory where she was supposed to park my car and it looks like someone took her."

"Took her?"

"I'm sorry, Harriet. The cakes were on the floor along with her phone and purse."

"Did you call the police?"

He sighed. "Not yet. I wanted to call you first. She was adamant not to involve the police in case Troy came for you."

"I don't care. We need to involve them."

"I agree." He let out a sigh of relief.

"I know someone on the force here. Let me call him. He can be discreet. Where are you now?"

"I'm in my car outside Poole Hospital. I'm not sure where he would have taken her, but I want you and Lucy to be safe. Can you go straight to the police station?"

"I'm at the school with Lucy now but we'll head there right away. I'll let Georgia know." Harriet sounded like she was running.

"I'll check Sophie's calls and texts from earlier. Let's keep in touch."

"Sure. Now I'm relieved she ignored me and never put a passcode on her phone. Let me know as soon as you figure anything out. Be safe." Harriet ended the call.

Lord, I feel helpless.

Miles took a deep breath and checked back through her earlier calls, but only saw his own number and Harriet's from this morning. Texts. There had been several today and one caught his eye. He read through the details. Camille Clement? Troy's fiancée? Surely not. This was ominous. The text said they were meeting here in the parking lot. He jumped out of the car and scanned the area. Nothing suspicious. He paced between the rows of parked cars and called her name. Only people heading in and out of the hospital entrance. What now?

Miles ran back to his car and scrolled back through the texts. Camille originally suggested meeting at her home. The mansion. He knew exactly where the property was. If Sophie wasn't there, perhaps Camille could offer some information or would at least know if Troy was in the country. It would be a start. He had to do something.

He knew Harriet was making calls so he quickly texted her and copied in Camille's address. When he swiped the screen, he noticed the voice memo app on Sophie's phone. She used the app all the time for tidbits of information with her writing. He could at least listen to the last few entries as he drove, in case there was anything from today.

He found his shades in the glovebox and revved up his car. A call came in and he glanced down at his phone on the passenger seat. The specialist's office. He was supposed to be up there discussing treatments.

The consultation could wait.

Sophie could not.

Chapter Twenty-Six

Sophie blinked back the glare of light that shone between slats of barn wood beside her.

Where am I?

Her head pounded and she swallowed down bile. Heavy, so heavy. Every part of her ached and felt bruised. She inhaled the sweet scent of straw and the distinct tang of manure. Her gaze followed a beam of light that illuminated the dim surroundings. A horse barn? Unable to pivot her head, she tried pulling her body to a sitting position.

Nothing.

She heaved herself up again but could hardly feel her limbs—as if she were paralyzed. Even her mind was foggy. Someone had stuck her with a needle. Lifted her. The cakes? She dropped all those beautiful cakes. Drifting, she'd sensed she was on a ship in the middle of the ocean but that couldn't be right...

Without moving her head, she peered down and saw her hands and feet were tied with thick rope as she lay in the fetal position facing the wooden slats. Her vision cleared and she made out thin strips of green pastures beyond her prison. Why was she even here? She didn't recall who brought her, but who else could her kidnapper be other than Troy Sanders?

A wave of nausea washed over her, and she closed her gritty eyes and waited for the feeling to pass. Pieces of straw dug into her cheek like pins in a silk pin cushion as she lay there helpless and alone. Was the fact that she could feel her cheek a good sign?

Maybe. She tried to open her mouth.

H-e-l-p.

Barely a whisper. Was anyone close enough to hear her? What if Troy—or whoever her captor was—came once they knew she was awake? Tears leaked and trailed down her face. Why was this happening? She dreamed of a new life, a quieter life in the serene English countryside. Well, she seemed to be in the English countryside now. In some kind of horse stable amidst a bunch of fields.

God, I know You're here. Please, please help me. I'm in a mess. I don't understand what's going on, but I need to get out of here.

Sophie heard of people bargaining with God when they got into trouble. Promising to follow Him all their days if He would help them out of their dilemma. That pricked her soul more than the straw on her cheek. No, she wouldn't bargain with God. Who was she to talk that way to the God of the Universe? The clay questioning the Potter. Bargaining didn't seem right.

Sophie opened her eyes and squinted through the slats to the great outdoors.

What do You want from me, God? I love You. I can't deny that. I've loved You since I was five years old. I've been burned though, and I think I let go of Your hand somewhere along the way. Instead of clasping tighter, I let go...

The realization made her chest constrict and more tears brimmed. God never changed. Sophie was the one who had been stubborn toward His love and hardened toward His grace. Where had she gone wrong?

Troy. Her downward spiral began when she put Troy before her relationship with her Heavenly Father. Believed Troy's truth, warped as it was. Now Troy was manipulating Camille Clement.

Her gut clenched. Camille—she'd forgotten about their meeting. Sophie lost track of time. She inched her head down to see her watch. Movement was returning, slow but sure. 1:30PM. Camille was expecting her half an hour ago at the hospital parking lot. Would she have thought to keep trying Sophie's phone? The last place she remembered having the phone was at the elevator with the cake boxes, when she was about to text Miles.

Miles. He would be in his appointment at the hospital and probably had no idea she was missing. *No one knows I'm missing...*

The heavy clomp of footsteps sounded outside the structure, and Sophie gasped as a door creaked and someone marched inside.

"Hey, gorgeous."

Sophie bit the inside of her cheek. Troy. No shock there. She attempted to heave her shoulders up so she could see him walking toward her.

"Having difficulty, are we?" He squatted down next to her, and she longed to slap the smarmy look off his face, inches from her own. How had she ever loved this creep? He was despicable. "Can we talk yet?"

She might not be able to slap him, but she gathered all the saliva she could muster and spat in his face. It hit the mark and he recoiled.

"That's no way for a lady to behave." Troy gritted his teeth and grabbed both her shoulders.

Sophie squeezed her eyes shut and held her breath, unsure what to expect. He yelled obscenities and slammed her head back onto the ground. Her skull ricocheted and flooded with searing pain. The hay did little to soften the blow.

"You're the devil." Her words were a whisper.

"What?" He roared and she blanched, fully expecting him to finish her off. Instead, he stood to full height and towered above her. "You have no idea. You're weak. This is nothing compared to what I grew up with. Nothing."

Troy always spoke of his father with a bizarre mix of admiration and contempt. She'd never understood and never pushed for details. Perhaps now. She cleared her throat. Maybe she could keep him talking for a while, at least. "Your dad?"

"My hero." He rubbed his mop of dark curly hair. "He's always got my back."

What? This was getting weirder by the second. Sophie went to sit up and fell back down, the back of her head throbbing.

Troy spat out a laugh at her display of frailty. "I warned you to stay away from my plans with Camille. She's going to be my greatest conquest yet. I know your boyfriend was snooping around here in that sports car of his. Dad saw him. I warned you, Sophie. I said I always have the final word, didn't I?"

His dad saw Miles? What was he talking about? Her vision was speckled with tiny lights as she tried with all her might to look at him and concentrate on what he was saying. He said Miles was snooping *here*? Was she at the Clements' residence? She knew from her investigations on the internet that the property included a fair amount of land. Likely stables and such. "Camille?" She was supposed to meet Sophie. Could she be coming back to the property?

Troy sneered. "Before you get excited thinking Camille's going to trot in here and save you, she's in Paris. The family rarely even come here, but I have a room as the favored future son-in-law and am free to use it whenever I wish." He folded his arms across his chest. "It was me who texted you. I knew you'd meet given the chance to share all the juicy dirt you had on me with my beautiful, wealthy fiancée. Couldn't resist it, could you?"

Sophie's heart sank. What was she thinking? Would Camille really have wanted to talk to her about Troy? She'd been foolish to believe for a moment that she might be in a position to help. This was Troy's trap and she'd walked right into it. Now she was stuck here alone with him. A lamb in the lion's den. Her pulse thrummed in her aching head.

"W-why? Why kidnap me?" Her words were slurred.

Troy snorted. "Having trouble with your words, are you, Miss Author wannabe? Fancy that. I couldn't take the chance you might change your mind about meeting Camille, could I? Or perhaps that stuck-up singer dude of yours would try to talk you out of it. Half-expected to have to take him down actually." He pulled his jacket open to reveal a knife.

Sophie gasped. "W-what are you going to do with me?"

"Well, let's see. Knifing you seems too kind somehow." He leaned down until he was inches from her face. "I'm pretty good with the knife, you know."

Sophie's mind cleared. What was the girl in the alley's name? "Madeline?"

"Ah, yes. Poor Madeline."

"Why?"

"She was a little too feisty for my liking. Seems her family knew the Clements, and when she got wind of my glorious engagement, she had the nerve to try to tell them about my less-than-gentle relationship with her when you and I were together." He pouted. "Sorry, I confess I was not exactly faithful."

Sophie struggled to take a breath. He was disgusting.

"Let's see, I seem to remember you being especially nervous of fire. Am I correct?"

Her eyes widened. *Please, Lord, no.*

He took a book of matches from his back pocket and began striking one. "The way I see it, a barn fire will get rid of you and this ugly outbuilding all in one go. Hasn't been used in years and no one's going to miss it. By the time somebody calls it in from one of the neighboring properties, you'll be ashes. Poetic, don't you think? Dying the same way your dear old daddy perished when he saved you all in the house fire back in the day."

Sophie couldn't stop the tears snaking down her face. He was heartless, using her pain against her. She struggled to loosen the ropes, her limbs now moving with a great deal of effort.

"It would make an awesome ending for a book, don't you think? Tragically beautiful." He shook the matches. "I'll make it a s-l-o-w burn. I'll be long gone by the time any of the neighbors see a hint of smoke—that's one of the many, many great things about being rich and owning extensive property. It'll give us a chance to go and tie up any loose ends before I head back to my perfect Paris life. Wish me luck, princess."

Sophie let out a strangled cry as panic wrapped its tentacles around her chest. Troy's footfalls faded and the barn door clicked shut.

Blood whooshed through her veins.

Muted thuds hammered the ground outside as he ran. A faint sound of a door slammed. A car started and drove closer to the barn. More footsteps pounded the ground.

Another male voice, lower than Troy's. He was doing something outside. Maybe beyond the barn?

The car door shut, and she listened as the engine revved and then took off into the distance. The driveway was long, she knew that. The vehicle paused, presumably at the double gates, and then sped off.

Silence. Did she imagine the faint smell of smoke in the air?

Every nerve in her body screamed. What now? Was this how her life ended? Miles. She missed Miles. Was Troy truly going to have the final word?

No. I'm getting out. Sophie gritted her teeth, mustered all the strength in her sluggish body and rolled onto her side. *Must keep moving.*

Wind whistled through the cracks between the wooden slats. She had to see Miles again. She let out a groan and pushed herself up onto one shaky elbow.

Slow, slow moves, otherwise she would pass out.

Adrenaline pumped through her body enough to sit for a few seconds. She was falling for Miles. He needed her as much as she needed him. They could figure out a future together. God would help them.

Trembling. She couldn't control the trembling. Not a soul knew where she was—not even Miles—so who would come looking?

Sophie bit back the sob that rose in her throat, licked her dry lips, and lifted her chin.

I'm not giving up. This is my story and Troy won't have the final word.

I will.

Chapter Twenty-Seven

MILES COULDN'T EVEN FIND THE WORDS to pray. His stomach roiled as he squinted at the road ahead, willing the traffic to thin so he could hit the accelerator. If only Sophie had told him earlier that she was meeting Camille, he could have at least attempted to talk her out of the decision. Asked her to come to his appointment with him instead. Would she have listened? She was strong and independent, but also tender-hearted. She would be willing to put her own safety at risk to warn Camille about Troy.

Miles loved that about Sophie. A fire burned in his belly. Loved? Yes, something special was blossoming between them already. He couldn't deny the truth. According to the voice memos he'd been listening to while driving, she felt the same. As he waited for the traffic lights to change, he flicked to the latest recording to re-listen.

"Tuesday noon. Send Miles an email re the meeting with Camille. I know he'll try to talk me out of going or want to come with me—but he needs to be at his appointment. Hopefully, I'll be back in time to be there with him. This afternoon will be... interesting, to say the least. I have to try to warn Camille. Troy will not have the final word this time."

The *click* was jarring after hearing Sophie's sweet voice. Of course, he'd checked his email as soon as he listened to the voice memo. The message had been moving. She'd intentionally sent an email rather than text, knowing he didn't check his email obsessively, and by the time he read her words, there would be no time for him to do anything about her decision. Would Camille really want to chat with Sophie about Troy? It seemed far-fetched, which is why Sophie sent the email. Just in case…

Miles swallowed the lump of emotion that stuck in his throat causing him more pain than any damaged vocal cord. Concentrate on the road.

The rest of the email was so kind, so open. She'd mentioned love at first sight. That no matter what his specialist said today, she wanted to be along for the ride. *I'm counting on you for my happily ever after.* She'd actually penned those words.

Now she could be counting on him for her very life.

Miles let out a groan. At last, there was a stretch of dual carriageway, and he could overtake the dawdlers out for a casual afternoon drive. He checked the signposts. He couldn't miss the turning.

Various scenarios played out in Miles's imagination. If Troy had taken her, would he really choose the Clement property to do with her whatever he had in mind? There was a chance he may take her back to Bramble Downs. Grab Harriet and have them both. Or could he smuggle Sophie back to France? Surely not possible. He ground his teeth. Troy may kill her and dump her body anywhere.

Nope. Not going there.

He recognized the turning he took last time to the Clements' place and slowed the car down as his heart rate sped up. The winding country road was familiar. Majestic beech trees lined the sidewalks, and stately homes were set back on long, impressive driveways. They all blurred as he drove by with one destination in mind.

Miles pulled to a stop outside the Clement property, the familiar set of ornate iron gates shut tight. What now? He grabbed

Sophie's phone and sprinted around his car to the gates. No latch. No visible way of getting through—this place was like a pretentious prison. How did a person gain access? Perhaps only from some mechanism inside. He peered through the railings and surveyed the area. A lovely sunny afternoon in the countryside. No vehicles visible. No movement at all. In fact, the scene before him was eerily still.

Sophie's phone rang out. Harriet.

"Miles? What's happening?"

He was reminded in that instant how similar the twins' voices were. "I'm at the Clements' property. The gates are locked and there doesn't seem to be anything going on as far as I can see."

"Okay. I'm at the police station. I explained everything and they have officers on their way out, too. Do you think she's in there?"

Miles scanned the mansion and the surrounding grounds with several other small buildings either side. The scene almost appeared peaceful, other than a stiff wind that ruffled his hair. He blinked. Was that...?

"Oh no."

"Miles? Are you all right?" Harriet's voice wobbled.

A soft plume of pale gray smoke floated up against the cobalt blue sky. Miles gripped the railings and shook them. "Harriet, I see smoke. I think it's coming from one of the smaller structures. A barn, maybe? I need to get in there. Call the fire brigade."

"*No*. A fire?" Harriet let out a sob. "I'm on it. Be careful."

Miles shoved Sophie's phone into his back pocket and scanned the perimeter. Amidst the perfect row of trees, tall railings guarded the property for as far as he could see. He had to get in there somehow. Fast. No way was he waiting for the firetruck. Every minute counted. He stared at his car.

Without a second thought, Miles scrambled back to his vehicle and reversed as far as he could go in order to give him a good twenty-foot run at the gate. "Lord, please let this work." He clicked the seatbelt, took a deep breath, clenched his fingers around the leather steering wheel, floored the gas pedal, and braced for impact.

Every muscle tensed as the front nose panel of his beloved vehicle crunched against the metal railings of the tall gate.

The gate was damaged but still intact. He peered through his windshield into the property and the growing tendrils of smoke snaking into the sky.

Again.

He shoved the gearstick in reverse. The crunch of gravel under the tires fueled his angst as he readied himself for a second attempt.

Come on. We've got this.

Miles set his jaw and dropped his foot onto the gas pedal, arms locked and body on full alert.

Oof.

He cringed as the car smashed through the gates, leaving them hanging on their hinges. *Yes.* He squeezed the steering wheel as he sped down the gravel driveway toward the house, as close to the barn as he could manage.

The car barely stopped before he jumped out and sprinted to where he presumed Sophie was being held, his eyes scanning the deserted property.

Probably should have picked up something to use as a weapon. Too late to worry about that now.

"Sophie." His booming voice seared his raw throat, but was

lost in the wind.

God, please don't let me be too late.

The drugs were starting to wear off. While Sophie attempted to squirm her hands out of the thick rope, her ears pricked at the soft crackling noise from outside the barn. A noise she associated with the worst day of her entire life.

She had no solid recollections, but certain feelings and sounds caused ripples of fear to squeeze air from her lungs when she thought of the day her daddy died in a house fire. She and Harriet had only been two years old, Georgia was five. She'd heard the story enough times from her mother and had the vaguest memories to piece together details in an ugly mosaic of pain.

Mom. Her sweet mom. How would she ever recover if Sophie perished in a fire, too?

God, please get me out of here.

She figured Troy set the fire a decent distance from the flammable barn to give himself opportunity to get away before anyone noticed the smoke curling into the sky. Although who knew how much time she had? The acrid stench of burning particles drifted in on the breeze, stronger by the minute.

Giving up on freeing her raw wrists from the rope, she bent over to her ankles and tried loosening the knot with her fingers. If this didn't work, she'd crawl like a caterpillar over to the barn door. Troy was definitely no boy scout, and she had a sudden surge of optimism when one strand loosened a little. Scouring the area, she spotted a small stick and leaned across to grab the skinny length of wood in her bound hands.

Got it. Blowing the curtain of long hair from her face, she shoved the stick in the messy knot of rope and loosened it enough to get things moving. Frantic, she tugged and tugged until the rope slithered from her ankles like an indignant snake. *Yes.* She steadied herself with her hands on the ground and went to her knees, then stood to full height and took a tentative step toward the entrance.

The barn spun, her vision blurred, and her body dropped to the straw. Sophie gasped at the pain in her elbow, which had taken the brunt of the fall. She took a couple of deep breaths and stood again, this time staring at the door and concentrating on placing one foot in front of the other. Her legs felt like tree trunks. Not part of her own body. She turned back—smoke seeped in from the rear of the barn. No time to waste.

"Help."

"He-lp."

Now at the entrance, she leaned heavily and pounded with her bound hands. Of course, the doors were locked from the outside and were solid. Heavy. Immovable. There was no way she could break through. Tears filled her eyes as she searched for anything that might prove useful. A large rake sat in the corner of one of the stalls, so she stumbled over to fetch it. Her throat was scratchy and her nose tingled, but she could still breathe.

The rake made a decent walking stick as she made her way back to the door. With all her might, she swung the heavy end at the door.

Nothing.

No dent. Not even a scratch.

She was working at half-strength here. Her escape was going to take forever.

Sophie didn't have forever.

She swung again. Again. Again.

Tears poured down her cheeks and she let them fall. Sweat beaded her neck and back from the exertion and the sudden onset of heat that radiated in the space.

Is this the end? She collapsed against the door, spent.

Sophie closed her eyes and listened. The fire crackled while the wind whooshed outside.

She inclined her ear and listened for God's calming voice in the chaos.

"Proverbs 3:5-6."

Her eyes popped open. She hadn't thought of those verses in years. She'd memorized them as a teen but now only snippets washed over her, "all your heart… submit to him… paths straight…"

Exhaustion and heat covered her like a weighted blanket. Sophie lay down on the floor and curled into a ball. The smoke was thinner down here.

God, help me.

Chapter Twenty-Eight

MILES PUMPED HIS ARMS AND LET his legs carry him as fast as they could toward the wooden barn. Smoke now poured from the back and sides of the structure.

"Sophie?"

She had to be in there, and she had to be terrified.

"Sophie, can you hear me?" He reached the door. "It's Miles. I'm here. Hold on…" He yanked a solid oversized bolt across and tugged the door open, half-dreading what or whom he might find. He raised his elbow over his mouth as smoke escaped past him into the wide-open space beyond, and he stepped inside.

"Sophie." Miles sank to his knees. She lay unconscious on the ground in front of him, her wrists tied with rope, her face grazed and tear streaked. "It's Miles. Can you hear me?" He cradled one hand under her head and winced when he felt the tackiness of congealed blood matting her hair. What had Troy done to her? She gave a soft moan and Miles let out the breath he'd been holding. At least she was alive.

His eyes darted around the dimly lit space. Empty. With all the hay strewn on the ground and flames licking the back area, the whole thing could ignite any second. They needed to get out before the precarious structure fell down around them. With the greatest care not knowing how injured she may be, Miles lifted Sophie's limp body in his arms, stood to full height, and hurried back through the open doorway.

Out in the fresh air, he coughed away from her face praying

there wouldn't be blood, and adrenalin kicked in as he took purposeful strides in the direction of his car. As they got close, he groaned when he spotted the badly mangled front of his Porsche. Would they make it to the hospital? The whining drone of emergency services pricked his ears, and he broke into a jog in the direction of the entrance instead.

"Everything's going to be fine, Sophie. Help is on the way."

She was out cold again. How much smoke had she taken in?

Close to the gate, Miles lay her on a bed of soft grass. Her eyes fluttered open as she turned onto her side while hacking coughs racked her petite frame.

Miles's heart swelled and he sighed with relief, his own breathing labored and his throat raw. "Hey."

A frown creased her forehead and she grimaced. "Where…" She licked her lips. "Wait, the fire?"

"You're safe." He turned to see the ambulance and police had arrived at the same time through the gate. He kissed her cheek. "Don't move. Help is here."

Two paramedics jumped down from the ambulance and rushed toward them with a stretcher.

Miles stood back with hands on his head and caught his breath while they assessed her condition.

"I'm fine." Her voice was thin as she spoke between coughing bouts. "Can you get this rope off me?" She attempted to sit up with hands held high and they lowered her back down onto a stretcher.

"Take it easy, you've been through a lot." Miles came close and squeezed her foot, the only part of her he could reach while others crowded around.

A police officer joined them. "Sophie Brooks? I'm Officer Parker. Are you able to give me any information? Your sister reported someone kidnapped you and has been threatening the family."

Sophie shook her head. "Wait. Troy. Where is he? Did you catch him? He murdered Madeline. In Paris. He told me."

"Not yet, Miss. What can you tell me? Who is Madeline?"

She let out a cough, which caused her entire body to shudder.

Miles stood next to the officer. "Take your time, Sophie."

The officer nodded at one of the paramedics. "I presume we're good to talk with her. Or do I need to come in the ambulance?"

"I'm perfectly capable of talking." She tried to sit up again and then had second thoughts. "Although I do need some painkillers for my head."

"We need to get her checked out." The younger paramedic strapped her onto the stretcher. "Concussion, for sure. Cuts and bruises. Smoke inhalation."

Sophie tried to protest but deflated. "Can I go to Will's hospital? Doctor Will Hughes? I can't think of the name…"

"I know Doctor Hughes." The police officer led the way to the ambulance. "That's the closest one anyway. I'll follow. We have a dangerous man at large." He turned to Miles. "Are you riding in the ambulance?"

"Please. I'd prefer not to let her out of my sight." He'd also be able to call her sisters and let them know what was happening. They would be frantic by now. He walked alongside the stretcher. Sophie's eyes were closed but it was obvious by her contorted face that she was in pain. His fists clenched at the thought of what Troy had done. Hopefully, she'd get a second wind once the medication kicked in and they could find Troy Sanders and put him behind bars where he belonged.

By the time the ambulance arrived at the hospital, Miles had texted Georgia so she could notify Will and asked her to contact Harriet and tell her that Sophie was safe. Sophie was now awake again and the paramedic assured him she was going to be fine.

Miles followed as they wheeled Sophie through the emergency department where he was told to wait on a gray plastic chair. His head spun. What else could he do to help? He exchanged several more messages with Georgia. Prayed. Not with actual words. More like shallow breaths and deep sighs. God would understand.

"Miles? You okay?" Will rushed toward him in his navy scrubs with an iPad in hand. "Can I have someone check you?" He put a hand on Miles's shoulder.

"No, thanks. Not necessary."

"You sure?"

Miles nodded. "I wasn't inside the barn long, and I have a follow up appointment at Poole Hospital anyway."

Will raised a brow.

"Long story. I'll fill you in later. How's Sophie?"

"Come with me." Will waved at the nurse on duty and Miles followed him to a private room. "She's doing remarkably well. We're checking everything to be sure. I'd like to keep her overnight but she's not so keen. See if you can convince her?"

"I can't make any promises."

"Miles." In the stark room, Sophie sat up in bed while a nurse dabbed her grazed cheek with a piece of gauze. "Are you all right?"

He ran a hand through his wayward hair. "I am now. I'm more concerned about you." When the nurse bustled from the room, he approached the side of the bed and took her hand.

Sophie's face was ghostly pale against her dark hair. "What's this about you wanting to break out of here?"

She pouted. "I'm not feeling that bad. My head aches and I've bruised my elbow, but nothing's broken. At least I've stopped coughing up a lung now." She looked beyond him. "Did you see that police officer? He left, but I'm not sure what he's doing about Troy."

"Officer Parker. No, he must have gone already. Did you explain to him what happened?" Miles spotted a cup of water on a side table and offered her a drink.

She took a long sip. "As much as I could. Honestly, it's all so blurry. Troy must have drugged me with something in the parkade and it's taking a while for me to piece things together." She blinked. "All I know is he wanted me dead. He pretended to be Camille and texted me this morning. I guess my guard was down as I jumped at the thought I'd be able to explain everything to her before she made the biggest mistake of her life. He must have seen me arrive at the hospital parkade and decided to grab me inside." Her chin wobbled. "The cupcakes?"

Her hand trembled and Miles took the cup from her.

"Don't worry about the cupcakes. The kids will have cake. Let's focus on you. Troy's desperate to keep you quiet. Did he give any indication where he might be heading? Back to Paris?"

Sophie squeezed her eyes shut. "I can't remember. He banged my head pretty hard. He said some stuff before he left but it's fuzzy."

"Maybe you'll recall more details later. You're safe and that's the main thing for now." Miles stroked the un-grazed side of her face and nodded over his shoulder. "Will's watching out for you here so you're in good hands." Where on earth was Troy? He didn't want to cause Sophie any added stress. She needed to heal and to rest. Yet once Troy discovered Sophie was alive…

She opened her eyes and yawned. "Officer Parker is posting one of his guys outside my room here, too. He said he's keeping things under wraps as much as possible though."

"How do you mean?"

"Keeping it out of the media for as long as he can, I think. He reckons they have a better chance of catching Troy if he thinks I'm dead and he has nothing to hide." She wrinkled her nose. "I'm pretty sure the officer said they were putting alerts out at the Chunnel and the airports. Probably the best place to catch him as he could literally be anywhere in England."

Made sense. "He has to make his way back to France and to Camille Clement at some point if he's going to follow through with this plan of his to marry her."

"Exactly." She blinked several times. "I don't know what they gave me but I'm so sleepy."

"Rest. I'll stay."

"You will?" She snuggled deeper beneath the thin blue blanket.

Miles placed a tender kiss on her forehead. "Promise."

"Thanks. Love you."

She drifted back to sleep and left Miles staring at her beautiful, bruised face. Medicated or not, he'd take that declaration.

Chapter Twenty-Nine

Swimming. She was swimming through the thickest water, crystal clear but heavy, holding her breath. Blissful and comforting yet something niggled. Agitated her insides. She needed to come up for air. Lungs burned. Her silent scream surfaced as she gulped oxygen, feet kicking, hands grasping for something, for someone…

"Hey, Sophie. Wake up, sweetie." Georgia's face came into view through the water. Through tears. "You were having a bad dream, but you're safe."

Sophie inhaled and filled her thirsty lungs, then coughed and let the air out. She pulled herself up to a sitting position and Georgia plumped a pillow behind her head. Oh, her head. The ache pulsated. Her throat was sore and dry. Before she could even ask, Georgia had a cup of water in front of her mouth.

"Here, take a sip and try to lay your head back down. Does it still hurt?"

"Mm-hmm."

"I'll tell the nurse you're awake. See if we can get you some meds." She disappeared and Miles took the seat next to her bed.

"You're still here?" She mustered a smile.

"Of course." His voice was strained. Oh, his voice…

"Miles—your specialist appointment? Did you go?"

He tilted his head. "There was a more urgent matter to attend to, don't you think?"

Sophie put a hand over her mouth. "You actually saved my

life, didn't you? I mean, you walked into a burning barn to rescue me."

Miles gave a half-smile. "I wasn't going to take the chance of losing you, if that's what you mean. Besides, I've already made another appointment with the specialist, thanks to Will."

"Well…thank you. Words seems rather inadequate, but seriously—thank you, Miles."

He leaned over to her and placed the gentlest kiss on her lips. "You're welcome."

Sophie longed to pull him in for a deeper kiss, but her twin sprung to mind. Her thoughts were such a jumble. She scanned the room. "Harriet? Do you know where she is?"

"She's safe at the police station, last I heard. No need to worry." Miles settled back into his plastic chair.

"The police station? Why?" A sudden chill caused the hairs on the back of her neck to prickle. "I have an uneasy feeling about her."

"She went there with Lucy as soon as we realized you'd been taken. Figured it was the safest place for them to be. I think she knows Officer Parker pretty well, and he let them hang out in his office until Leo could pick them up."

"Maybe he already has. You'd think Leo would do everything possible to get to his wife and child in an emergency like this."

"True. I think we all need to be on high alert until Troy's caught. We can check with Georgia in a sec. I meant to ask, did you speak with Harriet about Leo's connection to the Clement family?"

Sophie rubbed her temples. "She thinks it's all innocent enough. Leo's mom is the one who knows Madame Clement. Leo might be a workaholic and maybe he's been acting a bit out of character, but he'd never put his girls at risk."

"Good. Perhaps you should try to sleep some more."

She winced. "After that nightmare, I don't fancy going back to sleep."

"It looked like you were running somewhere before you woke up there. Your feet were going crazy."

Sophie licked dry lips. What she wouldn't do for some Chapstick. "It was the weirdest. I was actually swimming and then drowning and couldn't breathe…" Panic gripped her and she gasped. "Wait, how long was I asleep?"

Miles checked his watch. "Two hours. Maybe a little longer."

She tucked her hair behind her ears and clasped her hands together in front of her face. "I started to remember some stuff Troy said in the barn." A shudder rippled through her body at the thought of being tied up and left to burn to a crisp by that monster.

Miles leaned in. "Good. I know it's tough to think about, but anything might help. Officer Parker hasn't been in touch for a while so I'm guessing they have no leads yet."

She closed her eyes and pictured Troy's face. How his handsome features twisted with his final words to her. "He said he was going to Paris."

"That would be great if he tried—the police have alerts out everywhere."

She shook her head and then regretted the jarring movement. "But before the Paris bit, he said something about tying up loose ends."

She glanced at Miles. His face was pale. He should be resting, too.

"Loose ends? That's curious."

"I know. It sounds more ominous than curious to me." Her

voice quivered. "And he said *we*. Yes. He said *we* and not *I*. It didn't sound right and for a moment I wondered if Camille was in on it with him."

"Didn't he say he texted you pretending to be Camille though? Why would he do that if she was his accomplice?"

The antiseptic hospital smell turned Sophie's stomach. "True. It can't be her. It makes no sense. She's the one he's deceiving. She would never marry him if she knew who he is. What he is. Come to think of it, I'm pretty sure he said she was in Paris already." Why was everything so jumbled in her memory?

"Then who do you think could be helping him?" Miles squeezed her toes through the blanket.

"His… his dad?"

"Why do you say that?"

She sat up straighter. "Yes, I'm sure he mentioned his dad. He's here. In England. He has to be the one who's been following me and doing Troy's dirty work for him, I'm sure of it. He must be over from the States. When Troy said *we* have loose ends to tie up, he meant he and his dad."

"Can you think of why his father would do this?"

"It's messed up. Today, Troy said his dad was his hero, yet I know he was a violent man. Some of the things he told me before…"

Miles stood. "This is important. I should try to contact Officer Parker. Let him know what you've remembered and see if he has any updates."

"You've remembered something?" Georgia approached the bed. "The nurse will be here as soon as she can, by the way."

"Thanks." Sophie fixed the lopsided hospital gown on her shoulders, self-conscious about her appearance now that she was thinking straight. "Do you have the officer's phone number handy?"

Georgia reached across to the side table and plucked a business card from the surface. "He left it here in case you remembered anything."

"I can call him, if you like." Miles took the card and studied the details. "I could do with stretching my legs. I'll be right outside in the hallway in case he wants to speak with Sophie."

"Sounds good." Georgia patted his arm and then greeted the nurse who passed Miles at the door.

Sophie accepted the tiny paper cup and two tablets from the nurse. "Thanks. These aren't going to knock me out again, are they? I'm feeling much better now, and I only want to get rid of this headache. I need to be thinking clearly."

"Don't worry, dear. They're ibuprofen. Let me know if you need anything more later." The gray-haired nurse checked Sophie's chart and left the sisters alone.

Sophie swallowed the tablets with some water and sank back down against the starchy white pillow. "Has Miles been here this whole time?"

Georgia checked her phone and nodded. "Sure has. He's a good guy. He was super worried about you. We all were." She frowned.

"What's up?"

"Umm nothing." Georgia squinted at the screen. "I'm sure everything's fine."

Sophie clutched her thin blanket in both hands. "Georgia. Please don't keep anything from me or try to protect me. I need to know what's going on if it's anything to do with Troy."

"I'm going to check something out with Miles and Officer Parker." Georgia couldn't hide the quiver in her voice.

"What? I'm coming with you." Sophie pulled the blanket back and swung her legs around.

Georgia put up both hands. "Okay, okay. Please, stay in bed." She rubbed the back of her neck. "It's probably nothing, but I'm not quite sure where Harriet is right now."

"No." Sophie's head spun. "Not Harriet."

God, please don't let Harriet be the 'loose end' Troy was talking about...

"This doesn't make sense." Georgia tapped her phone again. "Leo says he picked up Harriet and Lucy from the police station thirty minutes ago. She wanted to come and sit with you and asked him to take Lucy on home as the poor little girl was getting tired. Leo pulled up outside the entrance and then he and Lucy walked Harriet to the elevator to make sure she was safe. That's the last time he saw her. Supposedly, safe in the elevator on her way up to see you."

Sophie's pulse raced. "Thirty minutes ago? Then where is she now?"

Miles appeared at the door of Sophie's room, his face even more ashen than before.

"Miles? Did you speak with Officer Parker?"

He strode to the bed and took both her shaky hands in his.

"I'm so sorry, Sophie. It looks like Troy has Harriet."

Chapter Thirty

"No. No. *NO.*" This could not be happening. Sophie balled her fists and thumped the bed either side of her legs. She swiped tears from her cheeks. "How can you be sure?"

Miles passed her a phone. *Her* phone. "I still had it in my pocket from earlier. Troy sent you a message about thirty seconds ago."

"He knows I made it out of the fire alive. How?"

Miles furrowed his brow. "You said he wasn't working alone. He could have someone watching the Clement place. His father? It was crawling with emergency services. The Clements probably have security footage he tapped into."

Her stomach clenched. "I feel sick." She clutched the phone in her shaking hands and studied the text.

PLOT TWIST. TWIN TRADE. NO POLICE. ONE HOUR. BRAMBLE DOWNS.

Georgia gasped as she read over Sophie's shoulder. "*No.* Harriet must be petrified. What are we going to do? We *have* to tell Officer Parker everything."

Sophie shuddered. "What if Troy panics when he sees the police? He could hurt our sister… or worse." She shook her head. "You guys, Troy is unpredictable. He likes feeling in control. I'm not taking any chances with Harriet's life. She's a wife and a mommy. This is on me. If Troy says no police, we have to let him believe I'm toeing the line. The police can be there ready and waiting but I'm going to meet Troy. Do the trade."

Miles shook his head. "You can't simply walk in there and let him… kill you. He's tried once today, isn't that enough?"

Georgia glared from Miles to Sophie. "I don't want to lose either of my sisters. There has to be a way." She hugged her torso as tears pooled in her eyes.

"I'll get Harriet out." Miles paced the small room.

Sophie scoffed. "What do you suppose he'll do when he sees you, Miles? Simply hand Harriet over?"

Miles turned to Georgia. "Could you give us a minute?"

"I'll wait outside, but please, hurry."

"There's nothing to discuss." Sophie coughed. "This is my mess."

Georgia ducked out of the room and closed the door behind her.

"Hear me out." Miles sat on the chair next to her bed. "You've been through an ordeal already today. You could have died." He took one of her hands in both of his. "Let me do this. I want to protect you, and today when I thought I'd lost you, I realized how precious you've become to me. Your family needs you. You're priceless to so many people. If anything happened to you, it would be devastating." A muscle jerked in his cheek. "It would be different for me. My family's dysfunctional at best. I may not be able to ever sing again anyway…"

"Whoa." Sophie pulled her hand from his grip. "Stop. You need to leave. Now."

"Excuse me?"

"Go. Please." Sophie's head pounded. "I can't do this."

"Can't do what? I want to help you." He narrowed his eyes. "Don't shut me out."

"I see what you're doing. You're pulling a martyr thing and offering to give yourself in my place because you don't think *you'll* be missed. That's ridiculous." She folded her arms. "Tell me I'm wrong."

He looked at the floor. "I'm not trying to be a martyr. I want to do the right thing."

"Go. Please. Do I need to walk you out?" Her breath hitched and she started to climb out of the bed.

"Fine. I'll leave, but you can't meet with him, Sophie. The man's a murderer. Imagine how Georgia will feel if she loses both of her sisters at once." He stood. "Please think rationally. I'll give you some space. You have my number if you change your mind."

She watched him open the door and disappear down the corridor. Would she ever see him again? Not if Troy had his way. Her heart squeezed.

"What happened?" Georgia rushed in and stood over Sophie. "Where's Miles going?"

"I told him to leave." Sophie's voice was flat. She was spent. Done. Empty.

"Why? Is he going to the police?"

"I hope not. For Harriet's sake."

Georgia checked her watch. "We need a plan. Otherwise, *I'm* calling Officer Parker. What did Miles say?"

"He's ridiculous. He can't take my place."

Georgia tilted her head. "That man loves you."

"That man is crazy. He thinks he won't be missed if something goes wrong."

"Did you tell him he *would* be missed?"

Sophie rubbed her face. "No. I told him to get out. I can't let him do this… he's known me for less than two weeks, for goodness' sake. He's sick and needs surgery and may never sing again and…"

"What?" Georgia sank onto the bed next to her sister. "Hon,

you need to get him back here and figure this out. Troy may be calling the shots, but Miles is proving how much he cares for you. Can't you see that?"

Tears trickled down Sophie's cheeks. "I know. He already saved my life once today. What have I done?"

Georgia leaned in and cradled her in a hug.

"Knock, knock."

They both looked at the door.

"Miles?" Sophie sniffled. "You came back."

"Where else am I going to go? Do you think we could work this out together?"

"Maybe."

"Do you trust me?" He took three strides into the room.

Sophie gazed into his steel-gray eyes and saw strength and kindness. "I trust you. Do you trust me?"

"Absolutely."

"Come over here." Sophie held out her arms and Miles walked into them without a second's hesitation. "Thank you."

He studied his watch and stood. "We don't have much time. There has to be a way around this. If I were Leo, I'd want the police involved, even if we keep it on the lowdown. Let Troy think he's calling the shots."

Georgia put a hand on Sophie's arm. "Miles is right. Leo's back at their house. He's trying to keep his cool for Lucy, but I just talked to him, and I can tell he's totally stressed. He ordered pizza to keep Lucy happy for a while, at least, but she's missing her mommy… Soph, he needs to know what's going on and he'll want to try everything possible to get Harriet back safely." She checked her phone. "He's seriously getting more frantic with every text."

Sophie scrunched her eyes shut. *Think. There has to be a way.*

Miles's cool fingers stroked her cheek. "Let me call the police again? Please? I know you don't trust them, but these guys actually know your sisters. Officer Parker seems like the real deal. We can explain the situation."

God, all this talk of trusting the police and trusting Miles… the big question is—do I trust You?

"I can speak to Officer Parker." Georgia wiped tears from her cheeks. "I would trust him with my life—I trust him with Harriet's."

Sophie swallowed down the retort she had on the tip of her tongue. This wasn't about her anymore, this was about her twin. "We need a plan. A good one."

Miles folded his arms. "Do you think you can be ready to leave in about forty minutes?"

"I'll leave now." She pulled back the sheet.

"Wait." He put a gentle hand on her shoulder. "We don't have an exact location yet, and we don't know if the hospital is being watched. Plus, you're still weak after your ordeal and another few minutes in bed while we figure out some details sounds smart to me." He looked up at Georgia. "If you can explain to Officer Parker that we are planning to meet Troy on his terms— with the police out of sight—he'll need to be ready to come to the location as soon as we know where it is in Bramble Downs. You be his point of contact."

"Got it." Georgia hugged Sophie. "Please, take care. I'll get Will to come with me to Leo's so we can explain without him freaking out. I can stay with Lucy while Leo and Will come to the meeting location. Will may be needed if…" She shook her head. "I can't go there."

Miles walked her to the door. "That sounds great. Thank you. One more thing… can you guys use Will's car? I'm going to have to borrow your Mini, I'm afraid."

"Of course. It's on the ground floor close to the elevator." She dug a set of keys from her purse. "I… I should get going. Keep in touch. Stay safe. Both of you." She blew a kiss and left them alone.

Sophie chewed on her thumbnail. "Wait. Where's your car, Miles?"

He winced. "I used her as a battering ram at the Clements' place."

Wow. "You did?"

"She'll be fine. Seems kind of trivial in the big scheme of things." He attempted a smile and sank down on the edge of the bed.

Sophie took his fingers and kissed them. "Thank you."

"You're worth it." He leaned over and planted a gentle kiss on her forehead. "For now, we need to take time to discuss exactly what's going to happen."

"As much as we can."

"Right. Troy must suspect the police are going to be notified. At the very least, he's going to know you won't be driving yourself, so someone—namely, me—is going to be with you."

"I guess so. Who knows if he's capable of thinking straight."

"Obviously, he realizes his plan A failed." Miles rubbed the stubble on his chin. "What is he thinking now though? He can't exactly carry on with his marriage to Camille after all this, surely. Even with the best lawyers money can buy, there's no denying attempted murder. He left you for dead. Now he's kidnapped Harriet."

Sophie bit the inside of her cheek. "He's manipulative. He may use our family's safety against us to keep quiet and not press charges. I honestly wouldn't put it past him. Plus, his confession about Madeline's murder in Paris is my word against his, and he has people in high places." The reality was nauseating. "If the barn is burnt down—I'm guessing it pretty much is by now—there's no evidence or anything to prove he held me captive there, it's literally my lone testimony."

"Mine, too. I found you there and then there's emergency services…"

"None of whom can say Troy was present. You don't understand." She waited until she had Miles's full attention. "He's kidnapped Harriet, but he's got a way with words. It's his poison. His weapon. He'll find a loophole." She trembled at the painful memories.

"Hey." Miles stroked the side of her face. "Are you forgetting our Weapon is so much greater than anything Troy can wield? We have God on our side. His wisdom and strength. The power of prayer." He leaned in and pressed a featherlight kiss on her lips. "And *you're* the one who has a way with words. Remember that."

Sophie closed her eyes. When she thought she was taking her last breaths back in the barn, she believed she was the one who had the final word in her story. She'd whispered that proclamation to take the power away from Troy. Now—now she needed to surrender her story to One who truly would have the final word. She needed to trust God with the next chapter.

"What is it?"

Sophie took both his hands. "It's not my story. It's God's." Verbalizing the truth made her insides warm. "I've been fighting it for so long and I'm exhausted." A single tear meandered down her stinging cheek. "Can we pray real quick?"

Miles broke into the gorgeous grin she adored. "I would love that."

She bowed her head. "Heavenly Father, I'm scared, but I know You are sovereign. I've always known that in my head, but now I accept it in my heart. You know all things and You know what we're facing. I surrender it all." She sniffed. "God, I give You everyone. I give You everything. My family, Harriet especially, Miles, and my life story. It's not my story… it's Yours." Her chin wobbled and Miles squeezed her fingers and took over.

"Lord, give us wisdom and strength in this situation. Keep us all safe. I surrender everything and everyone to You, too. In Jesus' name. Amen."

Sophie took one deep breath and released it. She wouldn't have wanted to share this precious moment with anyone else. "Thank you." Now they had to put that trust into action. "So, about our plan…"

They spent the next ten minutes figuring out various options, depending on where the meeting place might be and how Troy might react. Georgia called and so far, Officer Parker was agreeable to play along, but he had his limits. Also, Will had made arrangements, and Sophie would be able to check herself out of the hospital with minimal fuss.

"Good. Let's go with our plan until our guts tell us otherwise." Sophie eyed the room. "Any idea what happened to my clothes?"

Miles grimaced. "I don't think you'd want to put them back on, to be honest. Smoky is an understatement." He opened the door of the side table. "However, Georgia is super organized and grabbed some things for you from the cottage."

"She's the best." Sophie accepted a plastic bag and took a peek inside. Yoga pants, a white T-shirt, and tennis shoes. "I'm going to change in the en-suite." She swung her legs to the side of the bed.

"Might want to give yourself a minute before you stand." Miles took her arm while she steadied herself, and then helped her to the bathroom. "Shout if you need me. I'm going to give Georgia a call and make sure everything's okay. Maybe get you some snacks. I'll bet you haven't eaten all day."

"How did you guess? Thanks. I have my phone for when Troy texts again." Sophie shut the bathroom door and leaned her back against it, careful not to put pressure on her head. No dizziness. No nausea. Even her headache eased. This was good. She could do this.

God, we can do this.

Sophie stared through the windshield, willing energy to return to her body.

"You need anything else to eat before we get there?" Miles looked over from the driver's seat of Georgia's Mini, a frown on his handsome face.

"I'm fine. My stomach's churning, so I think I'll stick with water." She stared down at the phone in her lap. When was Troy going to message her? "The waiting is excruciating."

"I know." He turned his wrist to check his watch. "Fifty minutes since he texted. Won't be long now."

They had decided to drive to the edge of Bramble Downs so they could be at the mystery location in good time—they couldn't afford to get stuck in traffic or behind a herd of cows in the country roads. The police were ready to make a move. Leo and Will were awaiting news. Everyone was in a holding pattern until Troy revealed his whereabouts.

Sophie could almost hear the seconds tick by. She tried to stretch out her arm. The bruising on her elbow was already an impressive explosion of colors, but at least she hadn't broken her arm. Again. Her chest still felt a little tight, but the rawness in her throat subsided. Troy was pure evil. *Dear God, please don't let him hurt Harriet.* She had to be all right.

"Harriet's okay." She nodded as she watched the emerald fields fly past as they drove familiar country roads into the village. "I feel it."

"A twin thing?"

"Yeah. It freaks Georgia out sometimes. When I had a grumbling appendix last year, Harriet knew I was sick before I told her. The bond was stronger when we were young. I guess because we were always together. I would know if she was… not okay." Her voice cracked and Miles covered her cold hand with his warm one.

"You're both strong. We're going to figure this out."

Sophie's phone pinged and her entire body jumped.

Miles tapped his indicator and pulled over into a small lay-by. "Troy?"

"Yeah." She blinked and read the message aloud.

"BRAMBLES & BERRIES. TEA TIME. TEN MINUTES. NO POLICE. STRAIGHT SWAP. HAPPILY EVER AFTER."

Her stomach dropped.

Miles took the phone and re-read the text. "The tearoom? He's been watching you, big time. Will it be open?"

Sophie's heart pounded. "No. It shuts at five and should be completely empty by now." Unless Dorothy decided to stay on for some reason. *Please, God, not Dorothy, too.* "I-I guess we should keep driving. I don't want to be late."

"We have plenty of time, Sophie. We're almost there already." He gave her back the phone and pulled out his own. "I'll text Georgia quick and tell her what's happening. The police station is super close. Officer Parker can be there fast, right?"

"He has to stay out of sight. Maybe the road behind the tearoom? I think it's Bluebell Lane. He'll know. It's where Dorothy puts the garbage out for collection. They can access the property and be inside in seconds."

"I'll relay that to Georgia. Makes me feel slightly better knowing they'll be close." A muscle twitched in Miles's cheek. "I'll suggest they have someone out front but a little farther away, in case Troy's watching. Where do you want me to park?"

Sophie's brain scrambled for ideas. This was her territory, the kitchen at Brambles and Berries. She knew where everything was kept. Knives. Potential weapons. Unless he had a gun. Had she ever seen Troy with a gun?

"Sophie?" Miles set down his phone. "What's going on in that smart head of yours?"

She swiveled in her seat. "Let's park on Main Street a little way down from the tearoom. I'm guessing Troy will break in via the back entrance. Likely already has. Into the kitchen. The village is quiet at this time but breaking into the front would be too obvious. It's not quite dark yet." She swallowed hard. "We have to stick with the plan we discussed, Miles. No matter what."

"I know. Officer Parker and his guys will be there with more police on standby. Georgia's on it. They'll stay quiet until it's time."

"We can't wig Troy out. If anything goes wrong…" She let the sentence hang.

"Nothing will go wrong." Miles picked up her hand and kissed it. "I'm not letting him hurt you again."

"My priority is Harriet. You have to understand that." She motioned for him to drive and stared at her phone.

"My priority is you." Miles pulled back onto the road, his jaw set. "Are you texting him?"

"Yep. With a solution I think he's going to like. I'm appealing to his ego. Giving him an out." She tapped the keys harder than necessary. "Relying on the fact that he would throw anyone under the bus to save his own skin."

"Sounds ominous."

She pressed the send button. "I'm using my own weapon."

He glanced at her, eyes wide. "Which is…?"

"Words."

Chapter Thirty-One

MILES GRITTED HIS TEETH. *I DON'T like this one bit.* There were too many variables. Not to mention risking the life of the woman he had fallen for. Yet he needed to be strong for her now more than ever.

He parked on Main Street and texted Georgia again. Georgia already had Officer Parker en route—he would be on Bluebell Lane with his men any minute and had back-up prepped and ready to move in.

Sophie sat next to Miles in the passenger seat, phone in hand. She looked up at him and blinked. "Want to read it?"

He checked his watch. "Sure." He scrolled down.

"Troy. We can do it your way—but I have another idea.

Right now, you're in trouble, you know that.

How can you avoid a scandal and incarceration after this?

If you want a powerful future with Camille, let him take the fall. Your dad.

Call it payback for your childhood. You're smart… figure it out.

Let us get on with our quiet lives while you live out your happily ever after."

"Wow." Miles swallowed. Could this really work? "Do you think he'd betray his dad like that?"

Sophie stared at her phone. "You know what they say—the apple doesn't fall far from the tree. Troy told me his mom died when she fell down the stairs, but I always wondered how much of an accident it was. Especially after what he did to me." She rubbed her arm. "I figure if Troy's flaunting his upcoming wealth and power, he could talk his dad into helping him get there. Whatever it takes."

"Smart." Miles picked up her hand and kissed her cool skin, then glanced back at his watch. "It's almost time."

"Give him a minute to respond to this message. Or at least read it so I can go and attempt to reason with him."

How could a person reason with someone like Troy? Miles gritted his teeth. He'd like to go on in and "talk" man to man. Leave Sophie in the car. She would never let that fly though, not when Harriet was being held hostage.

"Pray for me? And promise you'll get Harriet to safety."

"Of course." Miles unlatched his seatbelt and leaned across the console. He took her beautiful face in his hands and memorized every square inch. "You are one brave woman. For the record, I'm falling in love with you, too." He closed the space between them and kissed her with all the passion he could muster.

A text ping interrupted the magic.

Please, don't let that be our last kiss...

"He replied." Sophie read the message and peered at Miles, a glimmer of hope in her eyes. "He likes my idea. I know it could be a ploy on his part, but it may at least give Harriet and me a chance to get out to safety." She unlatched her door and was out before Miles could get around to help her.

"You feel all right?"

She steadied herself and rested a hand on the car. "Yeah. All things considered. Painkillers are working. I'll go ahead, you stay back a little, out of sight. I'll dash around the back to the kitchen. It's dark there so you can follow and hide out. Grab Harriet when she appears and make sure she gets to the police cars safe and sound."

He nodded. "You know that if anything goes wrong, I'm barreling in there myself. You can't expect me to sit by and watch you or your sister get hurt."

Sophie leaned in and buried her head against his chest. Miles hugged her close. They fit so perfectly. He felt the softness of her T-shirt beneath his fingers. Inhaled the mix of scents in her hair—a subtle floral with a hint of antiseptic and an underlying reminder of smoke.

Lord, we need Your help, and I need this woman in my life.

"See you soon." Sophie turned and walked away, the streetlamps now flicking on as if to illuminate her path. She was a little unsteady on her feet, and no wonder after all she had endured today. This was one determined woman.

Miles followed at a distance, hugging the shadows in case Troy was on the lookout. His eyes were trained on Sophie's silhouette in the fading light. Would Troy listen to her idea? If he wanted to try to get out of this situation unscathed, her idea was his best shot. A son betraying his father. Not the first act of betrayal for Troy. He'd broken Sophie's heart and crushed her spirit. Until now.

He wouldn't recognize the strong woman she had become since he left his mark on her.

I'm not going to let him leave a mark on her again.

Sophie rubbed her bare arms as she approached Brambles and Berries tearoom. She'd been warm in Miles's car, but there was a nip in the evening air and a slight smell of burning twitched her nostrils. Was someone lighting a cozy fire indoors or was she still smelling the barn? She picked up a lock of her hair and sniffed. Yes, smoke. The memory of Troy leaving her there to burn pumped much-needed adrenalin through her veins.

God, let Harriet be uninjured. Please protect her and help her not to be too scared.

Her sweet sister had done nothing to deserve this. Troy had no right to involve her. Did he wonder at their identical features? He'd met Harriet once before and commented on how much more glamorous she was than Sophie. Jerk. He did everything he could to put Sophie down. To make her feel inferior and less than. She lifted her chin. Let him see how inferior she was now.

Up ahead, two young boys rode bikes and farther down on the next block, a man at the law office was locking up for the night. Other than that, the usual peace and quiet ensued in the village. A quick check over her shoulder. Miles walked in the shadows with hands in pockets, his presence a comfort and a concern. She would never forgive herself if something happened to him. He proved himself to be selfless and strong. By her side all the way. Did he say he was falling in love with her *too*? She had no recollection of declaring such a thing… but she couldn't deny the truth.

Brambles and Berries. Sophie eyed the well-worn, wooden door with its cheery welcome as she hurried down the thin alley at the side of the tearoom. She longed for the streetlamp's glow. Wild brambles scratched her bare arms. Her sharp breaths came fast and her pulse whooshed in her ears. Troy could decide to kill them both and be done with them. Frame his dad and get away with everything.

No, the police were outside. Miles was closer still. He wouldn't let that happen. She'd warned him not to follow her inside, but knew he wouldn't hesitate if he feared her life was in imminent danger.

Sophie slowed her steps and went to slide her phone into the thigh pocket of her yoga pants. Wait. Could she somehow record what was about to go down on her voice memo app? Worth a try. She pressed record and slipped the phone into her pocket with the mic end pointing up. A sword in its sheath.

The light was on in the kitchen, but she couldn't see inside. Dorothy always pulled down the blinds to stop anyone from eying her expensive equipment. No windows seemed to be broken so he must have used the back entrance. The door was ancient and wouldn't require much effort for anyone to jimmy the lock or force their way inside. Sophie stood on the mat and swallowed. *God, help me.* Without giving herself a chance to chicken out, she turned the handle and pushed the door wide open.

"Harriet?"

The brightly lit kitchen looked neat and tidy, as usual. Sophie scanned the room, her fists closed tight at her sides.

"Come on in." Troy marched through the door which connected to the eating area, a sick grin on his face and Harriet in his clutches. "Close the door, darling."

Sophie folded her arms across her chest. "Not until Harriet leaves." She noted her sister's disheveled hair and streaked mascara. "Did he hurt you?"

Harriet shook her head.

"Not yet." Troy stroked Harriet's bobbed hair in the same way he used to stroke Sophie's. Her skin prickled.

"Let her go. It's trade time."

Harriet let out a sharp gasp. "No. I can't leave you here."

Sophie clasped her hands in front of her chest and glared at Troy. "Unless you've decided to be smart and let me go, too. Frame your dad like I suggested."

He sneered. "I'll admit, I like the idea. He's going to be excess cargo once I have this all sorted out, and I was wondering what to do with him." He leaned over and smelled Harriet's hair.

"Mmm. You use the same shampoo as your twin. Cute."

Harriet quivered beneath his touch. Sophie had to get her out of there. She stepped farther into the room and stretched out a hand. "Harriet, it's time to go home."

Troy let go of Harriet but trailed a finger down her cheek. "Remember what I told you, beautiful. Ever say a word against me and I know where your little girl goes to school."

Harriet nodded.

"And don't touch your sister. Straight out the door. Understand?" He propelled Harriet toward the exit.

She nearly lost her balance, steadied herself, and paused when she reached Sophie. Her face contorted with fear and grief and confusion. "How can I leave you here?"

"It's okay. I'm going to be okay." Sophie nodded with more confidence than she felt. "Go and see Lucy."

Harriet shook her head, let out a cry, and ran through the doorway into the dark alley. Sophie closed her eyes for a second and pictured Miles's strong arms around Harriet as he led her back to the safety of the authorities. Her sister was going to be all right. The dominoes were falling and she needed to think. Now what?

"See how reasonable I am?" Troy marched over and slammed the back door. "What to do with you?" He grabbed her sore elbow and she stifled a moan. "How is this going to play out, princess?" He towered over her and squeezed her cheeks until tears gathered at the edges of her eyes.

"Where's your father?" Her words were muffled in his hand.

He released her face and shoved her against the island in the center of the kitchen. "Down the street." He extracted a phone from his jacket pocket. "Waiting for my command for our quick getaway."

Dread washed over Sophie. If the father saw Miles, he may intercept and grab Harriet. Or hurt Miles. Plus, if he got curious and checked down the street or out back, he would see where the police were situated. There was no time to stop those dominoes. An idea sprung to mind.

"Get him in here now."

"Excuse me?" Troy raised a brow.

"Call your dad and say you need him in here to watch me. Then you can go to the police and… report him. Say he coerced you into tricking me. Used you for his own gains because he wanted in on your future inheritance with the Clements. Come on, Troy, you have the gift of gab, you'll say the right thing." Flattery always worked with this narcissist.

He squinted. Loosened his grip on her arm and took out his phone. Turned from her for a mere second.

A second was all she needed.

In one swift motion, Sophie pivoted, grabbed a chef's knife from the wooden block behind her, and thrust the blade deep into Troy's back. The sound of gristle and muscle and tearing… she didn't recognize her own screams as he collapsed in on himself and blood spurted in every direction. His phone clattered to the ground. Was he alive? Had anyone heard her screams?

Sophie darted for the door.

She needed to get out of there. Fast. She yanked the handle and gasped.

There before her stood an older version of Troy Sanders.

Chapter Thirty-Two

With Harriet safe in Officer Parker's car and Leo on his way to take care of her, Miles turned toward the tearoom's back entrance. "I have to see what's happening." His voice was a mere whisper.

"Let the police carry on from here, son. More officers are en route." Officer Parker lay a hand on Miles's shoulder.

"No police." Harriet whispered from the back seat of the car. "Please, don't make that man angry. He's crazy."

Officer Parker silenced them, and Miles watched in horror as a second man ran up the side of the tearoom from the front and disappeared through the kitchen door.

Harriet gasped. "Who's that?"

"Could be Troy's father. I'm going to find out." Miles sprinted down the alley to the back door before anyone could stop him. He froze as two muffled male voices sounded from the kitchen. They could be doing anything to Sophie.

Miles clenched and unclenched his fists, unsure how much longer he could wait.

He couldn't hang around for the police.

"Son, trust Me."

Miles's eyes widened, every nerve on edge. The message wasn't audible, yet he knew God's whisper.

Lord, our lives are in Your hands here. I'm waiting and listening—but if I hear them lay a hand on her...

"He's bleeding out." The older man turned to Sophie. "What did you do to my son?"

Troy's father had pushed her back into the center of the room.

"He hit his head on the counter after I… I stabbed him." Her voice quivered. "You should know Troy was about to hand you over to the police to clear his own name. Let you take the fall for him."

Troy's dad stood over his son's body. "Is he dead?"

"No, unconscious. He needs medical attention."

"You a nurse?"

"I'm a writer. Listen you have a choice. Run and leave me with Troy to wait for the police—because they *are* coming. Or stay and both get arrested so Troy can talk his way out of everything. You know he will."

"Dad?" A mumbled groan.

He was coming around. Sophie winced.

"Son, we need to get outta here."

"Go." Troy sounded groggy. "I'll figure it out."

"You mean you'll give the police my name. Like she said."

"What? No. Don't believe what this woman says, Dad. She's a storyteller. Pathetic one at that."

A grunt. "Why do I have trouble trusting you, Troy?"

Troy took a ragged breath. "Do what I say, old man, will you?"

There was no way Sophie could take on two grown men, but this was her domain. Plus, one was horribly injured already. If only she could get one of them to the stove. She'd managed to switch on the huge griddle when she stood in front of it and now the metal was white hot.

Troy somehow managed to pull himself up to his feet as he held a hand to his knife wound. He was strong. The men argued with some choice words and then Troy lunged at his father.

Sophie jumped out of the way and let them duke it out.

A roar. A crash of steel on steel. Both men growled.

The older man dodged while pulling a gun from his jacket pocket, and Troy face-planted on the griddle.

Troy shrieked as he bounced back and collided with Sophie, taking her to the floor with him. She let out a cry and he screamed like a wounded animal. The smell of burning flesh permeated the air. Sophie turned away, her stomach heaving. Where was his dad?

A kick to her rib cage answered that question.

Steel pots fell on top of her. She covered her face with her arms.

"Sophie." Miles. Where had he come from?

She scrambled to her knees in time to see Troy's dad pointing the gun at Miles.

"Sophie, leave. It's your turn now. Go." Miles's mellow voice was steady and sure.

"I'm not leaving you." No way.

"Ain't that cute?" Troy's dad sneered. "One of you is my ticket out." He stared down at Troy and grimaced. "Uh-oh, pretty boy. Don't think your rich French lady will want you now."

Troy cursed from his fetal position on the floor.

Sophie couldn't bring herself to look at his burned face. She stood and clutched the countertop. "Take me."

"No." Miles stepped toward her, and she held out her arms for one last embrace.

A gun shot.

Miles collapsed and Troy's dad grabbed Sophie by the hair,

marched her through to the front of the tearoom, and kicked the door open wide onto the pavement.

She opened her mouth but nothing came out. She heard more voices at the back of the tearoom. Police?

"Run." He pressed his gun into her side. "Now."

Sobs caught in her throat as she tried to make sense of what just happened. Miles was shot. Because of her.

God, let him be all right. Please. Whatever happens to me…

Faint sirens filled the cool evening air as Sophie struggled against the rough grip of her captor. He might be older, but he was strong and fast—she couldn't argue with the gun.

"W-where are we going?" She spotted a familiar white SUV parked up ahead.

"You're with me as my hostage until I'm out of this wretched country. Or until I've had enough of you. Get in."

Dread washed over her as she watched him start the car. "W-what about your son?"

"I'm done with Troy. He's made his own mess. He can figure it out. Now shut-up." He waved the gun. "Try anything and you know I'll use it."

The quickest way to the highway was back past the tearoom and through the village. Surely the police would appear at any moment.

Against her rule-following tendencies, Sophie decided not to fasten her seatbelt. She was getting out of here as soon as possible. Had he planned his escape route? Speeding was almost impossible for a non-local in these winding country roads. He must know this wasn't going to be a dramatic getaway.

Lord, please don't let him do anything foolish.

Sophie clutched the edge of her seat. Could she jump out while the car was moving? Drop and roll? Her breathing came in fast bursts as he started the engine, the gun resting on his lap. His foot pressed the accelerator as they neared the tearoom. A dark figure. Two. Police? She eyed the gun on Troy's dad's lap.

A guttural growl and her captor sped up.

Sophie gritted her teeth and grabbed the gun. His meaty hand engulfed hers. A struggle she knew she had no hope of winning, but she wasn't giving up without a fight. With only one hand on the steering wheel, the car swerved. Crashing was preferable to being kidnapped. Again.

A sudden streak of red blocked the road, and the blast of a car horn caused a split-second distraction.

The gun fell to the floor at the screech of their tires.

Troy's dad shouted and turned the wheel.

Sophie took the opportunity, shouldered the passenger door open, closed her eyes tight, and rolled out of the vehicle.

Over and over and over.

A crunch of metal and glass close by. Too close.

On instinct, Sophie's hands covered her face in protective mode.

A jolt.

A gunshot.

Chapter Thirty-Three

Sleep. Glorious nothingness engulfed her.

Silence. Rich and deep.

Sirens. Yes, now the wailing of loud sirens like squawking seagulls at the seaside…

Sophie opened her eyes. How long had she been out? The curb must have halted her momentum. A paramedic was fussing with her pulse. She gasped for air and sat up way too fast.

Her head spun and her bruised elbow screamed with pain, but she needed to get away. Somewhere, she wasn't sure where…

"Try to stay still, Miss." The paramedic was a young man with glasses and curly blond hair. So curly. Her eyelids were heavy…

Shouts from all directions and flashes of blue lights. What was happening?

"Sophie?" Harriet sank to the pavement next to her and touched the arm of the paramedic. "Is she going to be okay?" She stroked Sophie's long hair and held her gaze with brown eyes, so like her own. "Sophie, are you all right? Is anything broken?"

At this point, everything hurt to some degree, but nothing felt broken. "I-I think I'm fine." Sophie got her bearings. They were a little way down the street from the tearoom.

"You rescued me." Harriet's smile wobbled, and then the tears came.

"And you were so brave." Sophie pushed the paramedic to one side. "I can sit up. I need to see what happened."

"Come here, you two." Georgia appeared and wrapped her sisters in a tight hug. "Mom will never let us live this down, you know. She'll be emigrating and moving into Bramble Cottage before you know it so she can keep an eye on us all." She burst into tears. "I thought I'd lost you both."

"We're all going to be fine." Tears leaked down Sophie's face as she tried to figure out what was going on around them. Police, ambulance, and so much noise. She feared her head might implode. She spotted the white SUV wrapped around a streetlamp, the front crunched in like balled-up, crumpled paper. Troy's dad. Was he injured? Dead?

A moment of panic. "Wait, Miles. Where is Miles? He's been shot."

Harriet scouted the street. "No, no he can't be—"

Sophie held onto both girls and pulled herself up. "Yes. He's in the tearoom kitchen." She covered her mouth with her grazed hands. "Is he—is he dead?"

"Sophie."

She turned at the sound of Miles's beautiful voice.

He sat in the driver's seat of Georgia's Mini, door wide open, and a paramedic crouched next to him.

Her heart swelled. He was alive. "What are you doing over there? I don't understand." She left her sisters with Leo and a police officer, and hobbled toward Miles, dazed and confused. "I-I thought you were shot in the kitchen."

He unfolded himself from the car and wrapped her in a tight hug. She buried her face in his shirt, closed her eyes, and trembled with relief, pain, joy, and a hundred other emotions that coursed through her body. Someone covered her shoulders with a heavy blanket.

Miles kissed the top of her head. "I *was* shot. Thankfully, it barely nicked my arm. Stings, that's all."

Sophie stepped back and he revealed a bloodied shirt sleeve.

"Ambulance guy says I should get a couple of stitches, but he's put some strips on for now. No big deal."

"Right. No big deal." This was surreal. She was having trouble piecing the details together. "I don't understand. You must have followed us out of the tearoom straight away."

"Yeah. Troy was rolling around on the floor and I knew his dad would have to drive this way out of the village— and there was no way he was taking you with him. My car was parked where we left it earlier. I sprinted out of the tearoom and prayed he wouldn't turn around or hear my footsteps."

"Risky."

Miles leaned back and cupped her face in his hands. "What else could I do? I knew Officer Parker and his men were behind me and I didn't have time to explain. Troy's father couldn't drive too fast along this road, and I prayed you would either be buckled in safe or would jump out when I T-boned his vehicle. He swerved and the streetlamp stopped him in his tracks." He held her close again and rubbed her back in circular motions. "Courageous move there, by the way. They wouldn't let me out of my car at first, but I could see you'd made it."

"I didn't really have time to think. I only knew I had to get away from that monster. Like father, like son." She blanched at the thought of what could have become of her if Miles hadn't stopped them. "Thank you."

"You're the brave one." He stepped back and smoothed her hair behind her ears.

"I did what I needed to do. God gave me the strength and the know-how. That's the advantage we had over Troy and his dad." She bit her lip. "What happened to them? Do you know yet?" Did she even want to know?

Miles looked over at one of the ambulances and drew her close. "Troy was in a bad way, and let's just say his face will be a constant reminder of his actions. Did you hear the shot after the crash?"

"No, or maybe…."

He squeezed her tighter. "His dad used the gun on himself. Before the police even had a chance to get to him. He's gone."

Sophie gasped. "He shot himself?" She was the last person he interacted with. The gun had fallen to the floor of the car…

"I know it's awful, but my guess is there's a lot more than your kidnapping and stalking he's responsible for. He likely didn't want to face whatever the police in the States may have on him. You said there was a history of abuse in the family, maybe the truth will come out somehow."

"I don't know what to say or quite how to feel about that." Numbness poured over her like a freezing waterfall, cleansing as frustration and fear were extinguished. She patted her thigh and pulled her phone from the pocket. "I almost forgot. This thing's hardy." She pressed the pause button. "Hopefully, it wasn't wrecked, and my recording will help justice to be served."

Miles took her phone and whistled. "Genius. Let's give this to Officer Parker and see what he can do with it." Miles turned toward Georgia and Harriet. "There will be time to process all this. Your sisters look ready to take you home, but I'm afraid we both need to go on a little date first."

Sophie cringed. "Hospital?" Her shoulders sagged. She'd had enough of hospitals for one week. "Again? I suppose we both need to get checked out."

"You hanging in there? You've been beaten up pretty hard today."

Sophie blew out a long breath. "As long as this is over. As long as we can get on with our lives now, I'll be fine."

"We'll both be fine." He put his uninjured arm around her shoulders and they plodded over toward a second ambulance. "We'll need to take the ambulance. I seem to have wrecked two cars today. I hope Georgia will forgive me."

"I think tonight she's just thankful her family's still intact. I'll help her figure it out. How about your beautiful Porsche? I know how much it means to you, especially as it was such a precious gift."

Miles stopped and studied her face with his fathomless gray eyes. "It's repairable. I'd willingly wreck the whole thing again if it meant keeping you safe. Truth is, I'd give myself for you." The feel of his fingers on her cheek made the surrounding chaos fade into the sweetest, safest silence.

"I think you proved that today. Twice. Thank you. You have no idea what that means to me." She stood on tiptoes and kissed his lips. "I'm willing to do what it takes for your wellbeing, too."

"You are?"

"I haven't forgotten about your appointment with the specialist. Whatever the verdict is, whatever your next chapter looks like, I fully intend to be there with you, like you've been here for me."

Miles returned her kiss with one that held a promise of an exceedingly happily ever after…

Chapter Thirty-Four

"Sorry it's not better news, Miles." Almost twenty-four hours had passed since their harrowing ordeal, and now the specialist could only offer him a risky surgery and little hope for a full vocal recovery.

Miles's chest constricted. "I guessed surgery would be necessary." He shrugged. "I appreciate you slotting me in for an appointment today."

"Not at all." The doctor stood. "Sounds like you've had an eventful week. I hope you get some rest and truly, I wish you all the best." He nodded to Sophie. "Both of you. I'm here if you have any more questions before the surgery."

"Thanks." Miles took Sophie's hand. *Fresh air. I need fresh air.* They stood and Miles led her out of the hospital in silence to the parking lot.

"I'm so sorry about the results." Tears pooled in Sophie's eyes.

"It's okay. I prepared myself for the worst. Want to go for a quick walk by the sea or are you exhausted?"

Sophie wiped her cheeks. "Let's grab a taxi. I should be tired after Georgia checking on me every hour last night, but I'm craving the ocean." She tugged on his arm. "There's one."

They climbed inside the taxi and gave the driver their destination.

"Missing your car?" Sophie whispered in his ear.

Miles stared through the window at the traffic. "I am, but I'll miss singing more.”

“Oh, Miles.” She lay her head on his shoulder.

This had been a week from the twilight zone, and now he’d received the news he’d been dreading. “I was secretly hoping God would pull off one of His miracles and have me all healed by now.”

“You’re not going to be doing any of this alone. We’ll make sure you get all the help you need, I promise.”

“Thanks.” He gazed down at her. “My bleak future doesn’t freak you out?”

She made a sound that was half-laugh and half-cry. “Do you honestly think this would freak me out after my life this past few days? I don’t want you to worry about me. We’re both going to focus on you now. Get you through surgery and recovery in the best possible way. That specialist is top notch. Will said he has a brilliant surgical team. World renowned. You’ll be in the best hands. I guess we have to trust that God has got…” She pressed her lips together.

“Hey, talk to me. We’ve both been through a lot. I value your thoughts.”

Sophie looked through the window. “I don’t want to sound trite, but perhaps God’s got something *else* in store for you, for a season at least. Maybe something better?” She smiled up at him and he couldn’t help but reciprocate.

A life with you would be a really good start.

They pulled in at the clifftop. The exact spot they walked last week. Miles paid the driver, and then he and Sophie strolled hand-in-hand to the black railings that served as a barricade. He sighed. “This is a perfect place to think. I like it here.”

Sophie turned to face him, her back leaning against the railing. She was stunning, even with grazes down one cheek and goodness only knew how many cuts and bruises over her body. Not to mention the trauma of being kidnapped and then stabbing a man. She licked her lips. "Do you like it enough to stick around here? Maybe even put down roots?" Mahogany highlights lit her long, dark hair in the afternoon sunshine.

"I've been praying about it. For a while, actually."

"A while? And there I was thinking it was all about little old me." She held a hand to her heart.

Miles pulled her closer and chuckled. "Well, of course you changed everything, but I've always loved this area. My happiest memories are almost all from time spent in England with Aunt Joyce, and my uncle before he passed. I guess my aunt has been my primary reason to spend so much time here up until now."

"As well as your car?"

He winked. "Maybe a little. Although I'm holding my vehicle with loose hands. In fact, I'm holding everything with loose hands—especially my health and my future."

"Surrendering your story." She nodded. "I know what that feels like. Seems like God's got us both thinking along the same lines."

"Weird." He attempted to tame strands of her long hair that whipped around her face, courtesy of the coastal wind. "It's as if He thinks we could be good together." Miles spun her around to face the vast expanse of sea. White caps frothed the surface in the breeze as the water deepened in saturation to almost navy blue near the horizon. "Breathtaking, isn't it? The ocean reminds me how small I am and how big God is."

"Mmm, I like that. The horizon has always fascinated me. One long line so full of promise. Never ending. Steady and sure."

They drank in the moments of solitude for almost a full minute.

Sophie let out a small sigh. "What would you do in your next chapter, Miles? I mean, if singing professionally is not a viable option for you and you could do anything at all, what would you choose?"

He rested his chin on her head as he considered answering her in all honesty. "You'll think it's silly." Dare he share this with her?

"Umm, you're talking to the girl who bakes cakes while she dreams up imaginary friends she can write about." She waited. Gave him time.

Here goes nothing. "I'd own a B&B."

"You mean a Bed and Breakfast? Here in England?" There was excitement in her voice. Genuine joy.

"Yeah. I had a real vivid dream once that I owned a quintessential English B&B in the countryside. It was pale yellow with white pillars. I even saw my car parked in the circular driveway in front. Green hills all around. Not far from the forest and the ocean. I could picture it all when I woke up the next morning. Never had a dream quite like it."

"Sounds perfect. Tell me more."

"I'd maybe give private singing lessons if my voice allowed and play opera music for the guests. I even thought it might be fun to have each bedroom named for an opera. Tosca, The Marriage of Figaro, Carmen, that sort of thing. This might freak you out, but I had a wife and a baby in this particular dream, too." He held his breath to see what her response might be.

Sophie turned back toward him and hugged his waist. "I love it, Miles." She looked up with tears in her eyes.

"What's wrong?"

"Nothing's wrong. Nothing at all." She let out a giggle.

"I'm not convinced. Are you going to tell me your grand

dream of dreams for the future, Miss Brooks? More exciting than a B&B, I hope."

Sophie leaned back against the railing, bringing Miles with her. "Believe it or not—and you can trust that I have this in writing and naturally, on my voice memo—but I have always wanted to own a property here in the countryside where I can host writing retreats and bake for my guests. It would be the perfect inspirational place for me to embrace my own career as an author while I encourage other writers, too." She blushed. "I'd be up for it being pale yellow."

No way. "Seriously?"

"I'm deadly serious."

Miles let out his loudest laugh and twirled her around—until he remembered his injured arm and her bruised elbow. "Sounds like we could be quite compatible. You know, if we end up following those particular dreams."

She reached up and ran her fingers over the stubble on his chin. "You're a special man, Miles. I'll never forget the first day we met. The first time I heard you sing on stage in Paris."

"That was possibly the last time I'll ever sing on stage…"

She put a finger over his lips. "Shh. You don't know that for sure. What I do know is up until that day, I never believed in love at first sight. I wrote about it, but I thought it fictitious. How could such a thing possibly happen in real life?"

"You changed your mind?"

Sophie reached up and kissed his mouth. The kiss deepened until they were both breathless.

"No, Miles. *You* changed my mind."

Epilogue

Nine months later…

"THEY'RE READY FOR YOU INSIDE." MILES'S voice had almost recovered to regular volume. "We should get you settled before everyone arrives."

Sophie slid an arm around his waist as they stood side-by-side on the circular driveway staring at his new home. "I can't believe this place. It's literally your dream come true." Right down to the pale-yellow walls and white columns flanking the huge front doors.

"*Our* dream come true." He let out a laugh, still rich and joyous even post-surgery. "I think you're going to like what your sisters have done with the place."

"They've been so secretive." She clutched the book in one hand, reveling in the weight of it. "I know Georgia had a spectacular vision for her wedding reception here next month, but you have to live in this place, and you've barely had any say at all. You're awfully trusting."

Miles put his arm around her shoulder and they began walking. "I think the Brooks sisters have impeccable taste."

"Let me guess—especially with men?" She raised a brow.

"Now that you mention it…"

"I'm not arguing." She stopped, reached up, and pecked his cheek. "You're a keeper."

"Glad you feel that way." Miles took her in his strong arms

and kissed her with a passion that caused every nerve ending to tingle. "I feel the same."

Sophie straightened and fanned her face. "Wow. You're making a remarkable recovery."

"Thanks." He ran a hand through his hair. "I think kissing helps."

"Really?" She continued walking and squeezed the book to her chest. "I'm grateful you're here with me today. It's pretty special." She turned to him and beamed.

"I wouldn't have missed this for the world." He tapped her nose. "How does it feel to have your own book in your hands?"

"Magical. Miraculous. It was the best decision, going with a smaller publisher so we could push everything through quickly to ride the coattails of all that happened with Troy and his upcoming trial…"

"Try not to think about that today, honey. He's already taken so much."

"I won't, but you have to admit, the past nine months have been like something out of a novel even I couldn't have written."

"We've had our fair share of highs and lows. Such is life." He winked. "Today, we celebrate you." He pulled open the wooden front doors and stepped back. "Go and check it out."

"Oh, my word." Sophie's jaw dropped as she walked into the foyer of Miles's dream home and future Bed and Breakfast property. Soft opera music played in the background as she spun around in a circle. "It's so light and airy in here." The paneled walls were painted a creamy-white and the wooden parquet flooring was in perfect condition. A wide staircase led to several large bedrooms yet to be renovated, but something else drew her eye. Sophie let out a shriek.

Miles laughed from behind her. "You like it?"

"You didn't tell me the foyer has a floor-to-ceiling bookcase… with a ladder." She stood on the first rung. "I feel like Belle in *Beauty and the Beast*."

Miles frowned. "Cute, but you realize that's not particularly complimentary for me, don't you?"

She jumped down and grabbed his arm. "Miles, this is gorgeous, and you're not in the least bit beastly. This foyer sure makes a good first impression. Look at my book table. It's so pretty." A long mahogany table held a tall pile of her books on one end and a crystal vase of fresh flowers in every shade of yellow dominated the other. "I see now why the girls wanted me to bake lemon macarons." A silver platter piled high with the macarons sat next to the flowers with a silver statue of the Eiffel Tower. "Where *are* my sisters?" She set her bag down behind the table.

"Surprise." Georgia, Sophie, and little Lucy came in bearing a huge balloon bouquet in pale yellow and white.

"Extra surprise." Sophie's mom stepped out from behind the balloons, her beautiful face radiant as always.

"Mom?" Sophie's breath caught in her throat. "You're actually here?" She wrapped her in a tight hug. "I thought you were coming out for Georgia's wedding next month?"

"Did you really expect the professional party planner in the family to miss out on all this? I decided to come early and help with everything. I wasn't going to miss your book signing." She whispered into her daughter's hair. "I'm so very proud of you, darling."

Sophie turned around. "Miles, did you know about this?"

Miles glanced at his future mother-in-law. "Maybe. There may also be a certain Parisian baker who is due to arrive in an hour."

What? "Annabelle? She's coming here?"

"She said she wouldn't miss it for the world." Miles slid his hands in his pockets. "She also promised to bring her profiteroles."

"You guys." Sophie dabbed at the corners of her eyes and then hugged everyone in turn. "Thank you. All of you. For everything. For getting me through these past months. For giving me time to get this book birthed." She allowed her gaze to roam around the space that already felt like home. "This place looks stunning. You have no idea how happy I am in this very moment. I'm incredibly grateful."

Georgia kissed her cheek. "I'm the one who's grateful. Will and I can't wait to have our wedding reception here. You should see the dining hall."

"And you're going to die when you see the kitchen. It's utterly dreamy." Harriet picked Lucy up and kissed her cheek.

Sophie stroked Lucy's dark curls. "What do you think of this place, Mademoiselle Lucy?"

"I think it's like a fairy castle. Can I have sleepovers when you live here, too, Aunty?"

Sophie's heart warmed. "Of course." She stared at the beautiful oval diamond that gleamed on her finger. Their engagement still felt like a surprise every time she saw the ring there, even after a month. "You may have to wait until summer though. Does that work for you?"

Lucy pursed her lips. "I guess. Can I come to the cottage, too?"

"Yes, definitely. I'll be extra lonely once Aunty Georgia gets married. You can come stay with me anytime."

Georgia bent down and took Lucy's hand. "Bramble Cottage is always going to be in our family, Lucy. Nanny's going to use it when she comes to visit, and we're going to let friends stay when they need a place. Don't you worry. It'll always be our special home."

Lucy nodded and her frown transformed into a sweet grin that lit up her face.

Sophie checked her watch. "Well, I guess we only have a few minutes."

Georgia grabbed her camera from her purse behind the table. "I need to take some author pics. First book signing event."

"First of many." Miles raised his brows.

"Many events?" Sophie picked up a copy of her novel and stood in front of the table.

"Many books, honey." He pressed a kiss on her cheek and walked behind Georgia.

"I hope so." Sophie smiled and her soul sang as she posed for photographs. Not only because of this huge accomplishment in making her book dream a reality. As she took in the loving faces before her, she knew this was only the beginning of her own story.

A story where God had the final word. A story surrendered to Him.

This was what Sophie had longed for, even though she hadn't been aware of how much.

God, You've been so good. My restored faith, my sweet family, my phenomenal future husband.

Her very own happily ever after.

And now a published book. The icing on the cake. *That reminds me…*

"Can you give us a quick minute?" She winked at Harriet.

Harriet grabbed Georgia's arm. "Come, let's give the lovebirds some time before her bookish fans arrive."

Their mom took Lucy's hand. "Want to show me the rose garden, sweetie?"

"Yes, Nanny, let's go. I want to pick a yellow one for Aunty Sophie."

Harriet led them all out through the front entrance and pulled the door closed, leaving strains of opera music to fill the quiet.

"I do have a little surprise for you." Sophie scurried behind the table and grabbed a white cardboard box from her bag. "I promised you one of these a while ago."

Miles chuckled as he took the box and untied the string. "Is this what I think it is?"

Sophie perched up on the table, her feet swinging. "Opera cake." She hadn't made one since she lived in Paris.

He pulled down the cardboard flaps and held the pastry high as he studied the six layers of sweetness in a perfect rectangle, topped with chocolate ganache and decorated with his initials. "It's fantastic. Way too good to eat."

"Miles?" She blinked back tears.

"Hey, what's wrong?" He set down the cake, stood in front of her, and wiped a stray tear with his thumb.

She shook her head, allowing her long hair to fall on either side of her face. "Nothing's wrong. That's just it."

He tilted his head and waited.

"I wanted to bake you something special to show you how much I love you. An opera cake for my opera man."

He started to protest and she held up a hand.

"I know you may never sing again in a professional capacity. I realize this is going to be a hard adjustment. We both have a whole lot of new coming our way—but I'll never forget the first day I met you and heard you sing. It's the first page of our story and I'll hold it in my heart forever."

"Me, too." Miles took both her hands and kissed them. His gray eyes glistened. "I trust God and I trust you."

"Same."

"I can't wait to see what's next for us. Our life here." He picked up a copy of her book. "Quick, before your fans arrive, read me your dedication again?"

She grinned and opened the pages, inhaling the intoxicating smell of a fresh book. "Again? Okay.

'To the Author of everything, who always has the final word.

May this story give hope to every reader for their own happily ever after.'"

"Amen to that." Miles took Sophie in his arms, twirled her around until she was giddy on love and laughter, and lowered her into a chair behind the table. At the sound of the door knocker, he bowed. "I will allow your guests entry, my lady."

She giggled as he strolled over to the front door to welcome in her readers.

Sophie smoothed her hair and sat tall amidst the Eiffel Tower, macarons, and a stack of her very own books.

At home in her story.

"Trust in the Lord with all your heart
and lean not on your own understanding;
in all your ways submit to him,
and he will make your paths straight."
Proverbs 3:5-6 (NIV)

Author Note

"It is wonderful what miracles God works in wills that are utterly surrendered to Him." Hannah Whitall Smith

Thank you so much, dear reader, for traveling with me from the streets of Paris to the country lanes of England in this story of surrender amidst murder, cupcakes, opera, and fairy tales!

Those who know me well will often see something of my own personality, interests, or quirks in my characters—and Sophie Brooks is no exception. She has lived in both Canada and England, is an author, a sister, has a passion for baking, adores all things Paris, and is a romantic at heart. Thankfully, I do not share the more sinister aspects of her life—but a struggle with surrendering everything to God is a daily challenge for us both. The simple prayer she uttered in complete desperation is one I hold dear and repeat often:

God, I give You everyone.
God, I give You everything.

This reminds me of God's bigness and my smallness. That He is in control, and I am not. I pray this will bring comfort, peace, and hope to you, too.

I managed to work in a little extra research for this book whilst on a trip "home" to England in 2023. With my ever-patient husband along for the ride, we experienced a glorious sunny day in the beautiful city of Bath, where we spent luxurious hours in book shops such as Mr. B's, and enjoyed the best lemon curd "Bunn" at the oldest house in Bath, Sally Lunn's Buns—all in the name of research, of course. We also re-enacted the lunch-date scene between Miles and Sophie at The George Inn… I seriously have the best husband ever! (Side note: He did not kick up a fuss about travelling to Paris either. Being married to a writer has to have some perks!)

You may have noticed that the utterly charming Bramble Cottage, which made its debut in Book 1 (Captured in Frame), is also featured in this novel—how I could I not include the pretty pink cottage complete with thatched roof, adored by all the sisters?

So, as a story within the story, on my most recent research trip to England this year, I decided to visit the actual pink cottage in my fictionalized country village that inspired me back in 2019. Taking my sister Heidi for moral support, I bravely knocked on the rustic wooden door and met the kind, elderly owner, explaining how her sweet home was my inspiration and that my publisher even featured a similar pink cottage on the cover of Book 1. She was surprised and delighted to accept my gift of a signed copy of Captured in Frame, knowing her home played a part in the story. What a treat for us both!

In case you missed Book 1 in this Bite of Betrayal series, it's not too late to read Georgia's story in Captured in Frame—and look out for Harriet's story in Book 3: Ribbons of Guilt, coming in 2026.

As ever, my ultimate desire in writing fiction books is to encourage and inspire you in your REAL life with stories of hope, leaving no shadow of doubt that you are loved by God. Always.

You can contact me and find details on all my books, blog, writing coaching, and my free monthly newsletter at:
www.laurathomasauthor.com

Books by Laura Thomas:

(Bite of Betrayal Series)
Captured in Frame
The Final Word

(Flight to Freedom Series)
The Glass Bottom Boat
The Lighthouse Baby
The Orphan Beach
The Christmas Cabin
Snow Globe Secrets

(Tears Trilogy)
Tears to Dancing
Tears of a Princess
Tears, Fears, and Fame

The Candle Maker
Pearls for the Bride